YELLOW

NOVA

YELLOW

NOVA

—

by

GREGORY FITE

STREET
PRESS

ISBN 978-0-578-29670-8

First paperback edition April 2022

Printed in the USA

Cover design by Lynn Andreozzi

For more info: www.gregoryfite.com

For Ronnie,

Thank you for being the man I aspire to be.

Acknowledgements

—

Authoring a book has always been a dream of mine and without the love, sacrifice, and dedication of my family, it wouldn't have been possible for I am nothing without them. They believed in me when I went to war with myself thinking I could write, and I am forever grateful for their undying support.

So, to Mom, Bob, Deb, Owen, Serena, Diesel and Wildman, thank you for being my strength when the impossible felt impossible. Because of you my life is complete and filled with eternal hope.

I also owe an immense debt of gratitude to my partners in this endeavor, named and unnamed, who gave of themselves wholeheartedly to ensure this story will live on forever. In many ways, they are more responsible for its destiny than I am.

—

To: Sophia Dembling, my editor. Thank you for lending your linear voice to my complex prose and for showing me no mercy. Your tough love made all the difference in the world.

To: Morgane Leoni, my designer. Your patience is a virtue. Thank you for the beautiful layout and the grace you showed me as I stumbled through the many changes, I threw your way. Your good-hearted nature made this a wonderful experience I'll not soon forget.

And to my amazing cover designer, Lynn Andreozzi, may your work inspire millions of hearts and minds to change the world.

Prologue

—

Have you ever heard that voice? You know the one. The voice whispering that death will ease your suffering. My name is Lori, and I have; I've heard the voice of death. One early fall evening, lost in a rather vocal meltdown, she came to me as a friend. As a caring mentor with an answer to all my worries. Imagine death with a conscience for the living. She sounded eerily familiar. Like I'd known her forever. And like a gentle breeze, the softness of her invisible touch was a mystery I longed to solve in my quest for anything resembling absolution. Yet night after night our soulful connection filled my mind with a world of troubling possibilities. Much of my life to that point was privileged. From designer fashions to expensive toys, I had it all. Though I wanted for nothing financially, life felt temporary. Like an exploding firework fizzling into obscurity seconds after lift-off. A calamity I thought much too dangerous to continue pursuing as failure upon failure turned my once-promising future into a battlefield of regret until the night death became my refuge. She was my shelter from the storms that crawled into the back of my eyelids, forecasting sin's consequence. When she found me, my heart was a haunted house full of secret chambers and hidden screams. I had all but given up. I was naked, crumbled like a pile of decaying bricks, sobbing uncontrollably for forgiveness on the bathroom's cold Spanish tiles. But her message was simple: Those responsible for my unconscionable suffering must be punished.

I was barely nineteen the night grave silence first consoled me with an offer I couldn't refuse. One frightful enough to rewrite the course of history and forever end the wide-eyed insomnia keeping my nightmares awake. But I wasn't afraid. Like a moth drawn to a flickering flame, I clung to her every word. They played my despondent aspirations like an eerie symphony, beautiful and devastating. She brought me peace, not fear. At first, I dreaded her macabre glimpses of hope, but eventually I grew to crave our fatal exchanges.

Not because of some divine intervention but because I wanted to. I wanted to more than anything. Some might call this a death wish. I called it freedom. Now before you run screaming for cover, I beg you to reconsider as what I have to share could save someone's life. Maybe even your own. But I know what you're thinking. You're thinking *Whoa, who the hell is this crazy girl, and what's her problem*? I mean, I look harmless enough. Nothing scary about a short body topped with freckles, auburn hair, and hazel eyes, right? It's okay though. Heck, I'd be thinking the same thing if I were in your shoes. I mean, it's not every day a stranger corners you with a mouthful of doom, so I totally get it. Though many years have passed since death's last visit, I've not spoken a word about this to anyone until now. There are countless reasons why, but we'll get to that later. Who am I, you ask? Well, that's easy.

My story, however, is something else altogether. As a child, I forever dreamed with a dirty face and oily hands. I knew from an early age, wrenching alongside my grandfather under the hoods of his many fine automobiles and blue work vans, that I wanted to spend my days knee deep in horsepower tuning engines to perfection. His passion for excellence taught me the importance of handling heavy iron with delicate intentions. When my excitement to help him boiled over, sometimes spilling his tools all over the shop floor, he'd say, tugging on the shoulder strap of my denim overalls "Lori girl, sometimes slower is faster." This made no sense to me at the time, and he'd laugh himself silly watching me dive to the floor in a desperate attempt to clear my mess. But he was patient and let me find my place in his world of nuts and bolts. There amongst the soiled rags, some drenched in the sweet pungent smell of gasoline, almost begging me to take a deep breath, I was his equal. His one true partner. In those moments, he gave me the greatest gift of all: hope.

Our greasy connection didn't sit well with Grandma who all but broke down at the sight of me with black grime under my little fingernails. "Girls don't work on cars" she'd say, her wicked eyebrows scrunched together in an angry frown while I grinned from ear to ear, watching her unravel at the one true thing that made me happy. "Girls can too" I'd shout with fire in my eyes running to Grandpa heartbroken for reassurance. He was awe-inspiring. Exceptional. Polished. With a warm, welcoming smile that exuded a level of confidence foreign to most. I knew deep down grandma meant well, but nothing was going to keep me from messing with those cars. Nothing!

Sadly, she never gave up the fight until my hot little hands wrapped themselves around the steering wheel of my own hot rod some years later. At her expense no less. A brand new 1970 Chevy Nova painted bright lemon yellow. Talk about a dream come true. I cried for a week straight disbelieving something so beautiful was mine. But she was and I treated her like a queen, just the way Grandpa did with his favorite cars. Now I thought wheels of my own and the free rein of adulthood would make me happy. I mean, what teen doesn't? And before love arrived, I was happy, mostly, give or take. From seventeen to eighteen, life was Bliss, with a capital B. But then sleep became elusive - dare I say an estranged enemy. What should have been my most carefree years turned into a daily battle to keep my fair complexion and sunny approachable demeanor from turning stone cold.

Unlike my beautiful sister, I spent most of my romantic nights in those days staring into a shroud of blinding darkness, searching for a light at the end of the tunnel. See, when you're born a square peg in a round world, you can't help but question everything. Even when hair-raising backlash says you shouldn't. Of course, there were signs of the dangers that lay ahead, but the hopeless romantic in me couldn't help but fall for the love that dare not speak its name. Not once, mind you, but twice. Yet, the debate rages on and has since the dawn of time. I guess because we're all victims of reckless desire at some point and anyone who tells you differently is obviously lying through their teeth, because with the size of my silver spoon, I should never have felt neglected by my emotional needs. I know this must all sound petty and dramatic. But I pray the journey we're about to embark upon will change more than your mind.

Chapter 1

–

To this day I struggle to understand why death chose to share her message with a nobody like me. When I needed her most, she would vanish—a test; perhaps as the pain she muzzled deep inside me made existing impossible. Like timeless poetry, the faithfulness of her silent reverie shattered my past regrets and future fears with each tender prompt. But nothing flourished outside her empowered counsel. Nothing, that is, until one tired afternoon on a cluttered downtown street, when a barefoot face thick with matted hair and puzzled eyes screamed in passing along a warm sunny sidewalk "Time waits for no man." The old fool couldn't have been more wrong, as destiny is sometimes an inside job. "For some, the reverse is true," I chided, louder than the creak of a passing city bus reflecting in my mirrored sunglasses. His psychosis spun around, but it was too late for either of us to retreat. As I'd already slain the jaundiced street poet with his own words. Not bad for a chronic nail-biter from the shy side of town. Who knew being cute could be so ugly? The gloves were off. Seeds of knowledge planted at my weakest were now mighty, dark, and enlightened. For a moment, I wasn't vapid. I was unconquerable. Omnipotent. Death was me, and I her. It was the best and worst of times. Funny, because time, like stolen moments, doesn't exist. It's a formula measuring rotational distance used to chronicle one's life against a fickle universe. Clocks and watches are real, not time. However real or not, the precious time I refused to acknowledge marched forward unchecked, past my wayward soul underestimating forever's eternal price, leaving me to worry the immortal shadows of good love gone bad would never leave. And when the voices outside my head became too much to bear, death was there to heal my divided self. Her emotional intuition was staggering. Like light into light, only dark. Heaven-sent straight from hell. She was the key and I the lock. Looking back, I was so naïve—a failed honor student. Stubborn. Yet confident in the life death bestowed upon me. Only I feared whatever intimacy might toss across my happy gullible path.

I hate coming across this heavy so early on. But I have to be honest because my truth is all I have left. And nothing, and I mean nothing, is more important or beautiful than the truth. But I had opened Pandora's box running from mine and needed to close it before it was too late.

Chapter 2

—

Believe it or not, this is a true story. And it hit a desperate point shortly after turning twenty. I battled my demons hard back then, but I carried on as if I was the happiest person alive. I did so because I wanted to be the world's best friend.

Disguised as summer, mid-January 1974 caught me in pursuit of September birthday wishes dripping yellow wax onto Grandma's hand-whipped vanilla frosting. Unwrapped Christmas dreams, now a distant memory, wasted away in the regret of my forgotten New Year's resolutions while outside, sporadic holiday reminders twinkled across the southland on jolly rooflines throughout the day's night sky. I, for one, rather enjoyed the extended merriment most attributed to lazy dads unwilling to climb ladders in the timid afternoon sunshine. But not mine; his egotistical entitlement worked tirelessly to taunt neighbors he thought might call his manhood into question for being afraid of the sharp winter cold.

My sister said the festive abodes still adorned with garland and trees bright with comfort and joy belonged to devout Catholics who often display their decorations beyond January seventh, the day after Epiphany, celebrating the manifestation of the divine. She had married an East Coast

Catholic three years prior and came to love his church's centuries-old traditions. Unlike her husband, my sister's Mass attendance was sinful at best. I think, like me, she found the church's formal nature overwhelming to an antsy mind thirsting for a foundation rooted in peace.

Church attendance aside, the early seventies were rambunctious—America's melting pot stewed with demands for equality from coast to coast, fighting for justice in a corrupt and prejudiced system. There was an atmosphere of hatred across the country for anything progressive or different. This fear of diversity began years before with the assassinations of Martin Luther King Jr., and Senator Robert F. Kennedy.

The fusion of ideas and cultures responsible for shaping our nation endured spirited public debate meant to balance the power a select few held over the masses. These bloody clashes cost lives while survivors fought on, inhaling tear gas grenades fired in the name of law and order. Without this passionate revolt clobbering the streets, oppressive history would surely repeat itself. In Washington, DC, President Nixon faced impeachment while shell-shocked soldiers, recently home from the battlefields of Vietnam, returned to legal abortions and the occasional bra burning. Change was in the air, but it felt more out of reach than not. But politics never interested me. Nor did the government's discriminatory ways. All I ever wanted was a fair shot. Nothing preferential. But for each door that opened, two more would close. Talk about discouraging. In some countries, they still pummeled women to death with stones for independent thought. I got slapped and kicked. Other more so-called civilized people once preserved an adulterous woman's honor by burning her alive at the stake as a warning to others tempted by the same sinful desires. As you might imagine, I buried my combustible troubles deeper than hell itself.

When tension blew my way, you'd often find me fourteen miles due west of the claustrophobic bedroom where I'd dreamed of floating facedown between leaky walls until the wet swallowed me whole. Troubled people often crawl into a bottle when life gets tough, but not me; I ran to a parking lot guarded by rails and a flimsy chain-link fence. Why? The big city view, of course. Including the Coronado Bridge and the massive Navy aircraft carriers anchoring the bay. But if you were to ask me, the scalable eight-foot barrier securing the airport seemed a silly deterrent. While there, I'd stretch my teenage frame across the hood of my yellow Nova and lose myself in the sheen of blue taxiway lights, imagining faraway places free from everything I imagined.

My favorite spot sat directly behind the international runway, where jetliners rocket down its nine-thousand-foot center line every few minutes. I can't explain why, but life felt gentle, trapped beneath the crushing downforce of a three-hundred-ton DC-10 descending from the sky. The explosive shock waves created by these gravity-defying beasts still pound the air, where I hung my tears out to dry. Though I'd never spun a lap, I wanted to climb the twisted barbed wire and stow away to the race-crazy Carolina's red clay ovals, never to return. I saw a segment on them once watching the Daytona 500 on ABC. Plus, Grandpa was from the south, and everything about it felt like home. Being deathly afraid of heights stopped me in my tracks, but I found the liberating idea delicious. I visited this dreamers' cove so often, my sister would pretend to gag, complaining I reeked of oily kerosene. It was here on a stormy Monday evening where I found myself lost at the tail end of four regrettable days, being pelted by hostile arctic winds blowing upside down. I stood forsaken, anesthetized by pain, watching winged silhouettes disappear into a tangerine horizon three hours before coming face-to-face with the phone booth meant to save my life.

Once the last flight of snowbirds from Alaska's frigid tundra rolled onto the tarmac towards the terminal, I poured my questionable innocence into the driver's seat and backed away from the fence for a flight of my own. After a planned detour, a stifled sob accompanied me down Harbor Drive to Market Street, where I cut through a red arrow, dodging my perverse quest for love. Now in the city's heart, I aimlessly circled left, then right past dim alleys, and bleak corners ripe with failure. The tragic spaces revealed nothing new about the forgotten swaths of urban decay eyeballing my somber route through the echoes of wasted potential. I worried non-stop about becoming a vagrant. Forever bound to the gutters of these stubborn blocks, without friends or family to love.

Ridiculed by stale wine and squalor, these hardened streets weren't strangers, having passed their jaded whiskers and crooked smiles many times with little thought. But tonight, the butterflies were on my mind like never before. They cautioned that the weight of emptiness was upon me. So I pulled over to confess my unspeakable crimes. Crimes so vile, I shudder to think. I needed help. Yet forty-five tearful minutes dragged on before I summoned the courage to dig through my scatterbrained purse for the ten-cent premium standing between me and survival. A lifetime of misplaced emotions drove me to this random phone booth on Logan Avenue in Chicano Park, where history and Mexican pride color the walls. I didn't need eyes to see trouble had found me. Malevolent spirits I adored walked me backward with each forward step I took. They left me tucked away in plain sight. And stranded amongst the living with nothing but my shame to lean upon. I had unknowingly come to fear my shadow and what it represented. Illegally parked at the end of my rope, I curled myself into a shivering ball on the front seat of my Nova and prayed for enough nerve to dial the saint willing to call this sinner home. The longer I stalled, the deeper death's chilling warmth reached inside. She had come back for me. But why? This spiral into death's murky web of lies quietly sunk me for over a decade, leaving my quintessence littered with deceit. Like so many of you, my circumstance and happenstance struggled to coexist. Such an existential existence often lacks the courage to hope, to love, or survive. In middle school, this wrecking ball of confusion was little more than a slight irritation. Fast forward to age twenty. Thoughts of self-destruction sustained the assault battering my brittle self-esteem. This left me saddled with feelings of inadequacy and vulnerable. Being different made it easier to make enemies than friends, so lying about my truth became the standard. And I would have shed years of life for a sliver of acceptance. Society preaches each life matters.

This same society labeled me a mistake, a pariah. I find it ironic my so-called immorality affected others so horribly; they sinned themselves to declare me damned. Regardless, I believe we are all equal in God's eyes. Our color, or who we choose to love, makes us unique, not flawed. I know to some God is a sticky subject fraught with danger, but I regret not trusting in the mystery of faith. A bold statement, considering I introduced myself by sharing bedtime stories with the grim reaper. So whatever God you do or don't pray to is okay with me, so long as we can agree that love-inspired unity is the soul's nurturing essence. For without love, we are blind to the blessings of our purpose. From the melting snow cascading down a fresh mountain stream to an unkind gesture from a disheveled stranger, every facet of life carries a meaningful purpose.

But I know change and acceptance aren't always easy for in my post-pubescent days, when I was searching for my voice I too learned the challenges of living one's purpose, one's undeniable truth. For years it was one day at a time, until my desperate unhappiness exploded and punched back, stunning the knuckled innuendos used to control me. My blows never drew blood, but my double-fisted heart swung hard, fast, and true.

Chapter 3

–

While uncomfortable to discuss, intentional surrender often comes when life's bent, not broken. The easy way out is never easy, and it guarantees unforeseen consequences for those left behind. Trust me: a troubled life is a worthy gamble more precious than the pain we sometimes covet. I hate to think about it, but who here amongst us hasn't flirted with surrendering to momentary madness? Because whether life's blessings have paved your driveway with gold or dusty gravel, no one, including your strongest, most grounded friends and family, is immune to the suffocating hopelessness brought about by racism, bullying, relationship or financial ruin. You can look away, pretend not to hear my voice, but I trust everyone has considered giving up once for the pain-free glory thought to exist on the other side of an unhappy life.

As for me, I'll never forget the night God first sent his shepherds to intercept my fall from grace. Eyes heavy, I drove east through the smell of juniper-fired heat, warming the cold cross streets of Campo Road when the reality of midnight's unfulfilled promises stirred. This quaint patch of suburbia dubbed Casa de Oro and its famous yellow-orange striped Taco Barrel served up the best taquitos north of the Mexican border. A favorite lunchtime hotspot, this revered eatery sold deep-fried delicacies priced five for a buck that crunched a cheesy spice no other rolled tacos could match. Unable to feed my grieving appetite, I awaited a miracle in the new morning darkness of Friday, January 18, watching the reliable black hands of my silver wristwatch sneak past the witching hour. The impeccable timepiece had kept my late grandfather running ahead of schedule, chugging across the country in a steam locomotive whistling clouds of mechanical energy thick enough to chew from an elaborate funnel-shaped smokestack, wearing his gray and white striped conductor overalls. A far cry from today's electrified bullet trains run by college-educated engineers in military-style uniforms. Colon cancer took my grandfather's life in May 1970. After years of faithful service, his watch's metal band hung loose, so I wore it up my left forearm to keep it taut. By then, extreme pressure to please everyone but myself had me on the road hunting for clarity in a life hammered by toxic ridicule. I ran my gas tank dry twice in as many days, chasing cloudy stars from the beach to the rocky slopes of Devil's Canyon, searching for answers without questions. What started as a quest for the ultimate banana milkshake somehow evolved into a walkabout on wheels seeking the path of enlightenment. But boy, does a plugged straw complicate matters when life cuts both ways. Yet anyone who saw me would never have thought to question my happiness. I excelled at hiding from the truth with an innocent smile that told you exactly what I wanted you to hear.

The problem was I didn't refuse to be confused. Even the trio I rode with consisting of me, myself and I, couldn't help but roll their eyes. Misery had become lousy company.

Something had to give. But I didn't recognize that the power of change rested solely in my capable hands, steering the Detroit muscle growling under my yellow hood. Was my ignorance bliss? Did I secretly enjoy my naysayer's tyrannical enslavement? Whatever the reason, me, myself, and I grew tired of nursing a busted-up heart. I desperately want to tell you I was a victim, and I probably will more than once, but the truth is I played the starring role in my martyrdom. Who am I kidding? I was more than the star. I was the whole damn cast. But in my defense, there were factors out of my control—or so I thought.

Before I continue, let's talk about burning one's candle at both ends. To this, all I can say is my romantic purgatory rained infernal terror over everyone who cared for me. I always believed love is the answer but couldn't acknowledge to which side of the aisle my preference belonged. I share these ugly truths because I, more than anyone, know the danger in turning out the lights. Maybe, like me, you too lie awake at night, afraid to face the reality that dwells where the lies live. With any luck, I thought, this latest gas-guzzling introspection would end my lonely nights when I snuggled up to death's comfortable reassurance. Ten hopeful miles later, nerves afire, I signaled right from La Puerta and eased onto Costada Court, a working-class cul-de-sac in Lemon Grove. Four houses down from the corner, parked outside the tan, single-story rambler with the red brick chimney, was my dear ex-husband's sexy black pickup truck. A flared short box Ford custom. It was larger than life. But so too was my bearded tall drink of water. All six feet of him. Everyone called his scruffy brother Bigfoot, but Ronnie isn't a giant like Jimmy.

He's slender, casual, and well-groomed with an easy-going disposition and a calm, soothing voice. Seeing his truck for the first time in months, a wave of emotions washed over me, and I cried an hour's worth of tears in seconds. "It's not too late," I said. "He'll forgive you; he always does." Though not fond of labels, I admit to being the tortured lesbian who duped this honorable Navy man into holy matrimony for eight impossible months. Next to my sister, Ronnie was my best friend and has always held space for me. After cutting the lights, I circled his silent dead-end with the radio off, hoping he would sense my despair and rescue me from myself. While still lucid, I had little doubt his goofy smile would have altered the night's course. Then again, maybe not. He'd smiled upon my freckled rust before, and I walked away. He was more victim than a husband and our demise belonged to me. My Ronnie deserved a love I could never afford.

Doubting myself and ashamed, I sped off, fleeing the site of our nuptials, climbing Massachusetts Avenue in a face-tugging hurry to my sister's apartment in La Mesa. But instead of continuing past Broadway to her, I jerked the steering wheel hard left with both hands and screeched sideways towards reflective-green destination signs reading: FREEWAY ENTRANCE, CALIFORNIA 94 WEST. As I drove beyond the limits of the car, tires, and gravity, I slid across the seat, hanging on for dear life. At first, I drifted wide before breaking traction and nearly spinning around. Once through the empty intersection, I swapped side to side, almost tipping at one point, fighting the wheel for control. With the on-ramp fast approaching, I somehow stabilized before senselessly crashing my brains out. Next time I might not be so lucky.

With the danger safely behind me in the darkness, I exhaled my relief and shifted into third, merging behind a checkered cab carrying a drunken sailor dressed in white.

And when I say drunk, picture a sloshed face with a cadaverous stare smashed against the left back-seat window smudged with layers of old grimy fingerprints. I feel bad about it now, but I had a merry laugh at this poor fellow's expense. I mean, he looked awful; so bad, even my blurry eyes could see his unconscious drool fogging the glass. It appeared he would have some explaining to do in the morning. Nine miles ahead, an inhospitable postcard paradise awaited us. Above, where the freeway transitions into narrow city streets, the soaring skyscrapers disappeared into menacing, low-hung clouds. Eager to test my metal against the storm, I began pushing my Chevy Nova for all she was worth against a Boeing 727 thundering overhead on final approach to Lindbergh Field and the corner lot that knew all my secrets. The sleek blades of its three turbine engines whined at the speed of sound as she stretched her silver wings in a fog of jet exhaust laid across my path to defeat.

I am sorry to report that United Airlines bested me in a matchup rivaling David and Goliath. Neither planes nor my beloved hot-rod seemed able to deliver the nirvana I read about in the leatherbound Bible Grandma had kept stored in her wooden nightstand beside a green bottle of medicinal Irish whiskey.

As suburbia drew closer to coastal dreams, salty ocean air blanketed the cityscapes, glistening urban appeal like nourishing spring rain. But nothing out of the ordinary for a winter's night in sunny San Diego, California. Outsiders think we slather ourselves with coconut suntan oil every day, but that's not true. We also endure Mother Nature's moody seasons, when she blocks our fresh-squeezed sunshine with soggy cold funk. But who am I to complain? It's not like I had to shovel out my car after a blizzard or worry about driving on black ice. What even is black ice, anyway?

Downtown, brick and mortar now surrounded me, a far cry from the lazy palms and mission-style churches roaming the chaparral covered hills of East County. As I continued my pilgrimage to nowhere, capeless vampires, some without teeth, appeared drifting about in silence as if tomorrow had already passed them by. Thankful for the company, the slap of their shoes jaywalking in front of me, now louder than the whir of passing cars. Highway 94 had given way to F Street, near a gutsy corridor littered with high-heeled streetwalkers and greasy spoons serving up tasty conversation against a hushed backdrop of moonlit graphite. It was breezy, and I could taste the smell of warm sewer flooding my open window. Wasted after days of pretending to matter, I welcomed the gruesome air, keeping my slow prowl awake.

Chapter 4

—

I once heard that depression is the great equalizer because we've all suffered its wrath. The preacher also said that the lowest could rise above the highest if only they'd submit to God's will. These words spoken by a man of the cloth championed divide and conquer and completely turned me off. Not the throaty growl of my tuned race exhaust though. Those cherry bombs sounded recklessly divine, even at a dead stop. Lighting my journey to nowhere this night were vintage gas lamps giving life to the vacant passages towards Harbor Drive and its piers reaching into the Pacific Ocean. Their antique patina painted the sluggish overcast with a spooky golden hue. I wondered if heaven had a glow and if death was a black hole consuming our dreams while we slept. As usual, my mind brimmed with curiosity. Too tired to debate another narcissistic circle jerk with my current ex, I yawned and sang over dear Elton's piano, motoring past storefront windows splashed with vibrant, whimsically designed advertisements showcasing the latest and greatest, most fantastic deals. Though we never met, there was something awfully familiar about the Rocket Man filling my empty heart with joy.

One sign in particular stood out above them all. To my left was the facade of a rusty brick building—the City Rescue

Mission. On the second story, next to the black fire escape stairs looking down on Gene's Card Room below, was a six-foot white cross with Jesus Saves illuminated in red. Just what I needed: another reminder of my wicked ways. For once, couldn't well enough leave me alone to fend for myself? The fabled icon hung directly over the cement rectangles of sidewalks, facing two lanes of one-way traffic. A short must have caused the neon message of salvation to malfunction because I could hear it buzz every time it flickered.

A hundred yards beyond the color-blind sanctuary, past a row of expired parking meters, rose a competing cue from the bowels of the city's inhumanity. Unamused by those cowering behind false pretenses, demonic steam began hissing at me from a manhole cover, offering visions of Hades. Panic-stricken behind the wheel, my once-relaxed ten and two choked the blood flow to my ashen fingertips. I wanted to stop and run inside for help but feared no one cared to answer my cries. Little did I know my fate was about to be sealed at 529 Fifth Avenue. Seconds later, a glance in the rearview mirror startled me. I looked away, but it was too late. My blank stare spoke volumes. The hollow eyes staring back at me were flat, like buttons on a doll's face—no depth or perception. If the eyes were the windows to the soul, I was doomed. At this point, the luxury of hiding from my benefactors was no longer a choice. Nor was finding happiness where I lost it. Suddenly my throat tightened as the first drop rolled down my pale cheek to the mud-brown corduroy hugging my thighs. After years trapped behind my defenses, the floodgates burst open, freeing me from the responsibility of shielding others from the truth.

I refused to continue denying the inevitable. Never

again would life's discriminating power brokers control me. Triggered, I floored the accelerator, unleashing 155 restless horsepower through sullied intersections staffed with the nocturnal. My Chevy's excitable speedometer needle rose with purpose towards a labyrinth of helpless red lights as my yellow reflection raced by in slow motion. Denied "liberty and the pursuit of happiness," I rumbled east on J Street, past office buildings devoid of life, running from deafening-silence screaming '*Faster, whore, faster!*' In a way that defies logic, the depraved superpower pumping through my veins ensured I'd never know hurt again.

Unfazed by the bridge's dreadful reputation as a killer, I continued to accelerate, speeding faster and faster. I'd fantasized about this moment for months. A harbor cruise two weeks earlier with my sister and her three-year-old son had confirmed its drop-dead gorgeous potential. Tunnel vision now blocked the unsuspecting world around me, focusing my aggression on the black sky rushing the windshield.

The closer I got to the bridges peak, the more my despondent heart pounded with determined anticipation. Showtime! I speed-shifted from fourth to first, mashed the brake pedal into the rubber floor mat and screeched to a sudden stop. A violent force shook the steering wheel. My lungs slammed into my chest, knocking the wind out of me. I wheezed and gasped for air. A surge of orgasmic adrenaline unhinged the door, freeing me from my grandmother's token gift. Without hesitating, I launched from the sterile black interior, more determined than ever. The bite of winter stung my face first—a stark contrast to the heated cockpit that carried me to the point of no return. My quick feet floated with each stride. The edge was near. Thirty-four vertical inches were all that remained between me and the freedom I sought—one last step to the rest of my life.

246 FEET LEFT TO LIVE!

A recent dream saw me falling from cups and saucers stacked a mile high. I awoke happily and well-rested. This leap of faith was not my wobbly cups and saucers—

IMPACT!

Something was wrong. She promised I would grow wings and fly. Instead, razor-sharp claws tore at my raw flesh. Hot breath covered my face in hate. The beast poked and prodded, tossing me left to right. With each gulp of boiling air, blood-curdling screams emanated from my lifeless lungs. Romantic dreams of emancipation now a nightmarish smokey pit lined with embers of jagged retribution. To save myself, I kicked at the tentacles binding my legs, but it was no use. My worst fears had come true. The mortal judgment I died to avoid now tortured me in the afterlife. Death had betrayed me. Where was the peace my fallen angel promised? The sentimental liar, tender and majestic, laughed as I cried out, asking the heavens if this was hell.

"You're not in hell! Stop fighting, dammit!" These were the last words I heard before the world went dark. The stern voice demanding compliance was right; I wasn't dead. A hellhound wasn't mauling my charred remains—no raging flames, only high beams. Instead of letting me execute my best-laid plans, an alert California Highway Patrol officer lying in wait for speeders spotted my desperation and gave chase until he tackled my suicidal sprint across the Coronado Bay Bridge's summit. Time: 12:35 a.m. Once again, I had failed. Even at killing myself.

As life rebounded, I could feel the antiseptic snarl of mouthwash-flavored breath ruffle my shoulder-length auburn hair. Flat on my stomach, my impacted anatomy begged for release. The louder I screamed, the deeper his chrome utility buckle dug into my supple, fleshy hip. This was combat, primitive and barbaric. I tried to crawl away, bucking the officer wildly. He fought back, matching my pint-sized aggressions move for move. "Give me your hand, goddammit! Do it now!" In a last-ditch effort to escape, I let out a battle cry and thrust myself upwards into him right as he swept my arm out from underneath me, face-planting me for a second time. All while wounded pride reminded me that suffering is not for the weak.

My captor must have felt me surrender, because his bone-crushing chokehold relaxed the moment I yielded for air. Like ashes in the wind, we lay breathless between the profane and divine, entangled in suicidal chaos. The weight of his concern became a refuge from the destructive pleasure trapped in my mind. However, death was not pleased. But she would be back, I was sure of it. The bridge she used to tempt me was no longer a proud landmark. We had taken the heroic stranger to his edge. The exhausted disbelief blowing from his belly to my ear told me so.

Within minutes of hitting the asphalt deck, the anxious tread of radial tires skidded to a stop a few feet from our heads. Backup had arrived, and they came packing an attitude. The wild card responsible for grounding my flight had radioed a panicked "*Failure to yield, Failure to yield,*" to dispatch as he raced to catch me. I was the young officer's first, but unfortunately, not his last.

In my euphoric state of mania-fueled rage, I missed the flashing red-and-blue emergency lights atop his black-and-white cruiser chasing me up the bridge. Death had blinded me. I wouldn't have noticed an angry rattlesnake coiled on my lap, let alone a pursuing highway patrol officer. What sounded like a herd of wild mustangs was gung-ho footsteps. One after another, polished military-grade boots wearing royal blue ties stomped through the stench of hot angry rubber to aid the arresting officer holding me down. Heavy hands from all directions piled on top of us, grabbing at everything in sight. Dictating their moves was a cadence of grunts and groans commanding one another to "Get her ass up." My knees buckled, as I stood to face their judgment. The officer's choreographed brutality was useless against the numb, safeguarding me from their practiced aggression. What I saw upon opening my eyes disgusted me.

Life, the one I'd tried to annihilate, now mocked my downfall with a horrific display of disorienting lights sworn to serve and protect. I was the belle of the ball where no one and everyone wanted to dance. My wrists awaited the pinch of cold steel. I'd seen criminals handcuffed a million times on television. But something else happened. Instead of the expected ratchet clicks, an officer behind me draped his seasoned leather jacket over my slumped shoulders. Its forgiving black mass offered my hysteria a warm embrace. They were protecting, not arresting me. Amid the aftermath, the night's MVP babbled, speaking in tongues to arriving colleagues who worried there might have been a second jumper. It was all he could do to shake his head and point in my direction. Then, in the shadows of the waterfront's luminous skyline that stretches beyond view, he gently waved for me to come closer. With my first step came a heaving hurl, and the sour scent of last night's chili dog puked across two lanes of the heavily trafficked road.

"Whoa!" he shouted, leaping sideways to avoid a direct hit. "We got a bleeder." A classic alpha male, he snapped back into character without missing a beat. "Here," he said, speaking softer than before. "Let me help you." I pushed back, almost shoving him. "Don't worry, ma'am, it's clean." But I didn't care. The look of confusion he flashed confirmed death was right. I was the dumpster fire who shows up for a first date spewing plumes of emotional baggage. Suicidal manifestations aside, I promise that to know me is to love me. At least that's what I told myself whenever doubt squeezed the bile from my bubbly disposition. Rendered useless by fate, I still coveted freedom from small-minded people but surmised the khaki-clad crusaders swarming the bridge would die living their oath. The burden of their calling felt disheartening, which is why I ultimately accepted the officer's crisp, neatly folded hanky to dry my tears.

But what I needed more than a snot rag was an exorcist, or maybe a fortune teller, to yank the curse out of my temple of skin and bones. My God was absent. Had I run him off too? Being open to positive energy felt pointless, although a slice of cheese pizza dripping in grease sounded heavenly.

Chapter 5

—

A growing crowd of khaki uniforms wearing bushy mustaches and sideburns pleaded for me not to cry. The whine of an approaching siren ricocheted between us and the heavy metal clogging the bridge. "Ma'am, what's your name? We need your name." My stupor persisted, screaming "NO" at the flashlights shoved in my face. Chaos was in control. You couldn't see the city's brilliance for all the noise. Then, a powerful voice in the distance hollered, "Lori! Her name is Lori Elizabeth Vogt!" A backup officer had run a check on my license plate and exposed me. Hearing my grandfather's proud name broadcast with such authority haunts me to this very day. In all the commotion I faded away, when suddenly my hero grabbed hold of my arm and stretched forward to peek over the waist-high wall at the open sky below. "Holy fuck!" His honesty was frightening. Inhuman comes to mind. He looked as though he could weep. I did, but not loud enough to drown my sorrows. "Lori is it?" he asked. "I didn't hurt you, did I?" He was the first black police officer to know my name. After handing me off to a fellow highway patrolman, his sturdy mocha frame circled my paranoia. Slow at first, then faster. Each step louder than the next. His cropped afro led the way headfirst. Over and over, he clapped his hands together in rapid-fire succession. I could see his mind was struggling to untangle itself. Shaken, he continued to pace the expanse beneath us, trying to stabilize the mayhem of my depression. Finally, after several figure eights, he halted his frantic analysis long enough for me to read "Johnson" etched on the golden nameplate opposite his shiny badge. "*Wooooo!*" he shouted with a mighty voice, looking both hypnotized and astonished by the moon's phantasmal glow radiating through the clouds above us. "We almost took the long ride down, baby, but there was no way I was letting you go." He meant it. There was a foreign sincerity in his mind-bending, honey-dipped eyes.

Officer Johnson's passionate character spoke of understanding. How could I deny a person willing to surrender their heartbeat for mine? Especially one with a baby face. Like me, he bled and felt pain. But hate was never in my nature. So I collapsed into his powerful arms and begged him to release me. But before I could fall to my knees, he grabbed hold of my dead weight and grunted out with all his might. "All in a day's work, ma'am." I didn't believe him. I knew our collision would plague him forever. "What's going on tonight?" he asked, holding my imbalance steady. My sloppy butterscotch eyes pleaded for mercy. In defiance of the sadness driving my anger, I lifted my buried chin and yelled in his face, "*Everyone hates me!*" Trained for just such a moment, he doubled down, pressuring me the way cops do. "C'mon, now how can anyone hate a nice girl like you?" Was this some kind of joke to him? Desperate to be heard, I looked upon him darkly and blasted his good nature. "Because I'm a piece of shit, that's why."

He couldn't see me, but I could see him. I saw his color and the struggle it represented. His crisp features softened staring into my eyes. I wanted to trust his camouflaged scars and expose my frightened inner child, but feared doing so would yield another emotional gut punch. So to protect myself, I lashed out. "Have you ever tried loving a philanderer? If not, you should try one on for size. We're a real treat; just ask my father."

"Wait, isn't a philanderer a man?" he asked, dumbfounded, with wide, surprised eyes.

"You're just like them," I stammered, between gasping quivers, struggling to stay afloat.

Calmly, he disagreed. "Miss Lori, I don't care how funky you and yours get behind closed doors. Besides, I hate everyone equally," he smirked, smiling just enough for his boyish charm to say *Gotcha*.

"Well, would you love your daughter if she were a dyke?"

His childlike eyes widened.

"Without a doubt. I'm my daddy's son ya know, and family's family."

It was clear Officer Johnson's parents had raised him with humility and respect. His uplifting response left me uneasy because it's near impossible to trust what you don't understand. I'd not spent much time around Black people before, but his reverence destroyed all the stereotypes I had learned as a kid. Concerned for my privacy, he seated me in the front of his patrol car next to a locked shotgun bolted to the dash. The idea of an explosive ending never crossed my mind. The end result seems crueler than the act itself. I remember sitting there, oblivious to the trouble I'd caused when a plump seagull landed on the wall next to the car, searching for a handout. A tad hungry myself, I poked around under the passenger seat of the immaculate interior for a breadcrumb or stale chip to toss the hungry beggar, but no such luck.

"Hey, who's your friend?" asked Officer Johnson, slamming the driver's door shut behind him. "Brrr," he said, rubbing his hands together. "How about we crank the heat?" Not interested in mindless chitchat, I ignored him and watched the girthy gull fly away towards greener, more nutritious cement pastures downtown. With escape on my mind, I scanned the suicidal carnage for an opening when I noticed my lemon-yellow hot-rod glaring at me through the windshield. Wedged between CHP black and concrete gray, she sat eerily silent, with my keys on the roof. She felt distant, like a heartbroken stranger. "Sorry about that," said Officer Johnson, leafing through a stack of legal forms under the light of a flexible mini lamp snaking from behind the shotgun. In his haste to reach me before liftoff, he'd forgotten to shift his speeding cruiser into park. As our deadly foot chase ensued, it had rolled into my baby and pushed her into the crash barrier, running alongside the outer lanes, securing the bridge's edge.

"You're a crappy driver for a cop," I said, wobbling between resentment and half-hearted gratitude for saving my life. "You already owe me for scuffed pants, so don't push your luck," he said. "Besides, the great state of California equipped my trusty battlewagon here with a padded push bumper to avoid damaging anything needing a shove." Sincere in his approach. I begrudgingly looked ahead at the miracle before me, unwilling to force even a tearful smile. Nothing had changed; I still sorta wanted to die.

It felt unfair to stonewall such a genuine person. I didn't see the good Negro versus the bad Negro other people brooded about when talking about the "coloreds." No, I only saw kindness and substance. That anyone could see him any other way floored me. I appreciated Officer Johnson's sense of duty, although it wasn't enough to compensate for the unconscionable pain fueling my heart. Without warning, the police radio crackled, broadcasting an update to my failed suicide across the graveyard-shift airways. Reeling from the dispatcher's amplified breach of peace, I mumbled through my tears, with both hands covering my face, "No more. I can't take anymore. Please make her stop." Maybe two or three years older than me, Officer Johnson was helpless to stop the electronic ambush disturbing our moment. It was his work after all.

"Hey now," he said, half lowering the volume. "We're all here because we care, even the dispatcher. And if the ambulance isn't here soon, I'll take you to the hospital myself."

There was no going to the ER; the doctors would call my father. Melvin. A fiery death from the inside out was a better choice than a visit by him. His brand of parenting didn't welcome "niggers, spics, or queers." He was the kind of mean that could scare a serial killer into confessing. His broad shoulders walked ten paces behind his hateful nature whenever he entered a room. The naked lady and dagger tattoos on his bulky arms only made him more intimidating.

"No ambulances or doctors, they'll electrocute me!" I shouted.

"They'll what?"

Didn't he know doctors cured people like me with a hefty electric shock? Well, that and deadly treatments like insulin coma therapy. Isn't that what diabetics try to avoid if they want to live? You know, because of its fatal consequences?

"Lady," he said, "I don't know who told you what, but no one is going to electrocute you. Now relax and go along with the program, or I'll cuff you and stick you in the back."

What the baby-faced officer failed to appreciate was that Melvin, my sympathetic father, would finish what I had started, only worse.

My face flush with desperation, I called his bluff. "Just please don't call my dad. He'll kill us both."

Unimpressed, he leaned in closer, eyes narrowed.

"Better tell papa to pack a lunch."

I recoiled from his guttural tone. My breathing became squeamish, then ragged, as his harsh response slithered around my neck, suffocating my belief in the kindness of strangers.

Below us lurked the black abyss, gently rocking back and forth, awaiting its next victim. Officer Johnson made a crucial mistake, seating me next to the edge with nothing but a door and lane of travel between me and the intensity of my lethal mindset. Sweat from my racing pulse popped. Calculating the prospects of success against an army of police, pondering a heroic end to the night's festivities. Four strides, I thought, my mind already screaming at terminal velocity.

Battle-hardened officers standing in packs outside the idling cruiser replayed the night's events in dramatic fashion. Among them was a statue of a man about six feet tall with a square jaw who spoke more with his hands than his mouth. He was the boss and the only one not wearing a jacket. He was easy on the eyes, yet hard to look at, but I couldn't help myself. Some of his men chain-smoked cigarettes while others gabbed about me, almost "killing the kid." I found it funny the other officers called my savior a kid. Was I really so bad off they sent a kid to rescue me? Watching them act out my despair in view of a shiny red fire engine was surreal. Over and over, their flailing arms highlighted my demise. Using their peripheral vision, they peered at me in search of the monster behind my blubbering, suicidal eyes. Were they thinking of their wives or daughters, or had my presence spoken to the voices in their own heads? Either way, I felt their hearts break for me.

If only I had continued past Broadway to my sister's place, or snuck around and tapped on Ronnie's back bedroom window. What would they think if they could see me in police custody? And why had death instead of life spoken to me? I was neither controversial nor sinister, so what made me unique in the eyes of the underbelly of the universe? The reality of my actions had yet to sink in. I was neither dead nor alive. No longer was I the most positive person I knew—all I ever wanted was love; but the only suitable affection I found wore halos in hell. Where did I go from here—damaged goods forever scarred with the mark of the beast?

Chapter 6

—

A strange sense of relief unsettled me as a new danger emerged. "Yo, TJ, get her outta here before da Action News gets hold of this." My heart sank. Action News? What Action News? Surely he wasn't serious. Alone in my panic, I listened to Officer Johnson repeat his sergeant's orders to dispatch, careful to enunciate each word into the handheld microphone. He held a special trust in this man of few words giving him directions. This pleased me. To celebrate, my nervous feet tap-danced against the floorboard, knowing I was at least safe from the hospital.

"All set?"

I feared my safe passage home was about to be impounded by the man with the iron jaw.

"Wait, what about my car?"

My armed chauffeur widened his smile.

"Not to worry; the Godfather will have her run down before he clears."

The Godfather? His answer felt loose. I needed more.

"He won't tow her, will he?"

His response besieged what little remained of me.

"If you had died, yeah." Ninety seconds later, he spoke again. "Seven David, 10-97 Coronado with one, mileage 01.2."

"10-4 Seven David, time, 1:06 a.m."

The dispatcher sounded metallic, robotic, almost antiquated. With keys in hand, Officer Johnson stepped out into the tingle of fresh eucalyptus. His movements seemed deliberate, with life-preserving intent. Lacking cop-car etiquette, I sat catatonic and awaited instruction face-to-face with the killer bridge rising into the broken sky over America's finest city.

Beside me, the futuristically styled toll plaza housing the Highway Patrol substation resembled a white Frisbee atop a shoebox. Its windows were framed in the same baby blue as my dad's pick-up truck, to match the thirty bridge girders connecting mainland San Diego to the island. Back and to the left, Old Glory stood guard at the rear of the building. Her vibrant beauty gave purpose to the intergalactic structure lined with cold concrete sidewalks and flower beds flaunting manicured shrubs and cheerful flowers. The thoughtful landscaping was a colorful surprise in the officers' black-and-white world of policies and procedures.

Beyond the glass entrance door marked Highway Patrol in block letters was a makeshift lobby. The burnt-caramel scowl of day-old coffee and a brass ashtray scarred by a thousand discarded memories decorated the cramped space. Awkward silence swung with Officer Johnson's scuffed wooden nightstick, pacing our rhythmic steps down a nondescript hallway dressed in chronic underfunding. Overhead, a soft fluorescent glow hummed like Mrs. Lange's sixth-grade homeroom class at Dale Elementary. "Ladies first," Officer Johnson said, escorting me into Room One as he flicked on the lights, which immediately drew me to the dried blood wrapped around the knuckles on his right hand. I'd hurt him. Swollen and raw, those injured knuckles directed me towards a broken chair held together with mounds of silver duct tape. I didn't know how to feel at that moment. Seeing a tattered California penal code next to an awaiting typewriter alongside a basket of blank arrest reports certainly didn't help matters.

I took a seat as instructed near an oversized wall clock that hung above the door beside a loudspeaker squawking cryptic police-radio code into the tense air. The clock's red hand ticked past 1:10 a.m. and continued without stopping. Watching the future arrive was the first definitive sign; I wasn't dead. What happens next? Was I going to jail?

Would they force a confession from me playing good cop, bad cop, or was my release inevitable? The mystery surrounding the immediate future was killing me. Most concerning were the whereabouts of the roving Action News team in search of a story to die for. As I sat, insides churning, the organized clutter of Room One went from still to turbulent as chatty officers from the bridge with nicknames like "Pork Chop" and "Dorf" trickled in.

Their interest in me conflicted with everything I thought I knew about cops. The inquisitive peacekeepers asked about my yellow Nova, work, and if I had anyone special at home. They presented themselves as average guys just doing their job—nothing more, nothing less. But there was something else—something cautious and mysterious, but also familiar.

These diehard cops and I shared a secret. It turns out we all lived opposing public and private lives, concealed but visible to more than the naked eye. Sharing either with the wrong person could prove fatal, so we disguised our true selves as a survival tactic, simply to get by. To say this unprecedented discovery shocked me would be a colossal understatement. This was the part of the job they hated. Being caught out of uniform with their families or alone made them vulnerable to anyone wishing them harm for enforcing the law. Like me, they were wary of everyone who crossed their paths. And I'll tell you, nothing hurts more than mistrusting everyone you meet. Especially when they come with good intentions.

To better understand myself, I welcomed the hospitable fathers, sons, and brothers struggling to reach me. By embracing our like-minded differences, the commonalities between us dismantled the authority and mistrust crowding Room One. Like Grandpa said, "Keep your friends close, and your enemies closer." After about ten minutes chit chatting, sweet, smokey nostalgia began filling the air with chivalrous sophistication.

The warm tobacco notes awoke memories of Uncle Buddy in Idyllwild. Our fireside ghost stories birthed many sleepless nights in the brisk mountain air. One difference: Sergeant Zafuto's smile-transforming dimples chewed his cigar on the left side of his mouth, unlike Uncle Buddy, who preferred the right. A thousand Lori's must have been responsible for wrecking his handsome bloodshot eyes. "Call me Sergeant Joe," he said with a wink. Tough as the Brooklyn streets that raised him and never one to take a backward step, he was the man-child who matured but never grew up. A diamond pinky ring and slick black hair with wisps of gray said gentleman while his demeanor screamed cops and robbers.

"Is there someone you'd like ta call? Maybe a friend or family member?" he asked, leaning against a dark-brown doorjamb—metal, not wood.

"I don't have any friends."

Bewildered, he looked at me quizzically as he counted off the four other souls in the room. "Well, ya do now," he insisted, folding his muscle-bound arms across his chest.

I wanted to jump out of my chair and hug him but held back, fearful I might come across as needy. "Jesus," he murmured, shaking his head. "I look at you and see my caboose, Bella. She's my youngest of three, and even she knows death is not da answer ta life." While he spoke, I zeroed in on the charged veins bulging from beneath his short khaki sleeves emblazoned with matching blue-and-gold highway patrol patches.

"Lori my friend, nothing is worth dying over, especially some jerk-off friends or family. Look . . ." he said, rubbing his tired bloodshot brown eyes. "I know you're hurting, but we've all seen da closure jumpin' brings, and I do not want ta see da body snatchers draggin you outta da drink soaking limp.

"Not a pretty picture my dear. Never come back because da bridge you put your faith in is a goddamn liar. You see badge 4240 here? It reads sergeant, not headshrinker," he continued, pointing to the gold seven-point star pinned to his chiseled chest. "Listen," he said, commanding, not demanding, my attention. "Ya can't let a few rough years from da past kill da future. I survived two tours in Nam and an onslaught of drunk punches from an alcoholic faddah, which makes me twice as likely ta stumble. But I keep going, and so can you. Capeesh?" Sergeant Joe, moved by his own apocalypse, didn't realize his story ended where mine began. Completely preoccupied, I digested the heartfelt expression, both deep and humble, with one eye open.

After his sermon preaching intestinal fortitude, the good sergeant made me promise to seek help and avoid the booze, dope, and hippies pushing their flower power.

"Remember kiddo: da wacky tobacky will make ya stupid," he said, thumping the side of his forehead. "As for being a lady philanderer, don't sweat it. For Chrissakes, it's 1974, not da stone age. Besides, Dandy Randy, with da buzz cut, behind you, is queer, and everybody loves him." His last syllable hadn't yet breathed when an eruption of unbridled belly laughter shattered the uncertainty bubbling at the room's surface. My stiff face cracked, joking alongside these dry-cleaned warriors. For a fleeting moment, I felt respected, a welcome part of their secret world. Officer Randy Walker wasn't queer, but I understood the message woven into the welcome slapstick humor. While elated, even if temporarily, I didn't want to overstate the obvious, so I kept my cool as best I could. I felt so damn alive, but also defensive, scared, confused, angry, sad, hurt, disgusted, and the happiest I had ever been. The good Lord had spared me from death's hand, but why? He obviously had a plan for me, but what? I had one too.

"Alright, knock it off." Signaling the fun and games were over, The Godfather, as Sergeant Joe's men called him, slapped his knee and rose to his feet before placing a multiline phone on the table in front of me. Though I'd never agreed to call anyone, I knew to refuse his obvious conditions was futile. There was someone I could call. My big sister Karen would never deny me anything. When life kicked me into the dirt, she was there to dust me off. No questions asked.

I can make it past five cops and two doors, I thought, counting my earlier steps in reverse. But instead, I pinched the receiver's dial tone between my stage fright and bruised ego to prepare for the toughest call of my life. The red hold button below the dial yelled *stop!* How was I going to tell my best friend that her undying devotion wasn't enough reason to live? What do I say? *Hey Sis, I was going to call earlier but tried to hurl myself off a bridge instead.*

There was no reason to fear my beautiful sister. She wasn't blind and accepted my unspoken lifestyle with open arms, so why worry about her now? Besides, the cops had my back. The anticipation around my next move was palpable. I never pushed my beliefs, nor did I want them to define me. My suicidal dash was no political statement. Before tonight, love and life were the goals, not death. Barely able to stand, my tearful hands trembled. "Here goes nothing," I said, twisting the room's five other weightless stomachs into knots. Against my better judgment, I ignored the danger and absorbed the hypnotic tension between us with each pull of the rotary dial—seven first, then four. *Please don't answer,* I prayed, my heart thumping wildly inside my chest. Twenty excruciating rings passed before she did. "Erika, hi, it's Lori. I tried to kill myself tonight."

Chapter 7

—

I always considered myself the happy-go-lucky type, not prone to fits of rage or rash decisions. In fact, nothing about my slender girl next door looks said troublemaker. I was anything but confrontational. My Grandpa Vogt once described me as a smiling freckle stacked five feet high. Anger was never my bag. Only love. Yet not five minutes into my come-to-Jesus moment with Erika, I slammed the bloody phone into itself, spilling a half-empty cardboard cup of cold coffee drowning in powdered creamer. If I had not been standing with my chair pushed back, the milky brown river flowing towards me would have soaked my crotch as well as the war-torn décor in languished caffeine. In our heated tussle over my disappearing again, I'd forgotten about the police officers supervising our conversation. Sergeant Joe had flat-out refused my request for privacy. "No way, Jose," he said, his husky big-city accent not budging an inch. Five minutes later, he was singing a different tune. "Holy Mary Mother of God, talk about a bent lever." My lover had claimed another victim. A rush of guilt bowed my shoulders. Sergeant Joe scrambled to make sense of Erika. Too late for explanations, as the noose was already around my neck.

Utterly confused to the point of disbelief and mad

enough to see double, he fumed "I thought Karen was your sister." I wanted to laugh; I couldn't even cry. The feet I fell before in search of healing continued to kick and kick and kick. Our abusive truth, spoken aloud for all to hear, was difficult to accept. Plus, I could never again deny being gay, and I was angry with myself for letting things get so ugly. But I had a right to remain silent, and this conversation wasn't happening. Not now. Never. In a bold move, proving desperate people do desperate things, I cupped my mouth with my hand. "Sergeant, I'm going to be sick again." He winced. "Alright, shit." I wasn't sick; I just needed some time alone to get my head right.

So, I puffed out my cheeks and made a mad dash for the door, pretending to swallow a flood of imaginary vomit. Sounds and everything. Cheering me on, several uneasy voices shouted in unison, "Go right, go right, the head's down the hall behind the vending machines!" rang out as I stumbled, almost tripping over my exhausted two left feet.

Privacy at last. Since getting sacked on the bridge, I'd been under the suspicious, watchful eyes of a platoon of armed law men, who guarded my every move. As Officer Johnson, who'd followed me, jived R&B melodies, padding back to his paperwork, I watched him toss a red jelly candy into the air. Grape, he said, was his favorite. Another man deserving of more than I could ever offer. A sign on the bathroom door read: Police Business. Police? Oh boy, was I in trouble? I checked the doorknob for resistance—nothing worse than interrupting someone pinching a loaf. With the coast clear, I pushed open the heavy door to sex appeal on a budget.

Oh, God! The air smelled like a cheap pickup line. I recognized the astringent love potion from Karen's bathroom—except her guy didn't use the tangy cologne as an air freshener. The flammability factor was so high, a wet spark could have ignited a seductive fireball hotter than a sultry piña colada for two. I scanned the room for evidence to support my suspicion when I spotted the guilty party. Next to the sink's hot water knob, below the wall-mounted mirror, sat a green bottle of Hai Karate Oriental Lime. Squirming, about to pee my pants, I dropped trou and sat in silence to relieve more than my bladder. "Police business, my ass," I snickered.

The dirty ashtray atop a pile of nudie magazines belonged in a dive bar, not a police station, where the taxpayers expect moral cleanliness. I loved learning these cops were human like me. I found the naked *Playboy* centerfolds taped to the ceiling added some class to the joint—nothing like tits and ass to set the mood. All that was missing were a disco ball and the warm psychedelic bubbles erupting inside a gooey purple-orange lava lamp. You could tell countless smiles and cries had visited this living tribute to a bygone era of free love yet to happen. Now, I dig laid back, but this was ridiculous. I wanted to scribble a message on the tobacco-stained walls but figured the officers had enough to remember Lori was there.

How did I wind up facedown between attempted murder and suicide? And why were the cops everyone loved to hate offering me hope when the world outside their Freudian tribute masquerading as a bathroom held unfettered contempt for me. I had normalized the unthinkable without knowing the cost. I needed to figure myself out before someone besides me got hurt or killed. I'd hurt no one before and wasn't about to start now. With my anxiety calling the shots, the question was whether I'd find strength enough to deserve my next breath. The odds, I discovered, were double stacked against me. Triple stacked if you could see what I didn't.

Fifteen hours earlier, I was late for work. It was my sixth tardy of the month. Driving up to the red-and-white security gate off the main highway nearest the secure complex, I imagined the portly guard with mirrored sunglasses who waved and smiled each morning, making an example of me on my knees, execution style. These visions of capital punishment were new and terrified me. The day before my sixth tardy, I took an uncomfortable walk through a daunting set of double doors to my supervisor's corner office. After a proper thrashing, my nauseous penmanship signed a pink document marked FINAL with black ink, warning that further attendance issues would terminate my employment. I couldn't bear the carbon copy reminder offered to me. Now I held the dubious honor of being the unemployed daughter of a dog killer, unable to end her own miserable life.

I wondered if being locked in a bedroom closet after having your glasses beaten off your face by a coworker carried the same weight as a doctor's note. Who would have believed me, anyway? Surely not my boss, who labeled me the weak link. But the Lori he knew wasn't me. My self-indulgent lies were living on borrowed time. Everyone but me denied the anguish of my pre-death bereavement. I grieved alone with a million neighborly neighbors, who were blind to the fact I was safer dead than alive.

The initial plan was to kill myself on Valentine's Day,

1973, after my divorce from Ronnie was all but assured. I pretended to want it, and I did to an extent. But I hated that he hurt because of me. But instead of dying, I ran away with Erika again, only this time for good. I tried to stay with Ronnie, but I had to go. The heart, I learned, wants what she wants, no matter how much pain it causes. Along the way, sweet nothings whispered into my ear coagulated and rotted. Everyone has pet names, I thought. Dyke, ball-breath, four-eyes, faggot, and homewrecker were some of mine. I disguised the hurt and overlooked the horror, but a steady stream of caustic titles became impossible to contain. The crushing blow of uncertainty these tags fostered was downright savage. Who knew words could render me invisible? I was aflame in hate, but no one could smell me burning. When those I loved would strike me down, I covered my ears and choked on a lack of understanding, able to explain how life was not my fault.

I was the ugly painting plagued with beautiful brushstrokes only death could erase. Sure, I could have hung my troubles on the family tree. A more sensible approach might have been to declare myself an alien space invader. Or maybe a housebroken gargoyle born of immaculate conception as there was no end to the conspiracies surrounding the heathen world outside our perfect utopia. Don't believe me? Dig this:

Growing up, Grandma Vogt told me tongue kissing a boy would get me pregnant. She was as you would imagine—short with white curly hair and dark poodle-like eyes. Her disciplinarian stance and snappy attitude let you know she was in charge. Imagine her response to me wanting to kiss a girl. I envision her going blind from such a revelation. Try outliving that one at the next family reunion. I can hear them now as I walk past distant cousins sipping fermented courage. "Look, there she is, the girl kisser who blinded Grandma." Old-fashioned was in fashion, even if outdated and dangerous. In our world, ladies didn't fight, fart, or cuss. We were to clean house and marry within our race to procreate, not screw. You get the picture.

Interestingly enough, my best friend in high school and first love was a blonde-haired, blue-eyed all-American boy named Nipper, of all things. The son of proper Christian parents, he was perfect. Dad hated him for answering to a name he reserved for the yellow-bellied slant eyes. "Only a goddam gook would call himself Nipper," he'd say. His ignorance was astounding. I knew that behind closed doors certain members of my cherished bloodline would betray me if given a chance. To them, I was Grandpa's favorite, and they hated me for it. Should my secret have ever come to light, they would have outed me in a split second to Grandma to ensure their financial destinies. My grandfather would never have allowed this behavior on his watch. You either worked for it, or you went without. Though spoiled, I was never motivated by money. I'd seen it used as a weapon too many times and wanted nothing to do with its selfish allure.

So, there I sat, atop discount government porcelain, sorting a laundry list of woe in the middle of the night, when reality hauled off and slapped me across the face. I was gay, divorced, and barely twenty, with a brighter past than future. In the time it takes to watch half a bad movie, I went from rocking out with Sir Elton John at a cool fifty-five to a bare-assed veteran of a fresh suicide attempt, rummaging through a lifetime of sins consequences in a cop confessional fit for a sleazy Tijuana whorehouse. It wasn't fair how life was trying to kill me when I was so much fun. Clicking my heels together didn't work like those ruby red slippers. Trust me; I tried twice.

The last dribble had plopped five minutes earlier, so I wiped and wiggled back into my white cotton panties to avoid alerting concern. Standing at the sink, I couldn't believe my eyes. Neither could the mirror because it turned away when I did. Not once, but thrice. I was repulsive, cloaked in failure, wishing I were anyone but me. The loveable Hai Karate was no help. Even the dutiful powdered soap stationed next to the sink basin stood unwilling to scrub away the self-hatred molesting my low self-esteem. I felt sorry for myself. Yet an unusual urge to break death's stranglehold overpowered my irrational problem-solving skills, to the point where I declared an impromptu war on my depression before ceremoniously plunging three rounds of washes from the clunky soap dispenser to avoid a false start. And so began a new cycle of positivity sure to lead me astray.

Maybe there was hope for me after all. Down but not out. I knew survival depended on having my life's purpose revealed. And by purpose, I meant loving Erika. If I could survive long enough to get to her and smooth things over, she would see I wasn't a loser. And to prove my love, I'd take her hand in mine and shout it out to the whole wide world. The hairs on my neck stood on end. I'd made a breakthrough. But what about her abusive backstabbing ways? Or my family and her friends? Neither would ever approve. Not in a million years. Still, I had to try.

Suddenly, a shadow illuminated my broken reflection. The air became stale and hard to breathe. *She's not real*, I told myself. *You don't really want to die*. Plotting my demise. The blurred image in the mirror growled a stern warning, louder than a silent corpse's strangled cry.

This wasn't a dream, after all. Or was it? Only time would tell, but I hated the way death cheered me on sometimes. As I closed my eyes and stepped back from the mirror to process what I believed to be true, muffled vibrations climbed the surrounding walls while two doors down, frustration and wisdom debated my state of mind, unaware that the life they'd preserved was already frozen in time.

"She almost killed me, sir. Isn't that reason enough to lock her up for the night?"

"Technically, yes, but da quacks will just kick her loose anyway, so why bother?"

"Really, Sarge?"

"Hey, write her a ticket if it makes ya feel better. It's called bureaucracy, kid."

"But she's 5150."

"Maybe, but I doubt it. Either way, it's a slippery slope."

"So, you don't think she's . . . ?"

"What? Crazy?"

"Well yeah, I mean . . . She sounds a little, you know . . . and that look in her eyes . . . whoa."

"Crazy, no. Confused, yes. Crazy in love maybe, but not crazy."

Hearing a man I'd trusted ask if I was crazy devastated me. He didn't seem judgmental. But then again, maybe I was crazy. Earlier in the week I watched water flow backward from a glass to a pitcher, so perhaps he was onto something. Still, his concern gave me pause. Our fortuitous connection celebrated life's possibilities. But I couldn't help but wonder if his kind words were part of a bigger, more sinister plan. He carried a loaded gun, after all. A six-inch blue-steel revolver. I know because my dad owned the same model, Smith & Wesson.

But somewhere deep inside, I wanted the officers to help me. Just not tonight because tonight Erika needed me more than they ever could. With my mind made up, I arched my feet to tiptoe along the slate carpet towards the legalese happening down the hall. It turns out I'd make a lousy spy. The intense cross-examination I heard curling under the door softened the closer my intrusion came to the officers' heartfelt conversation. One thing for sure: These guys were in it to win it. You knew right away with them there were no points for second place.

"Better?" asked the gregarious sergeant, watching me slink back into the room, no more impressive than a waste of space. My voice no longer small, I came out swinging. "Wow," I chuckled. "Who's responsible for that mess?" My relaxed expression said I was glad to be there, but at the same time, was also unsure of who or where I was. With time ticking away above us Sergeant Joe warned me to respect their bathrooms, Zen-like healing qualities, or enjoy peeing in the bushes from now on. And to start thinking about my next move so as to not lose this momentum. The affable humanitarian ended his admonishment with a lackluster smile minus the dimples I'd become accustomed to and declared, "All who christen our honorable shrine should bow and pay a toll." Was he serious?

It was hard to tell sometimes. While comfortable, there was little doubt my trip to the bathroom now qualified me for an emergency tetanus shot. Yet I didn't want to disrespect their coveted throne and the peace it afforded me, so I played along to keep the vibe trending upwards.

"I'd bow, but your roll of sandpaper in there left my undercarriage wounded."

The sergeant's electric response was immediate. "You and me both, kiddo. You and me both," he chuckled.

"That's funny, but who's responsible for the Hai Karate stinking up the place?"

"How da hell does a suburban princess like you know about terlit water?" he shouted, throwing jovial hands into the air. "Where yous really from? Liddle Itly? I bet you're one of those closet Catlics, like me too, huh," he laughed.

"My brother-in-law is from the Big Apple, like where you're from."

"From Brooklyn? Don't tell me your sister fell fer da same line my Trudy did."

"No, not Brooklyn. Maybe Buffalo or Long Island. All I know is, Vinny's Italian."

"Ayyyy, Vinny! Well, if he's a Pisan, he probably laid on da upgrades pretty thick."

"Upgrades? What're upgrades?" I asked, hoping he'd say liddle Itly again.

"Hey, fuggedaboudit! You're barely past da birds 'n' bees, fer cryin' out loud."

In an about-face, he switched gears out of respect for Karen, and with one hand, rubbed the five o'clock shadow, scratching his face. He thought for a moment longer, smiled, then delved into a snake-charming incident at a fuggy stripper bar in Bangkok that ended with a bucket of vomit and a chipped tooth. The rest he left to my imagination with a message: War is hell.

Chapter 8

–

Life wasn't always this complicated. There were plenty of memorable moments along the way, and yes, some included my dad. This occurred to me at the most inopportune time, standing where I never thought I'd be. One particular Christmas comes to mind. The snowy switchbacks of old Highway 395 had all but shut down the road to the mountains where a family tradition would begin. Dad, back home in sunny La Mesa, swore he wouldn't fail me. And for once in his life, he was true to his word. This gave me hope that he wouldn't let me down when I needed him most. Though I was a little girl back then, his gesture has stayed with me all these years. Regardless of his past indiscretions, I wanted to believe there was a kind heart underneath all his gruff. That Christmas morning after Santa had delivered his goodies felt like a dream. Outside, six fresh inches of crystal-white snow blanketed the ground beneath glassy icicles, some at least a foot long. The rocky cathedrals surrounding our frosty winter wonderland granted all my holiday wishes except one: Mom. I hadn't seen her in years and wondered if she ever thought of me. I worried she was alone and prayed Santa left her a reason to smile because everybody deserves to be happy on Christmas. Thinking of her sad made it hurt to breathe. Dad assured me she was fine and quelled my holiday sorrows with a box he had wrapped himself in candy cane colors with a shiny green bow. I tore into the decorative paper like a wild animal, tossing it into the air with the force of a tornado. My little Christmas hands spotted the slanted riding heel first. "Jackpot!" I shouted. Dad, being the sneak that he was, didn't tell anyone about the cowboy boots sure to send me into orbit. Butterfly-inlaid cowpunchers, conveniently in my size. Grandma wasn't pleased and thought it unfair that she would have to correct people who'd confuse her darling girl for a boy. But I didn't care for I had a hero named dad.

Chapter 9

–

Sergeant Joe, like my dad, had these hard-boiled eyes that could make anyone doubt themselves. Besides a million other things, the major difference between the two men was that my dad likened himself judge, jury, and executioner. Officer Johnson on the other hand had kind eyes that smiled alongside his athletic build and all-around good looks. He could have been a model had he not been so humble. I believe Sergeant Joe saw his daughters in my struggle and protected me with a father's love. If only mine had looked upon me with the same reverence. I never pictured cops as people. I saw them as power-hungry bullies sent to sanction the sinners and ticket the stupid. I imagined being in the sergeant's shoes. What would I say to me if I were him? While he swung the same blond baton as his uniformed brethren, he wasn't a representative of a justice system known to fall short policing its own mistakes; no, he was a force of nature unto himself.

He was an emotional fortress. A blunt force you could appreciate, but I could tell stories like mine had taken a toll. His unique policing style paid homage to the gritty neighborhood, where he grew up playing stickball in segregated streets shouldered by brick row houses with arched windows and wide pitted concrete stoops weathered by decades of despair. To him, his corner of Brooklyn wasn't a ghetto. It was Shangri-La. A place where the roots of his heritage mattered more than the trappings of California's sun-kissed obsessions. A proving ground where there was no substitute for blood and guts. He confessed that if it weren't for his beautiful native-born wife, he would have returned home to "da city," as he called it, before the ink on his military discharge had dried. The way he gushed over New York City made me homesick for a place I'd never been. How amazing, I thought, to feel such a connection to a place in time where wonderful memories of life lived in poverty outweigh the bad.

I had interacted with a few cops over the years, mainly for "exhibition of speed," as they called it, but nothing this intimate. Grandpa was friends with the local fuzz in La Mesa, who often stopped by his workshop while on duty to shoot the breeze over free bottles of Coke from the showroom's nickel machine. But I kept my distance when they came to call.

Sadly, my Erika was out there in the world, fuming mad. Nothing new, of course, but this was different. This was the week we planned to confront my grandmother with the truth. For once, I needed her to support me and stop Dad from continuing to blame Ronnie. To him, our divorce was soft-spoken Ronnie's fault for being a "spineless dweeb." His condemnation was wrong on every level. Besides my grandfather, Ronnie is the greatest man I've ever known. Above all, he was kind when it mattered most. A rare quality in a world of me first, then you. Grandpa would have adored him. He was a hard worker too with the hands to prove it. I know in my heart that if Grandpa were still alive, none of this would be happening. But he wasn't, and I needed to face the music once and for all.

Three of the five officers who took the time to know me were missing in action. They had left while I lounged in the bathroom without so much as a good-bye. But where had they gone, and why? Was there something I didn't know about happening? Nervously, I tugged at the black leather sleeves that were longer than my arms.

"Whose jacket is this?" I asked.

"That's Webber's, but duty called while you were in the head."

I could tell Sergeant Joe was nose blind to the wild aroma of worn leather. But not me; I inhaled its unique memory like an exotic perfume. It smelled of musk with hints of sage and smoked citrus.

The earthy treasure reminded me of my purse, now wide open on the table between my keepers. It was reddish-brown with thick leather stitching and a matching strap, and just feminine enough to keep me out of trouble. My mind was with the missing officers, who had vanished to rescue someone else in need. They had moved on and were going about their lives as though we had never happened. I'd grown used to such feelings by now, but no one likes to be left behind. With each invisible second that ticked by, you could feel the rumination getting thicker. Time was again having its way with me. The once-playful sergeant's gloomy mood wallowed about, making no excuse for my behavior. Busy with his paperwork, Officer Johnson looked up, holding my driver's license, and shocked me with a list of intrusive questions. Starting with "Do you have any tattoos? If so, what, where and how many?" This bothered me. His trespasses slingshot my frail emotions around the room crippled with bright light. It warmed my once cold face leaving my insecurities no place to hide. My first instinct was to snatch the license from his hand and run, but I had already lost that race before it started.

How could my hero commit my name to the system, knowing what he did about my father? I answered no about the tattoo, of course, but what lie would they force me to tell next? "Thank you," he replied respectfully. "It's a standard form question, so I have to ask." Life was coming at me fast. Faster than I expected, with no sign of slowing down. The stakes were higher and fiercer than ever before. Like my brothers Allen and Paul, I, too, was now on the wrong side of the law. A regular Bonnie without a Clyde. I had fooled myself into thinking the officers and I were old friends. Fishing buddies you might find sharing a cold one after a tough day on the lake. Trauma has a way of distorting our memories as they happen, but I couldn't ignore the uniformed stranger documenting my truth on form after form in perfect capital letters.

In the years before tonight, both my brothers ran afoul of the law, trying to flee our father's loving hand. Dad beat those boys ferociously. Karen too. For only a look, he would rip off his brown belt and raise it high into the air to ensure every square inch of skin-blistering leather made its mark with a mighty crack. Karen tried repeatedly to protect Allen and Paul, but such brazen disrespect subjected her to an avalanche of hate, enough to make evil blush. I was a freshman when Allen was first arrested and sentenced to prison. As the story goes, after dropping out of high school, he'd stolen a car and fled to a Southwestern border state where, after a crash flipped him end over during a high-speed police chase, prosecutors charged him with a myriad of felonies. But not before he had punished our father with extreme prejudice for all the horror he had inflicted over the years. See, by high school, Allen had grown beyond Dad's strength. Stamina too. The neighbors said it was the bloodiest, most brutal beating they had ever seen. Most, like Sergeant Joe, were war vets and had seen a fight or two in their day, making Allen's departure from home one for the record books.

Paul had the good sense to enlist in the army after a few arrests by the local sheriff for being a shoplifting runaway. But there would be jail for him too—hard time. Hard San Quentin prison kind of time thanks to a string of drug related robberies. When I looked in the mirror, I saw his fragile shell. I saw the shackles of sadistic pain that fed his need for the next fix of filthy satisfaction. Just because I was free didn't mean I was. But I wasn't doing time; time was doing me. It seemed odd that my grandparents chose me over my brothers and sister. I lived with them throughout school and, for all intents and purposes, they were my parents and raised me as such. Yet for the life of me, I'll never understand their motives in leaving my siblings behind. But this was no time to dwell on the past.

Surely Erika had blabbed to her friends about me being a pathetic attention whore by now. She refused to believe that the dispatcher's voice sounding from the overhead speaker in the background was the real deal. "Never call me drunk this late again, you lying pig," she'd said before unloading on me in a way Sergeant Joe confessed made him feel bad about himself. "Jesus," he said. "I think we all need a hug after listening ta dat monster."

As sad as it may seem, I half knew what to expect when I dialed her but rolled the dice anyway and bet on me for once. But I feared another beatdown at the hands of old friends. Erika's friends. I wasn't fond of the five tree trunks she welcomed into our lives in the weeks after we'd met for the first time. If she had tugged at their heartstrings turning my pandemonium into hers, painful days filled with punchy eyes awaited me. Our cycle went left, right, left, body shot, hug. Maybe, as she said, I was to blame for their violent outbursts. I was, after all, addicted to their positive toxicity. Like badly. The problem was they considered my sexuality temporary. A passing phase not tied to advancing their cause. Apparently, "Only a faggot would be with a man." Any references to physical abuse might have gotten Erika or her friends in trouble, so I kept my mouth shut to keep the peace. I wanted no one to suffer, not even the violent hands of those who loved to hate me.

"I'm curious," said Sergeant Joe, shifting in his wooden office chair. "How did you and this Erika meet?" Unable to hold the breath beating outside my chest, I froze, embarrassed; our connection read like a low-budget skin flick. Never before had I felt such pressure to respond.

"Check it out, Sarge!" It was Officer Johnson to my rescue again, this time holding a yellow No. 2 pencil instead of a blinding flashlight. Without a second thought, he took up a position beside me and went to work. "What?" asked Sergeant Joe with a twinkle in his eye.

He smiled innocently. "Hey, I'm just curious, guys.

No need ta get all hostile over here." He was in his rights to ask, but officer Johnson worried I might need to take a breather before answering, as one loaded question often leads to another.

"With all due respect, sir, you've been housebroken too long, and the rules have changed since the days of arranged marriages."

"Yeah maybe," he sneered. "But at least I don't wet the bed sunshine." I fought not to respond until my laughter burst into hysterics. Within a nanosecond, a menacing smile settled upon the sergeant's bad-boy bravado, now swelling with pridefulness. "Oh you two wise guys got a problem I see." Disregarding the polished chevrons pinned to his collars, depicting equal parts responsibility and burden, Joey Zafuto from Brooklyn stepped up to serve baby-faced Johnson a grown-folks lesson in respect. "You sayin' I ain't got game, kid? Hell, son, I could have a wife, a woman, and a girlfriend if I wanted."

My chair shook with amusement while Officer Johnson reloaded. "Sir, with all due respect, the only thing keeping your wife satisfied these days is the graveyard shift. Now cut my friend here some slack, or I'll let everyone know you moisturize."

While delightfully funny, there was also a method to their madness.

Sergeant Joe grabbed his chest and stumbled, awkwardly jinking to the left and right. "Damn, kid, take it easy. You know I got da pressure?"

"Depression?"

"Not depression, da pressure. High blood pressure. Ya

know, hyperwhatchamacallit."

"Ah, hypertension. Silent but deadly, like an egg salad fart."

On the verge of a verbal knockout, Sergeant Joe conceded and called time.

Officer Johnson, thrilled by this unprecedented turn of events, raised his hands over my head and invited me to high-five our victory over his fearless leader. The student had become the teacher. I marveled at the officer's ability to weave salacious humor into sensitive, sometimes life-changing situations. Another survival tactic, I suppose as wading through people's carnage day after day must get old. Their nurturing disrespect seemed to strengthen the brotherhood in which they belonged.

"Alright," quipped Sergeant Joe, lamenting his loss. "I'll leave da love triangle ta youse kids, but I expect Miss Lori's report will be nothing short of spectacular, rookie. Now finish up, 'cause some of us round here work fer a livin'." I'd be lying to you if I said Erika wasn't on my mind. Since hanging up on her, my despicable actions flooded me with guilt for being bothersome at such a late hour. What would it hurt to call her back and apologize for my regrettable existence? What, indeed? I took full responsibility for her aggressive nature, even though I knew there would be hell to pay. Although it would have been nice to matter from time to time when it didn't serve her needs. But I felt she deserved better. How could she not, when I was the one calling from a damn police station in the middle of the night, halfway between the slammer and cuckoo's nest?

It was hard to ignore Sergeant Joe's sarcastic comments

about Erika being a dehumanizing animal, and I knew the odds were slim he'd allow a second round of narcissistic phone wars on his dime. The only time she never gaslighted me was when she was in the honeymoon phase of her abuse cycle. That Sergeant Joe said everyone expected a sisterly reunion and not a brokenhearted tug of war with a jaded ex-lover made his position on the matter crystal clear. But he didn't know Erika smelled like cotton candy.

Still, there was no escape from the opposing views of those who thought they knew what was best for me. Like my family, these well-intentioned officers could never know how good Erika was for me. Yeah, she laced our conversations with contempt, but so what? We always forgave and forgot. I mean, come on—isn't forgiveness the very essence of love? Wouldn't the world be a better place if there were more of it to go around? I honestly believed Erika's love for me was genuine because she was forever telling me it's what she was born to do. She also told me to drop dead regularly, so who knows for sure, but I needed to find out—even if it killed me.

Chapter 10

—

A few months prior to my impassioned charge up the bridge, in the days after Thanksgiving, life took an unexpected turn. The holidays were in full swing, and the season's chilly nights replaced the repetitive sunny, seventy-degree days we sun-weary locals sometimes despised. Stocking caps and heavy coats warmed us cold-blooded Californians as fantasies of impending blizzards filled the minds of everyone longing for the storybook white Christmas. Would-be elves dreamed of frolicking in a marshmallow world of steaming hot chocolate and elaborately decorated Christmas trees wrapped in joyful wonder. The North Pole should seem so festive.

The unexpected Christmas cold favored cozy embraces, crackling fires, and songs that inspired happiness and good will. You could feel the magic in the foreign, frigid air. The mythical red elixir inside everyone's thermometers cured everything wrong with a warm sunny Christmas. With each dip of the mercury, twinkling lights glowed brighter, carol harmonies sounded merrier, and the nose-tickling sensations of a freshly hung wreath smelled sweeter. Jack Frost had delivered his cold spell just in time to warm the hearts of those longing to create the perfect Christmas. But as we know, life is not always perfect, and dreams don't always come true.

As Christmas-crazed herds of people merrily celebrated the season's festivities, others, oblivious to the illuminated Santa's and sparkly tinsel displayed across town, went about their lives working late, tending to family needs, or maybe nursing a breakup with a stiff drink at a dark lonely bar while cigarette smoke danced in the air like a forbidden temptress. All across San Diego different versions of holiday life played out. Some good. Some bad. But all unforgettable.

While others taught painful lessons proving that life is sometimes confusingly cruel with no change in temperature able to mitigate its debilitating effects. For two San Diego sisters, the Christmas spirit was about to be tested like never before. They say you never know which tragic event will have the greatest impact on a person until it happens. The IT moment I speak of is different for everyone. But when IT happens, IT hits like a runaway freight train, destroying everything in its path. The blank response on Karen's face when I told her Dad needed to know the truth about me said this was her IT moment.

"Please," she said. "Anything but that. Haven't we suffered enough the past two Christmases with all Mom's bullshit?" Karen's pain was obvious. But this would not deter me.

"Don't you want to see me happy?" I asked, not knowing this would strike a nerve.

Her tears spoke without making a sound. "Of course I do. But I'm scared, sis. She quivered. What if he flies off the handle and hurts one of us? And what about Grego?"

She had a point. And there was no ignoring the nervous

chill inside me. I knew everything I was about to stand for could threaten Karen and my relationship forever. Coming clean to my father would be no easy feat. But it needed to happen. Like, now, not tomorrow. Unfortunately, Dad wasn't the kind for casual conversation if you know what I mean. Especially when the topic didn't suit his rigid tastes. But he might compromise over my dead body.

I wasn't about to take no for an answer. "Look, he is either going to accept me or not."

Karen saw in my eyes that I was tired of apologizing simply for being me. And father or not, no man was going to abuse me like they did my mother. Further disrespect from anyone would come at a steep price I prayed most weren't willing to pay. However, the days of being everything to everyone else were over.

"Besides," I said to Karen, nudging her arm with mine, "don't you remember my Christmas boots? Dad had the Christmas spirit then, so why not now?"

After a long pause, she wrapped her arms around me in solidarity. Next came some careful planning at the expense of a couple of underage beers before I called Erika and told her the good news. But she was anything but happy.

"Are you nuts?" she asked, shouting her defensive posture through the phone.

"No more lying or hiding," I said.

"Yeah, and shit speaks for itself too."

My pledge to Erika was survival on a united front. I loved her hostage heart, despite all the reasons I shouldn't.

"You know what," she hissed, "if anyone's to blame it is that goddamn family of yours so yeah, let's get it on big mouth. And if they want war, that's exactly what they'll get."

Her words lit up my insecurities like a bolt of lightning cracking across the sky. But I wasn't the quitter she believed me to be.

"You're serious about confronting old Bluto, aren't you, tough guy?" asked Erika.

"Stop calling me a tough guy."

"Well, look at you."

"Yeah, look at me."

I knew any fallout from facing my father would breed a lifetime of rejection from my family and their associates, so a plan was needed to ward off World War III.

"I don't know," said Karen suspiciously. "Even if you do go through with it and he blows his top, do you really think he'll admit to anyone a god such as himself created a gay?"

Karen's innocence was adorable. But she had a point. Our father was so cruel if he were to learn of my failed suicide attempt, he'd drive me back to the bridge himself for a guaranteed second shot at success. With the vote between us three girls unanimous, there wasn't a dry eye in the room. Especially Karen. She was a mess. Happy. But a mess knowing the danger at hand.

"Oh, and no telling your friends, Erika, until the job's done?"

This did not sit well with her. "And why not, Lori?" I hated when she called me Lori.

"Because I don't need a head full of their drama ramping up to face my father."

At that point, I expected her to distance herself from the fight she'd claimed to long for since learning of my dad's threatening views. But she didn't. Being all talk, this was her chance to save face riding my confrontational coattails. And she took it. Hook, line, and sinker.

"Why now?" she asked with a twinge of bitter self-righteousness.

"Why not now?"

I knew where this exchange was heading. If I didn't stop it now, her tension-fueled judgement would slaughter me later in private. I was hyper vigilant, constantly bracing for impact over my thoughts and beliefs. Dating Erika forced me to be. I loved the sound of her voice, but only when she wasn't minimizing my worth. She would hurt me and then act like I was the aggressor. One time she went so far as to attack me for keeping her from making plans. That's right, making plans. It was bad too. Apparently, my occasional desire to be spontaneous didn't sit well with her control issues. But I couldn't let my Erika go. Her structured abuse institutionalized me almost from day one. I depended on it to feed the slow death happening inside me. After a while I guess the torment just became normal. While she filled my life with many ups and downs, I never lacked for scraps of attention under her gorgeous spell.

I feared Erika's friends as much as my father. They were big too. Double my size and twice as mean. Like Chicago Bears big. Okay, that might be a slight exaggeration, but a few were close. First you had Marsella. About twenty-five and shaped like a pear, she wore a black pompadour to compliment her manly biceps. Next oldest was twenty-something Renee. Or the black widow, as she was known. Blonde with perky boobs. She was the worst, but also irresistible. A terrific sense of humor was her one redeeming quality. Her dreamy aqua eyes weren't so bad either. I think they killed more relationships than alcohol and gambling combined. So while you wouldn't know it by the way she made you laugh, her mean streak ran a mile wide. She definitely cut both ways. Then you had Gretchen, the not so mousy brunette who thought herself a ten. Followed by nineteen-year-old Curly Kim who happened to be quite religious, plain old Julie Wilson Palmer, and my favorite, Sacramento's very own Barbera Weeks. Or Big Barb as she preferred to be called. She made no bones about the fact that she was a big woman. Her confidence never minced words, nor did her appetite. A blonde herself, she was the kindest of them all, but still a bully at heart because she never shut up about other people.

Now plain old Julie Wilson Palmer had a sister named Amanda. She was the most genuine person I ever met. Beautiful too, with long flowy blondish hair that draped over her smooth feminine shoulders. Spunky and vivacious, it killed me that she loved boys as much as I loved girls. She was the type of Gal I wished Grego would meet when he grew up. Occasionally she came out with us, but never once disrespected me the way the others did. While her sister played a role, she sometimes held back. More than once Amanda was my saving grace when Erika struggled to contain herself. At times I thought she might be as lonely as me. The logical part of my brain said she was. But I never worked up the nerve to ask about her personal life.

Now Barb was the group's designated drinker. Boy did she love her some tequila. The heavy-handed hard to swallow kind with a worm served in a dirty broken glass.

Hell, her drunken breath alone could knock you out. If we were sitting around passing the bottle, the first person she lit into was always Curly Kim. Because of her kinky hair of course. "Can you imagine me with one of these ridiculous Fozzie's?" she'd ask, grabbing handfuls of Kim's jet-black curls with her long tarantula fingers. Okay, so the fozzy is an extra-tight, super-curly perm nicknamed by Barb herself. Thank God Grandma never signed me up for one. I think it would have bent my jaw backwards they were so tight. To gain acceptance, I used Christine, Kim's aunt and long-time beautician, to style my bangs once. But Lord. What can I say? She spoke with a mouth full of hot garbage. To make matters worse, she was a talker. The entire twenty minutes she spent styling my already short bangs, her proximity to my face choked my gag reflex into submission. I'm not kidding! You can ask Karen. I feel terrible speaking ill of her, but her rancid smoker's decay was hideous enough to peel paint.

Fozzy or no fozzy, I was ready to face my father. Now that Erika was onboard, I felt as though I could fly. Soon Erika's bullheaded posse would disregard my triggers and welcome me into the fold as an equal. Important because I saw them as the family I never had. Dysfunctional, yes. But with qualities mine would never understand. Plus, they bore the same relationship scars caused by following what someone else's heart deems acceptable. The time had come to turn the table on their insults and demand the respect I deserved. For too much of my life I apologized to make a situation better when I wasn't wrong. Those days were over. I was about to show the world I wasn't that person anymore.

Chapter 11

—

Despite our connection, all of Erika's friends were a point of contention with me. An eclectic bunch, they wore their sexuality like a badge—but not a badge of honor. No, more like a warning that threatened the likes of anyone who dared to look the other way. They were heavy-duty partiers, except for Curly Kim, and proud of it. Before I was fired, five of the seven of us had worked for the same defense contractor, assembling classified communication equipment for the military. Marsella was our shift leader and section's brown-nose extraordinaire. She kissed enough butt for ten promotions, but could never quite advance past her paltry lead position. For eight hours a day, five days a week, I quality-controlled classified circuit boards of various shapes and sizes. It was steady work but hardly what I would call interesting.

I never faulted Erika's friends for their outspoken behaviors; I only wish they had respected my subtle journey with the same openness. Their bullish ways painted me as weak-minded from the start. Life got painfully abusive whenever their excessive drinking slammed into my head. Sometimes it kicked me in the ribs, bruising my already broken heart. Erika tried to intervene a few times, but she was the guiltiest of them all. I caught the brunt of her fury most days, I guess, simply because I was there.

Anyway, on the day we confronted my father, I picked up Erika first, then Karen. Though Erika lived farther away, I thought it important we discuss the details since it related to us in private before dragging my sister deeper into our mess. But not before Erika slammed two shots of Jack Daniel's. "And one for the road." She laughed nervously, tossing back a third for good luck. My mind was running wild, firing on all cylinders as usual.

"Promise me we won't fall into old habits," I said, reaching for her hand. It was cold and clammy. Mine too.

"Old habits?" she asked, rolling her lovely eyes.

"Yes, old habits. You know, how we squabble over my family then make love to forget what we said. After today, I want us to normalize a bit and stop fighting so much."

Her tact couldn't match mine. "Let's get one thing straight," she said, opening the passenger side door then slamming it shut. "This shit's your fault, not mine."

"Are we rushing into this?" Another foolish question I already knew the answer to.

Her sarcasm stung. "Rushed? What the hell do you know about rushed, miss late to her own goddam funeral?"

I didn't stop to think about what we were getting ourselves into with my father. We just went, dammit. We just went. The slow, cloudy drive to Dad's weighed heavily on us all. There was absolute silence as we drove past lucky people wearing smiles for days. Thoughts of Allen and Paul dominated my mind's eye. The ghosts of their troubled childhood awaited. Paul had made the biggest mistake of his life the day he robbed Dad's rare gun collection, wrapped in blankets under the bed in the master suite. When Dad caught him outside a local pawnshop, weapons in hand, he beat Paul within an inch of his life before the police arrived, guns drawn. His timid son lay half-dead in the gutter, strung out on drugs, while Dad's official statement listed himself as the victim of a violent robbery. After Paul's first major conviction, the harsh reality of California's penal system further dehumanized my tender brother, robbing him of his future. Eventually, he joined a gang for protection, but not before it was too late. By then he was a lifer, inside or out. My brother was such a sweet little boy. His soft blue eyes would never dream of hurting a fly. Poor Paul could never shake the monkey off his back, and I'm not talking about the drugs or the easy money.

After a quick pit stop at Karen's, we were on our way. Inching closer to Dad's, I pulled over several times to vomit. I was a wreck. My talking points felt like invitations to lash me. Erika was so attentive, holding my hair back and massaging my shoulder to keep me loose. Wrenched over in pain, I couldn't even make it to a side street without having to stop. Right there on University Avenue, a major artery that runs from downtown San Diego through La Mesa, I violently dry-heaved into the gutter. After the third stop, a passing squad car took notice, slowed, thinking Ms. too much to drink and her crime partners might call for a closer look. But he kept on patrolling and left me to it.

The short ride up King Street took forever, but not long enough. Sixty seconds, tops. The cute hillside neighborhood offered a sense of calm. A place where families come to grow, not destroy themselves. I prayed for no one to be home. But there in the side drive sat Dad's baby-blue Ford F-100.

"Any last words?" I said, creeping to a stop.

I exited first, then Karen. Erika, bringing up the rear, held her face to the gloomy sun no longer full of confidence. The slim stucco cottage at 4020 King Street made no statements other than to say "welcome." Dad had turned the previous owner's unsightly yard into a prized topic of conversation. The star atop the tree in the front window glittered silver flashes of Christmas magic. Even so, I was prepared for psychological warfare.

I sunk the moment Dad's hulking personality squeezed the light from behind the screen doors, mesh panels atop his lofty concrete porch that stood taller than me. He greeted us with a hearty chuckle. "Come on in, girls." Typical Dad, always putting on a show. "How are ya?" he asked, offering to feed us salmon fresh from his customized smoker out back on the porch.

My insides were at war with themselves. My demon's nightmare had awakened. But Dad's sorry butt was mine. I'd had enough. It was my way or the highway now. Not his. Any delay might have caused more harm than good, so I dove right in. "Thank you, but we already ate." His mood shifted. He pointed to Erika, grinding his teeth. "Who's this?" he asked, looking her up and down. Karen too, but for other reasons. "Well, spit it out." The three of us stood there looking at him speechless the eggshell-colored walls. The air turned thick with suspicion. "Oh no," he said, waving his large hand back and forth in my face. "I'm not a goddam bank, so if you're looking for money, you can take your ass elsewhere, sister." Already I was off to a terrible start. "Maria," I said, "you're welcome to join us." Maria was Dad's third wife. And he didn't mind telling people she was trustworthy for a border jumper. Boundaries were of no concern for him. Ever. Before she could move, a thundering voice blasted me in the face, ending my crusade before it began.

"Our business is our business, not hers, so leave her the hell out of this."

Dad's hateful eyes took no prisoners. But I stood my ground, swallowing his eye-popping disgust with a stone face. I saw the wooden handle of his pistol when I reached for Maria, who could have been my body double we were so similar in size. Behind us hung an oil painting of ancient Mayan ruins bathed in rods of broken sunlight. Dad used lemon furniture polish to clean the long pistol's walnut grip. The ready Magnum lay without a holster near a white box of bullets with orange stripes encircling its square corners. A red sign in the living room's front window read Trespassers will be shot. There were loaded guns stashed all throughout the house, but this one pistol was the most obvious. For all Dad's hatred of anything un-American, he had shocked the entire world when he married a full-blooded Mexican.

A dark Mexican with a green card, no less. But she was beautiful. I guess she was the one woman he could control. And the blessings of America meant enough to her to tolerate Dad's daily threats of deportation. But Maria was the sweet-est. She endured Dad's abuse with back-breaking busy work and menthol cigarettes. She said the cooling burn gave her a "smoother, more pleasurable smoke." Honey, as we some-times called her, had the pearliest white teeth of any smoker I'd ever seen. Karen and I loved driving Maria down to Baja to visit her sister at Rosarito Beach. The lively plazas full of culture and handcrafted items kept us busy for hours. It's where I found the purse Officer Johnson rifled through, looking to profile me. The purity of the blue Aztec sky scattered my worries with each visit. To cool those humid afternoons in the Mexican sun, we sipped sangria made with green apples ordered in Spanish near dreamy waves caressing the tranquil sand dollar-rich shores. Maria displayed many treasures from her village on the Yucatán Peninsula around the house. My favorite piece was the marble bullfighting statue kept on the coffee table centering the living room. "Better lock old toro up," I'd joke, pretending to grab him and run. She'd just giggle and brush away the black hair from the corners of her soft brown face. As Erika, chomping a wad of pink bubble-gum, took my hand, Dad shouted, "What kinda bull-dyke shit is this?" I knew right then my days were numbered. But I felt fortunate, having avoided this level of hate for so long. Others weren't so lucky, wearing their differences as color or disfigurement. Hopefully Dad took pleasure in watching his daughter take his insults like a man. My biggest mistake was caring too much about what he thought of me. So much so, I begged him to punch me in the face so the world could know he was a coward.

My empty gaze was transfixed. Unblinking.

"Come on," I said, closing the gap between us. "Do it, you bastard."

Dad's nostrils flared.

"Yeah, that's what I thought. You're about as much of a man as I am."

He averted my tirade with a seething glare. My presence was a lightning rod. A perverted body of poisonous gay quicksand. He hated me. But for once, he took the high road. "You're dead to me, you sick freak. Now leave and take this mute bitch with you and get the fuck out of my house. And if I ever see either of you again, you can kiss your lesbo asses bye-bye. And that goes double for you, Karen," he said, mimicking the action of a pump shotgun.

Great. The one thing I didn't want to happen happened. My sister was now in danger because of me. Like, grab your family and run for your life kind of danger. This was serious.

Within less than five minutes, the entire ordeal was over. Quick and to the point. Dad's violent aggression cast me aside, stripping himself of my burdens. As intolerable as he was, this was not the outcome I had wished for. Deep down I wanted his blessing more than anything in the world. But it never came. Never mind the gratuitous death threats—his lowbrow remarks bit like nails clawing at a chalkboard. Life was proving just how tough I wasn't.

And poor Karen. Her intense sadness drained through me. What had I done?

"C'mon," she said, pushing me out the door past the porch light that no longer welcomed us home. I thought the worst things imaginable standing at the bottom of the concrete steps I used to walk out of my father's life. Erika stood silent the entire time. Not once did she stand up for me, other than to hold my hand, which only angered Dad more. Everything I'd hoped for was falling apart at the seams. Dad's first call would be to Grandma. So much for my safe harbor, never mind the inheritance. My sorrowful tears wept for all of us. If he could hate Mexicans but marry one, then why didn't the same love apply to me? We were blood. The same.

Dad's send-off was much too humiliating to share. No one should ever have to hear something more painful than being skinned alive. Back at the Nova, Karen, huffing and puffing, walked a wide angry circle into the street, growling, her fists clenched. Sparks of mad electricity were shooting off inside her.

I felt queasy. "Sorry," I said. "Sorry for dragging you into my stupid mess, Sis."

She was breathing harder now, almost panting, making abrupt, painfully hostile sounds. I apologized again. But she turned her attention to Dad's house of horrors.

"No, screw you!" she screamed, facing Dad's house. "You hear me, you sonofabitch?" I was shocked because Karen never cussed. This was bad. "Screw you and the horse you rode in on, motherfucker!" she hollered. Then, with both arms extended high, she flipped Dad the bird, screaming, *I hate you*! over and over at the top of her lungs. I was beyond devastated. A future without a mother and father seemed pointless. And what about the girls? What would they think? I could feel the chill of death's piercing black eyes circling me. She laid her black hand upon my heart revealing a chilling insight into my future. I should have let Dad be. I should never have drug his life into mine. Or Karen's. Or Erika's. Or anyone else's. Melvin was a curse, and my father. The poor excuse for a man who treated me like one. He wasn't willing to give more than he received unless by way of hate. But I loved him all the same. Otherwise, why would I have come? Once again, my best intentions had tried but failed. Even to warrant my father's love.

Chapter 12

—

Much to my surprise, Sergeant Joe, who retreated after his absolute routing, returned holding two full cups of piping-hot coffee. His creased khaki persona was a comforting sight. "Freshly brewed yesterday," he laughed. "Here, I think this one has sugar."

"Do you not take sugar?"

"Nope, I'm sweet enough," he said, grinning between sips.

After setting his cup down, he asked if Erika had any siblings. "Yeah," I snickered. "Two gay brothers named Ryle and Scott." His eyes nearly popped out of his head. "Say What?"

"It's true," I said. Although I don't think he believed me. The flavor-rich steam warming his face couldn't hide the wonder in his eyes. "What are the odds?" he declared in jest, throwing his hands into the air before slamming them down on the table. His hands spoke a language all their own. They were as inviting as they were frightening. Soft but strong, with knuckles sharp as razor blades. One punch, I thought, is all it would take.

"Hey, grab your cup and let's take a walk. No, not you, giggles," he winked, shutting down an eager Officer Johnson already on his feet. "Settle down, buddy boy. Chics only."

It was clear our time together was ending. "You know," he said, walking beside me towards the lobby's floor-to-ceiling window walls that looked out on the bridge ascending into the fog that rolled in with the tide, "this island of envy and military might was once a mound of scrubby dirt, home ta nothing, not even a dream. Now, look at her." He gestured, inviting me to see for myself. "All grown up and doing da town. It took a lotta uphill battles ta get here, yet here we are. You understand?" My pouty lip said I understood all too well. His lack of skepticism kept me out of limbo when all I wanted to do was pretend I was someone else.

Nothing about him made sense. His yin was also his yang. Which made his complex ways even more fascinating. Never mind his scorching look, this philosopher was more poet than a gunslinger, whether he liked it or not. "See, it's all in how we teach people to treat us, " he said. "Without boundaries, our mounds of dirt stay mounds of dirt, no matter how much we water them. Now normally we don't have this much time fer damsels in distress, so while you're here, why dontcha let us help you?" I had never felt so safe and threatened at the same time.

This is the moment everything changed. I couldn't let him see through my bullshit any longer. My illusions were going to stay my illusions. I was comfortable with them. Relying on anyone else at this point was unacceptable. The only way to the truth was going to be through it, without the aid of competing forces. And there were already enough of those going around for two of me.

Usually, I'd fold under questioning, but I held my tongue, fearful I might still be prosecuted for a broken heart.

My vigilance was on high alert because at no point had I been told jail wasn't a possibility.

"Okay, full disclosure," he said, with a look that begged me not to disappoint him. "The reason I brought you down here is I'd like you to reconsider going to the hospital tonight."

All my muscles clenched. Face, hands, and feet. *For heaven's sake*, I thought. *Not again.* I flashed back to weary steps, pacing the creek of freshly tanned leather, rookie leather. Officer Johnson's rookie leather. Now brighter than before, the lobby felt less like a pale winter's day than I remembered and more significant and spacious, leaving me no place to hide.

"And if you're worried about getting jammed up, don't be, cause tonight, you get a pass. Capeesh?" Sergeant Joe lived to bust chops, but this was no happy hour routine.

"Well, how 'bout it?" he asked, standing with his arms folded across his chest, I could tell pulling Erika out of my hat didn't amuse him one bit. I should never have called her. The sound of her heart-piercing voice pinballed between my ears. I might be on my way home by now had I dialed any-one but her. He knew my bait-and-switch was intentional. Self-accountability was never my strong suit, so I chewed on the corner of my lower lip to keep my face from sagging with embarrassment.

I worried Sergeant Joe was about to turn on me. His serviceable grin apologized, saying "I'm sorry, but I have to do this." I replied by not saying a word.

"What is so bad that da better option is ta jump?" he asked, seizing the moment. "Be honest now. Because if you lie ta me, we're done."

Like before, I had nothing to offer.

"Please help me understand because I don't get it. Every-thing I see tells me you're loved. You have a beeyoodeeful car, a perfect smile, and behave nothing like da typical hoodlums we roust from time to time." I couldn't believe my ears. Nor could I believe what was happening to me. His irritation was understandable, though, considering I mistook his concern for a fool earlier by calling Erika instead of Karen. But didn't he understand the dangers in judging a book by its cover? A former Marine infantryman, Sergeant Joe's fierce thou-sand-yard stare told no lies. And it was easy to see he was still knee deep in the heavy jungle. The distress in his watchful eyes tracked me like a predator. What stood out, though, was how this delicate bruiser deciphered girl problems. Hands to his hips, muscles flexed, lips pursed. "Miss Lori," he'd said earlier, fishing for a laugh, "tell me, I don't make this polyester wool blend look good?" Officer Johnson's spewed response to his boss's outlandish theatrics left anemic coffee puddled everywhere but his cup.

His fun-loving tactics revealed much, but getting into a deep-state conversation about my personal life with the government scared the crap out of me. He was a cop first, after all. Then a father, and I had a problem with fathers. However, true to form, I caved. Perhaps it was his charismat-ic dimples, but something compelled me to trust Joseph G. Zafuto. Unable to swallow, I shoved my thinly veined hands deep into my pants' front pockets and fanned the flames.

"I wasn't really going to jump, Sir. I mean I was just... well...you know." Silence gripped the room. You could feel the walls hold their breath. Still, Sergeant Joe, ever the consummate professional, gestured for me to continue.

"I know you want to help, but really, I'm okay."

After a few more lies, his bullshit meter pegged.

"You might be selling it," he said, furrowing his brow, "but I ain't buying it."

On the defensive, I readied myself for battle. "You're not fine," he said. "Which is how you ended up here in the first place." Flying his arms through the air, "Look around, young lady. Do you not know where you are? Because last time I checked dis ain't da Four Seasons, and I'm not a bellhop named Willie." Now a substantial target, I had to stand my shaky ground. Unusually shy, but this was life or death, so I breathed in, gathered all my broken memories, looked him dead square in his eyes, and said, "I am fine, and you'll see that if you just let me go home."

Holy crap, I whispered, my eyes large enough to eclipse the sun. Did I just step to a cop with balls bigger than me? Maybe I was stronger than I thought after all. Sensing I had bitten off more than I could chew, a half-cocked smile consumed the streetwise grin bouncing about the sergeant's face. "Since it seems we're at an impasse and going to agree to disagree, let's talk about the ramifications of you not getting help," he said, firm in his conviction.

I had come to the proverbial crossroads. But this was my life, not his. I should have cared, but I didn't, although he wasn't going to relinquish me without a fight. Actually he didn't have to let me go at all.

"Don't do it for me," he said. "Do it for yourself and that young man knee-deep in paperwork who saved your life. Did you know today is only his fourth shift off probation?"

Flabbergasted, I struggled to respond in my natural voice. "Is he okay?"

"No, he's not okay. In fact, neither one of you is okay. Hell, I'm not okay." Sergeant Joe had most likely experienced every emotion over his career. Some good, some bad, and most not worth the tickets he scribbled them on. Now he contemplated the decision that would define the remaining days of my life.

"Do you know where my car is?" Without thinking, I drew a definitive line between us, setting the stage for what came next.

"Couldja forget about that car fer two seconds already?"

I didn't mean anything bad. I just didn't know how I was getting home.

"C'mon, have you forgotten you tried to rub yourself out not twenty-five minutes ago?"

I hadn't forgotten. Karen often reminded me that it's unhealthy to look back at what doesn't exist anymore. But she ate leftovers, so what sense did that make? Yet I couldn't help but fantasize about life without karma's loathsome influence. Shifting my stance, I looked into Sergeant Joe's plump disbelieving eyes. They were on the edge of tearful. Behind him, outside our warm, inviting space, a smattering of traffic packed with clean-cut faces on military leave laid on their horns, passing beneath the toll plaza's unmistakable concrete wing punctuated with flashes of amber light.

"What's going to happen if I let you go home tonight?" he asked. Up against an equilibrium still tethered to a dangerous existence I couldn't resist, he understood that all my roads led back to Erika. Because this wasn't the Four Seasons, nor was he a bellhop named Willie. He was slow to respond. When he did, his smile lines tightened, burning themselves into my memory. *Here we go*, I thought, bracing for impact. But the rebuttal I expected never came.

A turnback moment stood before me. This truly was my chance at a new beginning. After some debate, I conceded that our coming together was no coincidence. He wanted to believe I was safe, that I wouldn't continue to choose death over life. In the refracted spaces between us, he looked upon the floor with an empty gaze. "You wanna know what makes my wife so beautiful?" he asked, his thumb and index fingers split, resting atop his gun belt like loaded pistols. "Because she's average."

My mind stopped short. What did he mean by average? The frankness in his remark floored me. This was more than I could handle. There wasn't enough circuitry to process the suicidal, Erika, Karen, Action News, Nova talk, let alone riddles doled out by the police. Some jazzy elevator music would have been nice though. You know, to break up the awkward tension. The sounds of a great tune always helped me think more clearly. So why not rock out? It's why our ancient ancestors beat a drum—it inspired emotion and change, movement and gratitude. I don't know about you, but like oxygen to fill my lungs, I needed music to breathe. With his elbows locked sharply in an outward bent position, Sergeant Joe's fierce eyes grabbed hold of mine to pressure me the way cops do.

"Again, young lady, what's going to happen if I let you go home tonight?"

While he searched my harrowing grimace for an answer,

I circled about myself, questioning everything, including my existence, which screamed I was alive by the thunderous beat in my chest. To stop his lawful momentum, I looked upon him tenderly, wondering why he was fighting so hard for me, and with great care I said precisely what he needed but didn't want to hear.

"I can't promise you I'll be better tomorrow, but I will be alive."

Sergeant Joe gazed outside at the caution lights blinking between the toll lanes, then back at me. "You sure about that?"

His words cut to the bone. The way he stepped back into his official capacity was breathtaking. I didn't know what to say. I could tell my premonition had upset the balance between us. He had convinced himself I would fall in line and decide for him. How could the hospital help, other than to expose me further? I mean, what did they know about troubles like mine? I guess a lie isn't a lie if you believe it, right? But what would it hurt to accept his help? So far, he and his men had treated me with nothing but respect, so why not? But why was I also asked to defend myself when I was the victim? Where was the justice for my peace of mind? It's not like I drove myself to the bridge alone. I had help, lots of it. Many paved the way, practically drawing a map for me to follow.

As Sergeant Joe walked away towards room one, fearing the inevitable, I swallowed a lump of tears, with the knowledge that I'd just made the biggest mistake of my life.

Chapter 13

–

Back where we started minutes ago. "How's the report coming, Johnson?" asked Sergeant Joe, checking his watch against the wall clock, keeping score minute by dreadful minute.

"Almost done, boss. Just gotta update my log before I forget."

The look of seriousness on the sergeant's face desperately wanted me to reconsider his offer. It said *speak now or forever hold your peace*. Again, I braced for impact.

Standing erect cracking his knuckles, Sergeant Joe coughed an icy bark. "Ahem. Against my better judgment, I've made an executive decision," he said, watching me shut down.

The sum of my greatest fears shown across my face in an indescribable horror. *Here we go.*

"Lori, I'm going to trust that tonight was a mistake and that you'll use it to better yourself. And if you're okay ta drive, we'll escort you over da bridge. From there you'll be free ta go, at which point I'll peel off, and Officer Johnson will follow you home. And before anyone objects, I'm not asking."

"But know this," he continued. "I'm doing this for you, not me, as I trust what you've shared is true."

My jaw hit the floor. He wasn't really going to let me just walk out of there without so much as a warning, was he? How could this be? This was exactly what I wanted, but oh my, what to do? I could tell the sergeant wasn't comfortable with his decision, but I wasn't about to question his motives. I had my ticket home, and there would be no jail or hospitals tonight. And one more thing," he said, putting pen to paper. "Call me if things don't go as planned. Dial direct or collect, I don't care. Just make sure you call. Capeesh?"

And just like that, I was free and clear. Standing to stretch, Officer Johnson slid my driver's license into my wallet, which he placed in my purse before pushing it across the table. To speed things along before Sergeant, Joe changed his mind. I took off the leather jacket and hung it over the broken chair. I wondered how it wound up damaged. The taped leg, shorter than the rest, caused it to wobble slightly to the right, but it was otherwise sound. The rest of their equipment proved top-notch, almost surgical.

"This thing's a hazard," I said, rocking the broken chair back and forth against the floor.

"It was the night it flew across the room," joked Sergeant Joe, ducking out of the way to show me how he escaped injury. "I'm getting too old fer dis shit," he said shaking his head.

Before I could laugh, the phone vibrated, ringing against the table's faux wood surface. *Dear God, not Erika.*

"CHP, Sergeant Zafuto speaking."

My heart flipped. It was the Action News calling about a jumper. Sergeant Joe could see I was about to spontaneously combust. The importance of this moment would have lasting consequences. He covered the mouthpiece with his hand

and told me not to worry. With a straight face: "You gots it all wrong, pal. Da so-called jumper yer calling about was liddle more than a stranded motorist wit a flat tire." There was immediate pushback on the other end. "Yeah, dat's right, a stranded motorist wit a flat. She musta picked up a nail after she dropped off her hubby at da base. Textbook classic, no-fuss, no-muss." His lies rolled off his tongue with the greatest of ease. Dare I say better than mine, which is saying something because I was a terrific liar, almost pathological. Not because I wanted to be, of course, but because I had no other choice if I wanted to enjoy mainstream acceptance.

I knew about these reporters, and to them, where there's smoke, there's fire. My Uncle Bob once worked as an investigative photographer for several insurance agencies and kept a mind-blowing archive of countless bloodstained unhappy endings. Before he retired to the family business, I snuck a peek at his work one afternoon, nosing through his leather satchel. What I saw shocked me. Uncle Bob described the reporters he befriended over the years as relentless. Meaning I had to get out of there fast—like, yesterday fast. As Sergeant Joe hung up the phone, he chuckled. "There's a sucker born every minute, but I'll deal with him later. Now, let's beat it before this jag-off knocks down the door asking to see this phantom nail for himself."

Grave feelings of emptiness permeated my soul, shuttering the lights to room one. I had grown comfortable amongst the feared group of lawmen thought to be antisocial. Now on the move, I slowed my hurried steps down the hall, trying to extend our last moments together. I didn't want to leave, but it was time to get over myself and move on. Outside the safe confines of the officer's home away from home, everyday life was not so attractive. The brisk air swirling about the edges of downtown made the dark feel dangerous. I could feel the cold sidewalk through my shoes. In the distance, irritable winds whipped the flagpole and the rope pulley securing the Stars and Stripes banged and rattled against the aluminum shaft, shivering doubt up and down my spine. The more I ignored its goading, the louder and harder it slammed. The air was peaceful when we arrived, so why did it torment me now?

Sergeant Joe, always at the ready, worked to temper my uneasiness. "Careful, or you'll squeeze da heat right outta dat coffee," he laughed. Confused, I cranked my head to find Officer Johnson smiling. The goodhearted Sergeant then nodded back at me, half-consumed with the bridge loitering in the background.

I worried what this exchange might mean, but the tension eased seeing Officer Johnson run back inside to fetch his coat.

"Can't take that kid anywhere," laughed Sergeant Joe, shaking his head with a smile. While we waited, he dug a flashy square from his pocket that reflected a chrome shimmer in the compound's artificial light. It was a Zippo lighter. He flicked open the lid, exposing the grooves of the flint wheel beneath his thumb, and rolled it, igniting the air with liquid butane, turning the fuel into a flickering yellow-blue flame. It smelled sweet and fast, like hi-test race fuel.

"Lori, he said, "don't make a fool outta me now, you hear?"

There was something about pipe and cigar smoke that spoke to me. I can't explain how or why, but it did. The weirdest part is that I craved apple pie whenever I breathed its rich, leafy, wood-stained texture. Maybe the warm, comfortable smell reminded me of happier times. I could tell Sergeant Joe felt the same way. Smoking cigars wasn't a habit to him. They were a passion, a way of life. Along the water's edge, angry waves slapped the rocky shoreline. Across the foggy air mass smothering the bay came the thunderous roar of aircraft, landing lights blooming before touchdown at Lindbergh Field. The short runway sits between multiple military bases, high-rise buildings, and the Pacific Ocean, leaving the most experienced pilots zero room for error. Still in denial, believing I was going home, I stood by, acting calm, cool, and collected. Yet I was anything but collected, calm, or cool. The anxiety behind my smile had everyone fooled but me.

Sergeant Joe called my attention to the buttermilk glow in the clouds above the city. "Spooky, huh?" Leaning against the aluminum handrail bolted to the sidewalk outside the front entrance, he pulled a long, relaxing drag off his cigar before motioning for me to come closer through the veil of blue-gray smoke hanging between us.

"Have you been to Palomar Mountain to see the snow yet?"

"No, Erika doesn't like the cold. She says it dries out her sensitive skin."

"That's odd." He laughed. "I thought an ice queen would be comfortable below zero."

"Oh, and guess what: She doesn't like to watch the planes with me either."

Inside I was dying thinking of Erika all alone in her king-sized bed. The more I convinced myself she was terrible for me, the more I longed to surrender and apologize for

being such a disastrous brat. It was times like this I needed her most. I missed her fragrant face.

"You remember what I told you earlier?" asked the good Sergeant.

I nodded yes, happy to see my Nova safe and sound, parked behind two squad cars alongside the rear of the building.

"Good girl," he said, pointing towards the bridge with his smoldering stogie. "Da best kinda life is long, not short, capeesh?"

I was proud of myself. I think Sergeant Joe was too, but his concern was clear by the warmth he conveyed. A blink later, he tossed my braided leather key ring into the air and shouted "*Catch!*" as it nosedived into a faint puddle of water in the gutter beneath my feet. Was this a sign or my clumsiness at work? The idea of going it alone destroyed me, though I'd never tell. Try as I might to contain myself, I broke down. This almost cost me my freedom. But I convinced Sergeant Joe everything was fine. Trust me, easier said than done when you've spent a lifetime feeling bad about feeling good.

In a few moments I would be home free and right back where I started. Only this time I was starting from a place of experience—the experience that gets results if you know what I mean.

"Now listen," said Sergeant Joe, standing between me and the black and white cruisers. His gaze probing and intense. "When you get home tonight, I want you to think of three things other than Erika worth waking up for. If you can do that, then you'll be one step closer to life on your own terms." But I had a question of my own I needed answered before we parted ways.

"What did you mean about your wife being average?"

He paused.

"Tell you what—think about it for a day or two, then call me. Maybe by then, you'll have figured it out."

Stripped of his burdens and satisfied, he smiled and blew a cloud of smoke over his shoulder towards Officer Johnson behind us on the sidewalk before offering some final last thoughts. "Look," he said. "There's no way fer a raw dog like me ta truly understand how ya feel, but If I see ya around here again, I'm gonna arrest ya on da spot. I don't wanna. But I will because I'm not sure I fully trust ya yet. And hey—the Hai Karate is on a need-to-know basis, capeesh?" The word "arrest" caught me flat-footed.

"Ladies," he said, "shall we?"

The creak of Officer Johnson's gun belt was still audible in the wake of commuters making their way to and from. Its stiff newness was years from understanding the complexities of his unforgiving career choice. Listening to him walk gave me a reason to smile. I was alive because of his selflessness. I almost melted when he opened the Nova's driver's door for me. "Easy now," he smiled. "And remember, there's no shame if you can't go through with this."

Now I admit, riding in his cop car down the bridge was cool. Cool enough to make me jealous thinking about him commanding such a serious machine.

Complex or not, his job came with some far-out perks. These were not the Dodges parked in your mom's driveway. No, they were street-legal twelve-gauge race tanks reporting for duty. More spaceship than a car. The elaborate array of switches, lights, and microphones crowding the dash looked to require a license to operate. After double-checking his pockets, keys, and paperwork, Officer Johnson fired up the radio, notifying dispatch of his intentions to escort me home, and cranked over the 440-cubic-inch power plant. The amperage strained under the Magnum's heavy load. You could see the chassis twist as the starter roared the four-barreled monster to life. The ominous rumble was a call to action. From my Nova, I could feel his trusty steed's idling vibrations through the black seat shaped like me. I thought of people who didn't know my name. More infamous than famous, I rolled down my window and followed the officers onto the concrete apron leading to the bridge.

The climb from the island side was more subtle than from the mainland. Our slow approach felt like a Sunday drive. Calm and peaceful. But then my skid marks appeared between shadows cast by the bridge's overhead streetlights. I punched the accelerator. I needed off the bridge like, now. The sound of my acceleration cut through the damp air, echoing across the bay like rolling thunder. My escorts, a car length behind and ahead of me, pushed to keep pace. A look of warning from Sergeant Joe calmed my racing heart enough to ease my foot off the gas pedal. Approaching the split, on the backside with offramps facing North and South, Sergeant Joe flashed his red and blue emergency lights before banking right South towards National City. To the left, the congested city and her lamp-lit runways longed to see me home. We were old friends, the roads and me.

A bit overwhelmed, I rounded the northbound curve at

speed and laid down some serious rubber, mindful of the friendly young cop behind me. Five minutes into our journey, my suicidal insomnia had met its match. The officers and I had come full circle. They had given me their best, and I was grateful, but my dreams would have to wait. I was so exhausted by this point I had to close my eyes to wake up. Not having slept for several days had finally caught up with me in the worst way. But I feared never sleeping again. Time would tell—and if not, then what? Alcohol, drugs, suicide? The end game was apparently nowhere in sight. This wasn't, however, going to stop my racy adventurousness. Erika or no Erika, I was bound for bigger and better things, whether dead or alive.

Some celebrated the bridge standing behind me as art. A marvel of engineering lending panache to the industrialized waters of San Diego Bay. For others, it's a means to an end. A blessed curse leading to the promised land. Without my glasses, I had to squint in the mirror at Officer Johnson steering with his microphone in hand. It's weird when the cops know your name. Like when your high school vice principal greets you in the hall as a long-lost friend. Half asleep, I readjusted my seat to compensate for the previous driver's long legs and searched for the perfect song to carry me home. My yellow Nova was everything to me. Her mirrored finish shone so clearly, she could see the air rise beneath the wind. A new camshaft, racing tires, and exhaust system gave her the strength to challenge any big blocks that dared test her limits. With these few modifications, she leaped forward past speed limits with great ease when the mood struck. I found such raw power incredibly sexy. There is freedom in horsepower. Erika saw things differently, preferring instead the comfort of hand-stitched leather to cushion the torque of her imported chariot: a red 1973 MG Roadster with chrome wire wheels.

She loved the ease of an automatic transmission's hushed changing of gears, while I preferred the clutch-popping revs of a manual stick shift. We couldn't have been more different, me and this love of mine. We fought for weeks after I taught her to drive stick so her new car wouldn't go to waste. It was always something—never a dull moment with Erika.

My brief venture into living strong evaporated when I spotted the bridge riding along in the backseat. I wanted to feel different but couldn't. The amber glow arching through the rear window reflected without remorse for what she had put me through. I changed lanes, then back again, to shake her wide-angle perspective. A quick smack to the rearview mirror did the trick. Hard on the gas with my police escort in tow, I watched the city's green peaks and asphalt valleys roll by the tropical breeze swaying in the dark morning's hushed softness. The wide avenues and tight alleys looked nothing like I remembered from a few hours before. Maybe because my lesbianism was officially confirmed, on government documents no less. I knew before, but now so did everyone else. That, along with also being a documented half-wit. Both criminal and mental. And to think, this all started because of my desire for a stupid milkshake. *Never again*, I thought. From now on it was healthy foods only for me, eaten at reasonable times, instead of late-night junk food runs.

Far and wide there were only pockets of light. Houses, shops, and buildings along the way all stood ready for the new day to arrive. Each one responsible for its own success-es and failures. I liked knowing they had no idea of what a fool I'd become. Or that I had almost killed Ray Johnson's younger brother, California Highway Patrol Officer Tommy Johnson. He was a chef at a hip spot in La Jolla and I hated myself for almost destroying his life by snuffing out his heroic brother forever. Officer Johnson couldn't help but smile talking about their spirited chess games or how Ray wanted to open a Caribbean themed restaurant after he saved enough money. Ashamed doesn't begin to cover how I felt. In that moment though, my unforgiveable secrets were safe. But for how long? Come daylight, a new view would dominate the shadowy late-night solitude taunting my soul. I wasn't home free after all, not by a long shot.

Chapter 14

–

Euclid Avenue signaled the halfway point between home and Coronado. From either direction on Route 94, Euclid to Imperial takes you to my grandfather's crypt at the Cypress View Mausoleum. Aside from the massive showing of respectful mourners, his funeral had been a farce. A costly production intended for the living, not the deceased. But aren't they all? The convoy of stretched limos was a dramatic scene right out of a mobster movie. For two days, Grandma had him on full display in a fancy silver casket dressed in a handsome black suit, surrounded by enormous floral tributes and between a matching set of squatty double doors with gold push handles. The funeral director explained death as a renewal. A time to return to our creator as the water returns to the sea. Though appreciated, his kind words left me with more questions than answers.

The mortician used a white powder to make Grandpa's heavy makeup look more natural. Dad told me not to cry but I did anyway. Years in the desert sun had tanned Grandpa's skin like fine leather, yet he was white as a waxy ghost. The overstated rose lipstick used to liven him up looked phony, almost feminine. A private man with simple yet rugged standards, Grandpa Hank, would have hated the fuss made over his humble life. During his service, Karen and I clung to each other for support. The chapel's vaulted ceiling of slanted pine planks kept my claustrophobia at bay, but not the heat. The embalmed air hung thick like muggy thunderheads over the financial psychopaths bickering over control of Grandpa's wealth. The entire hour by his side was like an out-of-body experience. *Any moment*, I thought, *he would rise from the dead for his last act.* I wondered what people would say about me at my funeral. How would I be dressed, and would anyone be crying?

One thing was for certain: I preferred the natural look and would have absolutely died if they forced me to spend eternity with a face full of makeup. I didn't want to appear a braggart when talking about my grandfather with the officers, but he was more than a stand-up guy; he was an institution—salty, but a revered institution. The son of poor Arkansas cotton farmers, his strong, calloused hands and sixth-grade education built a fortune of millions. A Carpenter by trade, his word was his bond. Grandma Vogt ascended from a well-to-do Irish family in Boston and relished her local celebrity status. In her day, it meant something to be married to a master tradesman. Honest to a fault, Grandpa rebuked money's corrupting influence while Grandma embraced it. Honorable stewards of old-fashioned values, neither Hank Vogt Sr. nor Doris could understand the war raging inside me.

Thinking about my death, I recognized survival as a long shot. Erika held the power of my botched suicide in her hands and could destroy me. I thought of an awakening born of a secret high school crush, but my problems were not the result of steamy adolescent infatuation. If the truth was going to save me, I needed to be honest and start from the beginning, where life's troubles began, halfway around the world a decade before my conception.

I used to have this dream where my mom's father, Grandpa Virgil, would rock me to sleep beside a stack of freshly cut logs on a creaky old cabin floor smelling of sappy pine needles. Me on his lap, snuggled in red-checkered flannel, cheek against his chest, before the crackle of a stone fireplace insulating us from the frostbitten winds howling outside. Tragically, our fond memories together forever live in the boundaries of my vivid imagination because on July 30, 1945, at 12:27 a.m. Chief Warrant Officer Virgil C. Huntley died when his ship, the *USS Indianapolis*, sunk to the bottom of the Philippine Sea after two torpedoes from a Japanese submarine exploded into her starboard side five minutes past midnight, blasting wounds in her hull big enough to drive a Cadillac through. This tragedy destroyed more than our family because the Indianapolis had successfully delivered half the world's enriched uranium for the atomic bomb named "Little Boy," which had obliterated Hiroshima eight days after Grandpa Virgil died. Little Boy killed over 140,000 people, 39 percent of Hiroshima's population. Twenty-three years later, on November 6, 1968, my grandfather's captain, Charles Butler McVay III, an Annapolis graduate and second-generation naval officer, shot himself through the mouth with his service pistol, ending a twenty-three-year battle with survivor's guilt.

When I was fourteen, I asked Grandma Mary how she learned Grandpa Virgil had died. She directed my attention to the large window ledge above the kitchen sink overlooking her small grove of citrus trees, both oranges and lemons. On the ledge sat a black transistor radio. She loved to sing along with Bing Crosby and Frank Sinatra while elbow-deep in sudsy dishwater. It helped ease those lonely afternoons dreaming about her sailor bursting through the door with his seabag in tow, shouting "Honey, I'm home!" She said she heard a "BREAKING NEWS BULLETIN" the morning of August 15, 1945, with President Truman declaring, "THE GREAT WAR HAS ENDED." I fancy her relief, dancing in clouds of soapy bubbles tossed into the air, wearing those exhausted, hard-soled shoes that clicked when she walked. Several weeks later, a polite young man with a mouth full of smiling teeth handed her a yellow telegram marked URGENT from the Navy department. Unbeknownst to her, Grandpa Virgil had been dead for seventeen days. It was the last time she ever opened the front door for anyone. She turned to Jesus shortly thereafter and spent her remaining days hoping and praying for a reunion with her lost lover.

Mom described Grandpa Virgil as a warm spirit whose kindness could lift droopy wallpaper in the gloomiest of rooms. He was tall, too. Tall and slim. Not Grandma Mary— she was short with brown hair that turned white with age. The ship's clerk in Navy dress blues, his life of service to God and country, had swept Grandma off her feet fifteen years earlier when he was on shore leave in San Francisco. He used to tell Grandma Mary, "I hate the idea of killing, but good men must fight bad wars." One day, he was waving good-bye, blowing kisses from the deck of his proud ship, and the next he was gone without a trace—no body, no funeral, no closure. Only memories of what could have been. In hindsight, Mom was dealing with the loss of two parents, which is why I never blamed her for abandoning me. Broke and on her own, she married my father at eighteen. He gave her five children, including one who died at birth. I think losing a newborn baby was the straw that broke Mom's back. Grandma Mary said baby Frederick's death inspired Mom to drown her sorrows in twice-distilled Russian vodka. After divorcing my dad, she dated for a few months, then fled north to the dry, cracked lake beds of the Mojave Desert for a fresh start. There she married a gray-skinned, foul-mouthed little man about six-foot-three with a patchy red beard masking a sunken face. I met Neal twice, but once was enough. The day he slapped Karen for refusing his lewd advances was all I needed to kill his lascivious memory.

After a barroom brawl of a honeymoon in Bakersfield, Mom and Neal settled in Ridgecrest, California, population 12,500. Together, they enjoyed a whirlwind romance flavored with bottom-shelf bourbon and hair-pulling disagreements. The blasphemous loser whose name she took, slurring her words before a justice of the peace, loved to threaten her life publicly.

Next to pounding bruises into Mom with empty bottles of brown-bag vino, combing dandruff flakes from the waves of his greasy red hair was an obsession. Love existed between them I'm told, but only during jealous make-up sex inspired by rampant infidelity. I always thought Mom would kill Neal, considering he liked to ask unsuspecting women if they'd like to see his pet rock. He never asked me because I busted his sick ass the night he pulled his shy uncircumcised penis from inside his pants pocket for Karen to admire. I told her we needed to tell our brother, Allen, but Karen feared Neal would end us if Mom ever found out he tried to tag team her daughters. Dad didn't care because he liked that it made our mom look bad.

Like most families, we had secrets—dark secrets with violent tendencies. Maybe that's why I chose such a public forum from which to die. If they weren't going to recognize me in life, then I wanted to be recognized in my death. Aside from the bridge being a convenient killer, it's a path to paradise, a world of comfort lined with sandy beaches. Coronado Island, aside from its two active military bases, is anything but foreboding. There is no discomfort at any turn. Across Glorietta Bay, where the oceanfront golf course kneels into the tide, stands the Hotel del Coronado and her triumphant tower offering 360-degree views of heaven on Earth. In the sixties, celebrities like Marilyn Monroe and Walt Disney flocked to The Del in search of quiet sunsets far from the Hollywood spotlight. During World War II, armed sentries patrolled the now-famous, red-roofed Victorian turret for signs of enemy invaders in the foamy blue surf.

Almost ten stories tall, The Del's turret once served as a nautical and aeronautical landmark. Grandpa Vogt first shared the storied hotel's history with me at a Sunday brunch in the world-renowned Crown Room, where we dined like royalty under lofty ceilings covered in wood panels crafted from Oregon sugar pines.

Frank Baum, the author of *The Wizard of Oz*, designed the grand ballroom's famous crown chandeliers in the early 1900s. They still illuminate the vast hall to this day. Knowing the celebrated turret was used to help lost ships find their way home, I couldn't help but wonder—before I knew better, of course—if Grandpa Virgil could see the lofty lookout before he drowned. He died at night, so I thought maybe he saw the hotel's pristine reflection shimmering on the water's surface. "Impossible," said Grandma Mary. One, the distance; and two, the second torpedo sent to kill him ripped open a fuel tank, spilling thirty-five hundred gallons of black diesel oil into the sea. So thick was the water, one survivor about to be washed overboard dove onto a hearty oil slick before swimming away naked through seven-foot waves of gooey noxious fumes with a mouthful of flammable snot, hoping the pillar of fire behind him sank with the ship. The night Captain Hashimoto launched his six torpedoes, it was hot and sticky. Most of the crew were asleep on the wooden deck, stripped down to their skivvies, when the first blast sheared off the ship's bow, halting their seventeen-knot race to the Philippines, where they planned to practice invading Japan. This was wartime, and the enemy must die before he kills you. Twelve minutes later, every riveted ounce of Grandpa's heavy cruiser dove to the ocean floor with him, and 299 other waterlogged sailors, eternally trapped in sinking wreckage. Of the 1,196 crew on board, 900 survived the blasts, igniting the bloodiest shark attack in recorded history.

Dehydrated and blistered from the day's baking in the acrid swells, 316 out of the 900 survivors lived to be rescued. Most floated for days on the open ocean, waiting to die, while others took matters into their own hands. A hundred or more succumbed to their thirst and died from salt poisoning. They foamed at the mouth until their swollen tongues choked off their air supply, allowing for a slow, horrific death. The harsh conditions caused others to hallucinate. When they did, their minds tricked them into believing their friends were the enemy and they stabbed them to death to save themselves. These violent attacks chummed the waters already teeming with hungry sharks who came to feast upon the innocents treading water thousands of miles from home. After four days, a seaplane tail gunner spotted a winding oil slick and radioed the fleet for help. The heroic pilot some called a rogue, disobeyed a direct order and landed his plane amongst the bloody carnage. His decision saved lives. Without this dereliction of duty, the admirals in charge would have an added 316 deaths in their quest to lay blame elsewhere. The Navy never found Grandpa's ship. They stopped searching eight days later and shifted their efforts to court-martial the captain for not zigzagging or promptly ordering abandon ship. A false accusation considering the first torpedo cut the ship's power, thus silencing the intercom system.

To this day, nothing the government did to divert attention from their incompetence returned my grandfather or his dead shipmates home to their families. No, it tarnished a great legacy and turned hundreds on an innocent man. Fair winds and calm seas yawned open at the Golden Gate for America's most secret mission and the only one ever involving the use of nuclear weapons. A handful of days later, the Japanese violently laid Grandpa Virgil to rest in the crushing cold depths between Guam and the Philippines. Six thousand eight hundred forty-five miles in the opposite direction is where his terror became mine.

Being an explorer, my other grandpa, Vogt, a proud Army

infantry Veteran, loved everything about the godforsaken desert, especially Death Valley, the hottest place on Earth.

A lifelong smoker, he swore the hot, merciless air dried out his soggy post-nasal drip thickening his deep cough. Wide-open and mysterious, the immense static-free spaces were home to him. I think the mystical aspects of the desert intrigued Grandpa's hidden intellectual curiosity. Case in point: trees that grow from rocks. Nothing fascinated him more. While fantastic, the brilliant shooting stars at night captivated me more. The day my life forever changed began like any other. I awoke in grandpas beloved desert with the harsh sunlight in my eyes eager to play amongst the dust devils blowing across the nearby sandstone fortresses. In the kitchen, Grandma Vogt hovered in her blue cotton robe sipping black coffee over an empty plate covered with a napkin. On the stove, bacon sputtered and popped. "No school for an entire week!" I shouted.

Grandma was in some kind of mood. She stood about five feet tall and could break you with a single look. I knew better than to push her buttons. Everyone did but Grandpa. When she got too bossy for his tastes, he would turn down his hearing aids and parade around smiling. They were the cutest couple you ever saw and the least likely to agree on anything. She was relentless in teaching me the ways of womanhood. My future meant everything to her, and nothing but affluence would satisfy. "Never marry below your station," she would say, "No matter how much money they make." I think it embarrassed her that Grandpa was a proud Southerner. He was a family man through and through. And blue collar to the bone. But he never ever drank. Of the two of them,

I feared Grandma the most. If I followed her example, life was wonderful. If not, she, unlike Grandpa, would deny me anything and everything to make her displeasure known.

I may have only been ten, but I was a force to be reckoned with on the open water. If something was happening with the boat, I was first on the scene. Grandpa Vogt taught me to drive his triumphant vessel long before I could see over the steering wheel. I practically lived at the dock, bragging to anyone who'd listen. Nineteen feet long, Grandpa's custom Chris-Craft barrel back was one of 433 like wooden hulls ever constructed. She was shapely in all the right places. Each length of hand-cut mahogany was stained to perfection. Whenever I drove, Grandpa would fold down the Bugatti windshield so the speed could fly through my hair as we hopscotched over the whitecaps. The first thing Grandma Vogt liquidated when Grandpa died was our boat. Nothing I said guilted her greed for selling it at auction to a stoved up millionaire collector from Anacortes, Washington. Her selfish action changed our dynamic forever.

After a splash and go shower, I'd bounced back to the trailer's modest kitchen where I ate enough for two. With a full course breakfast of scrambled eggs, bacon, and apple juice down the hatch, I yelled to Karen, who was playing records in our bedroom. "The last one to the dock is a rotten egg!" and blasted out the single-wide front door, clearing the porch in one leap, towards the river across the street. I heard him once, then twice, before he repeated himself a fifth time. "Lori, get back here this instant! You weren't raised in a barn, goddammit!" I knew he would close the door for me, since he wasn't raised in a barn either, and continued sprinting towards the water without looking both ways, almost crashing into a thorny green cactus about seven feet tall. For me, the water was magical—the smell, the taste—and nothing beat the spray off the bow powering through the chop at full speed. From day one, I was hooked. That Grandpa Virgil died in the water never crossed my mind as a kid. His death lived a world away from my desert oasis where dragonflies, not bombers, patrolled the sunbaked mists shimmering against the rocky rainbows.

The first group of anglers to spot my impish glee that morning was loading ice chests with cans of Coors, Schlitz, and white bread sandwiches wrapped in cellophane. Dad said there was nothing worse than amateurs who pretended to fish wearing beer goggles. Grandma, not Grandpa, invited him to join us for the weekend, and I was secretly a little nervous. I had lived with my grandparents now for several years, and though Dad had anger issues, it was impossible not to love him. Since I hadn't seen him in about six months, I didn't know what he'd be driving, but I knew he'd be traveling with a spittoon full of wintergreen tobacco spit. From my vantage point near the water's edge, I could see pretty much anything that moved up on the road that led from the highway to the docks. It was a busy morning, and I labored, scanning the two-way traffic jam for the custom look only my dad would own. Purchasing anything stock off the showroom floor was unacceptable. Life was either his way or not. Grandma confessed Dad needed to make some changes but reminded me to watch my manners at the dinner table. Dad hated people using their fingers to eat and would demoralize anyone who manhandled their food in front of him. Running amok without a friend to pass the time, I waited anxiously for what felt like forever. To keep myself busy, I hiked the shoreline back and forth, skipping rocks across the water to the Nevada state line floating in the middle. Karen and Dad were missing in action, and Grandpa Vogt was busy smoking and reading his newspaper. Grandma refused to enjoy the arid landscape with me, choosing instead to iron Grandpa's Hawaiian shirts, as idle hands were the devil's workshop. Outside, the morning river looked frozen against the lunar-like qualities of the desert—dry, empty, and cold. But it was warm, about eighty-five degrees, and sunny. Soft as black velvet, the waters welcoming glassy surface hid many deadly secrets. Afternoons were a different story.

The dirt overhangs near the edge were crusty and dry. Rocks and scorpions were plentiful, but weeds and grass never survived long in the oppressive drought-fired rays. Busy adults meant I was free to explore, but not near the water's edge. Dad would arrive soon, and in a few hours, I'd show him how fast a girl could drive. I was ready to make history.

As I strolled in the forbidden zone hunting whiptail lizards, a beeping horn in the sun-drenched distance broke my concentration. Dad! I turned to wave when I felt the ground shift. Before I could blink, the bank crumbled. Fragile earth and petrified sand dumped me into the rage of the calm river's seductive curves. The shock of the cold water startled me, but drowning is anything but quiet—every fiber of my being screamed for oxygen. The indigo sheet of wet glass that earlier welcomed my dipped toes now swirled and hammered my body. The water no longer tasted sweet. It tasted polluted and foul. It seeped into my shoes, making them heavy and wet.

My eyes bulged wide. I could see the warm desert rippling on the surface above. I screamed for help two feet under as a maleficent force pushed me further down, away from rescue. Groggy and defeated, I succumbed to asphyxiated panic and inhaled the thin liquid, filling the spaces between my nose and mouth. As the last escaping bubbles of air silenced me, I floated away in the arms of glowing eyes. She had come for me. But why?

The swift water, cold and indifferent, was no match for my father's bear hug strength. Without hesitation, he had jumped into the river downstream and plunged his hand deep into my breathless world. In two forceful movements, he ripped me from death's eternal grip. Thanks to the man who abandoned me for less responsibility, I could now thrash about and gasp for air after a retired doctor boating with his family saw the entire ordeal and resuscitated me. While alive, my dead grandfather Virgil's frightful last thoughts took hold and never let me go.

Chapter 15

–

I felt a sickening sense of urgency as I slowed the Nova, pulling into La Mesa. Lose the cop, then sleep. There were a million questions afloat in my brain, but the officer trailing close behind me was the highest priority. No one could see me chaperoned by a police escort, especially a Black one. I planned to meet him at Drew Ford, the dealership atop the hill overlooking my apartment, and explain myself, so as not to offend him. I didn't have a problem with his color or being a cop, but those who paid my rent would. There was no way to avoid a problem if discovered together, especially when you consider the deadly origins of our connection. He had saved my life, so sparing him any further trouble was the least I could do. I think he understood. At least I hope he did.

Wilson Street lacks the infamous Southern California swagger known to inspire dreamers to reinvent themselves in the buoyant weather. Instead, it's an idyllic short stretch of Americana like you might find in small farming towns, where the sound of an ice cream truck awakens sugary excitement in children, young and old. Paved with a dirt-road charm between two significant boulevards and lined with trees that lose their golden fall leaves, it supports an interest in family values and traditional class status lost on the masses migrating south in search of new beginnings. There's even a church for those seeking God. Above all, La Mesa, and streets like Wilson, celebrate those who understand the difference between a house and a home. Save for me and my unholy suffering with a smile.

You might think it wouldn't be easy to lose oneself in a world built of glass houses. I did too, until I realized everywhere I went, there I was. Being home on Wilson Street, the stigma of my inequity was overwhelming, as there was a religious sense of guilt attached to my indiscretions. I couldn't help but feel I had brought this trouble plaguing me on myself. That being provocative with a woman made everything my fault. Life felt wrong, out of touch with the eternal plan whose eggs shed themselves in a bloody show each month to remind me I wasn't fulfilling my purpose. I was a thief, a bastard child, robbing the universe of life. Were my roadblocks to happiness punishment for sharing a love that shall not conceive? Perhaps. I didn't know for sure, but I had a fairly good idea it wasn't helping.

Officer Johnson was very protective. Also extraordinarily strong and incredibly determined. "You gonna be okay?" he asked one last time. How did I know? I could have loved someone like him. He was every bit of Karen, as he was Ronnie, only better and worse. But there was no fooling him. "We want you to take care of yourself, so make sure you do." In a choked voice, I reassured him his efforts weren't in vain. After saying our goodbyes, Officer Johnson drove out of my life as quickly as he had arrived. There was no fanfare or grandstanding from either of us. He said he understood my need for a discreet arrival and his promise to call and check on me in the next few days came with a demand that I connect with my sister and share the night's events in great detail before Sergeant Joe stopped by for a visit. I questioned what he thought driving away. Did he secretly hate me? Was he betting I'd be back for round two? Or had I made a good first impression? Only he knew for sure, but for now, sleep mattered most. As he shrunk in the distance, the exhaust vapor trailing his taillights said I may never see him again. This saddened me to tears. I knew then nothing about our lives would ever be the same.

My home was a place of consequence—a reminder I didn't fit the family mold. The goal that night was to sneak into my apartment undetected. Simple as it sounds, terrifying whispers and nauseating doubts wished me to tuck tail and run. I wasn't so much afraid of my grandmother as I was of what she represented. She was my father's mother and the driving force behind the false narrative of happiness I used to spread joy. I loved her dearly and never wanted to disappoint her, but I knew deep down she would never accept the person I was fighting to be.

If you blinked, you would miss Wilson Street. Grandpa constructed the apartments I called home in a U shape around a courtyard full of luscious tropical wonder. The units were spacious, with high ceilings, built-in bookshelves, and generous windows to fill the nooks and crannies with natural light. Everything about them was of the highest standards. A quick glance up the driveway at Grandma's dark second-story bedroom window signaled the coast was clear.

I felt sadness for Karen and how her continued involvement would only muddy the waters between us until resentment became the cornerstone of our relationship. She had confronted me about a month earlier after an anonymous call alerted her to my nightly beatings, but I refused her help, worried it might make things worse. Her support meant the world to me, and I couldn't afford to lose my sister, not like this. A mere two hours and some change had passed since my suicidal rage had almost killed an innocent man. *I can survive this*, I thought. But did I want to? I did, and I didn't, but that was for Erika to decide.

Before I made the driveway, I sliced through the dark, quiet as a mouse, to prevent the crunch of pebbles under the weight of thirty-two hundred pounds of race-ready perfection from sounding like boulders falling from the sky. Getting past a suspicious light sleeper like my grandma was no straightforward task—but then again, neither is drowning a fish.

Officer Johnson had pointed out my mirror's crooked stance, and after adjusting it, I could see St. Luke's Lutheran Church from my carport stall. The pasty chapel aligned perfectly with Mount Helix. Both display their massive crosses in a contemptuous, almost competing manner. Like my relationships with Grandma and Erika, the cross to me was a great contradiction. It was a symbol of death as much as life. When I looked upon its simplistic form, I saw love and hate, sin and accusation, but never forgiveness. Others see sacrifice—me, not so much. I considered the mountains my church. Their rocky outcrops, home to nature's abundance, rise from the depths through the clouds to naturally touch the heavens without man's sinful influence. The idea of such purity left me speechless every time it crossed my mind.

The concrete pad outside my back door smelled hauntingly familiar. There was nothing free about the apartment Grandma gave me. Flagrant hints of ocean breeze had followed me home to La Mesa, where I'd dabbled in happiness all my life. Look at me, I thought, daring myself to become a benevolent old dame. I took a moment to remember Grandpa's quest for perfection. Nothing he did was second rate, and you could always count on him to deliver, regardless of the obstacles at hand—like the apartments I called home. He'd scrutinized each step, from grading the foundation to selecting the exterior's sage green paint. Its robust manner complements the burgundy trim beautifully. The combination of colors memorialized a tranquil Japanese garden he had seen once in a *National Geographic* magazine.

It's funny the life we take for granted. You know, those imperfect moments we label insignificant that later become critical points of reference in our experience. Now, as I was deep in thought, the emergent flash of my spontaneous meltdown felt a million miles away. Over the years, I had become a master at concealing the truth, even from myself. A life teeming with abusers taught me to compartmentalize my pain, which allowed me to journey free, unimpeded by otherwise crippling heartache. I handled my sorrow as if it were ferocious crocodiles housed in glass enclosures at the zoo. They could only sink their flesh-ripping teeth into me if I placed myself in danger of being bitten. Similarly, I was safe from my demons so long as my boxes of grief remained undisturbed.

But death no longer trusted me. My stoic existence had become a problem. I was conscious of her movements, seeing monochromatic flashes of her shape-shifting presence walking beside me. With each step, the night deepened, inching closer to daylight. I feared my next move would sound the alarm. Then came a frightening cry from inside my apartment. Sounding like the toll rung from a haunted bell, the phone rang out, screaming *Erika, Erika, Erika!* The hair-raising sound pinballed off the cinder block and stucco walls around me. I yanked open the door to my apartment to silence her crosstown assault when the ringing suddenly stopped. My exhaustion struggled to compute. The tension filled my stomach with heaviness. Muscles rigid, my posture stiff, I boxed myself into an edge of darkness to avoid the observant streetlight raining down from above. The intensity of the moment seemed to amplify my compromised position. Does it ever stop, I gasped, this constant barrage of dramatic turbulence? How was I so lucky to have all my rights go so wrong? Seconds later, another call broke out like a raging inferno. This time, I was ready. There would be no more second chances. I grabbed the phone. My voice, tired and afraid, knew all hell was about to break loose.

"I fucking hate you. You motherfucker. I thought you were at the police station, you miserable liar." Erika was in rare form. "You're such a disappointment. You think you're such a saint, but you're not. You're a worthless nothing that contributes nothing to my life, and I don't care that you're nice. Nice is just nice, and it means nothing anymore. You have done nothing to support me, and, I hate you. All you do is use me." Her issues were old news. I'd heard this song and dance many times before. For God's sake if world peace broke out it woulda been my fault. She called me vulgar names so often, I practically forgot mine.

"You can plan all you want," she said. "But you're full of nothing but empty fucking promises. I fucking hate you so bad. I literally fucking hate you. I don't love you. This is the way you wanted it, so I hope you're happy, you wrecked bucket of fuck." I could hear her struggle to catch her breath. Yet this was no time to relax. But God, I loved her.

"You're no different than your father and fucking grandmother," she continued. "I hope you know that, you asshole."

I tried to calm her fears. "You mean the world to me. Please, baby, we can fix this," I said, desperately crying for her to stop.

"*Don't baby me!*" she screamed louder than before. "I guess we just have two extremely different understandings of what love is, and I'm just exhausted waiting around for this actually to be something, Lori."

What could I say that Erika hadn't already said? We fed off each other's insecurities with the knowledge that no matter how ugly things got, we were life partners forever. I had not treated her fairly and was paying a heavy price. In my darkest hour, she was most effective in her cause to destroy me. I was the nail, and she the hammer. But at times we were oh so perfect together.

Sick to my stomach, I spoke her name. E-R-I-K-A, but the angry sobbing on the other end of the line went silent and hung up. I feared the violence sure to come. If unhappiness were an Olympic event, I would have been a triple threat. To keep the walls from closing in on me and shake the feeling of being followed, I circulated, moving from one room to another. How must it feel to be loved unconditionally? *What's the use?* I thought, ambling to the bathroom. No matter how hard I tried, I couldn't shake the scourge of love. After a gushing pee, I stood to a garish caricature in the mirror and gawked at my grizzled features. I looked grisly. My youthful abundance looked burned beyond recognition. Wrinkled parachutes, not bags, hung under the whites of my cutie-pie eyes.

Clothed and dirty, I submitted to the merciful comfort of a hand-sewn patchwork quilt calling from the bedroom down the hall, where Grandma Vogt last hugged me. I bought it two years earlier from a local artisan while I was road-tripping through the fertile wine country outside Santa Barbara during a steady fall rain. The sweet autumn fragrances made for the perfect getaway. An abundant harvest allowed the widowed proprietor housed in a faded red barn to offer jellies and jams two for the price of one. The deep furrows of tractor-plowed soil behind the faded red structure reminded me of a freshly tilled garden, or maybe newly mown grass fertilized with ripe pumpkin seeds. While the quilt was neither overly ornate nor visually intricate, I loved owning something of substance that was not mass-produced. What my quilt lacked in fussy stitching it made up for in warmth, from layers of gold and orange fabrics sewn gently around blocks of red, purple, and rich scarlet browns. It was a promise, keeping me safe while I slept with my dreams.

Before yielding to the hijinks of dreamland, I told myself Erika loved me and didn't mean the horrible things she said. Then, well on my way to redemption, with Grandma safely tucked in above, I closed my eyes and crashed into sleep. Time: 3:00 a.m. sharp according to the reliable black hands of my silver wristwatch. As for Erika—she would call back in the morning. She always did.

Chapter 16

–

Four hours later there was an air of forgiveness in the pink sunrise clouds peeking through my bedroom windows as I lay suspended between insomnia and exhaustion. Another morning alone with a head full of the world was upon me. I knew Erika was out there, ready to defile my undug grave. I canvassed the room for proof this wasn't a dream. Piled on the brown shag carpet was a handful of coins. The two quarters, two pennies, a dime, and a trusty nickel were the only items of value in the entire apartment. They toyed with me, taunting their worth. Their silence was an unnatural lullaby welcoming me to rock bottom.

Erika and I had dreamed of sailing the world together on a boat with double masts named *Por Vida*. She would explore ancient wines and exotic cheeses in port towns welcoming free spirits while I tended to her every need. Her family was of Norwegian descent and owned a fishing boat docked on Harbor Island. We liked to say the enchanted sea brought us together, but why care at this point? She obviously didn't. Besides, I had a loving sister and two kick-ass brothers along with the greatest little nephew this side of anywhere, so why bother?

I should have known better, of course. My first introduction to love was pleasant and insightful. It was the first day of high school, and exotic Latin vibes were on display two lockers down. A year older and popular with the boys, Francesca's curves roamed wildly, calling out to me in the most beautiful of ways. Was intimacy with a girl possible? Maybe. My Latin princess could have been a one-hit-wonder. The jury was still out, but this newfound sense of self felt oh-so right. At the first sight of her, I would secretly pant and look away. She left me wanting more each time she flashed her gorgeous smile. I dreamed of her featherlight kisses until I couldn't. Zip code 91977 had delivered my first crush. I was sixteen and in love with a stranger.

For months her windblown aroma tickled my untouched desires. I loved the feeling of unbridled hormones teasing my body. Already graduated, Karen couldn't wait to hear if I'd met any cute boys on my first day of high school. My flippant response intrigued her, but I never shared a morsel of my mystery woman's voluptuous black hair and creamy caramel skin. A slip of the tongue nearly revealed that my crush dressed herself in plaid miniskirts with white knee-high boots. Of course, she wasn't gay, but the fight for my identity had begun. Thoughts of us together fortified me like when Elvis sang to Karen in 1960 during a break filming of *Kid Galahad* in Idyllwild. Chosen as extras, Karen and her girlfriend approached the King sitting alone when he surprised them with a song. Karen still blushes when she tells the story.

My apartment was cute, albeit empty. Almost everything I owned lived at Erika's. A corner unit, the apartment was warm and comfortable. Almond-colored walls with large windows made the cube-style layout feel larger than other typical one-bedrooms you might find around San Diego County. I kept a chair and television for special occasions. I had to; both were gifts from Grandma Vogt, and she would have flipped out had they gone missing, especially the TV. Housed in a beautiful oak entertainment console, it was the perfect blend of art and science. In high school, I had a small black-and-white TV in my bedroom—unusual in those days. I kept it until Grandma gave me the opulent Zenith Chroma-color monstrosity for Christmas a year earlier. Whenever she dropped by, often unannounced and sometimes late, she referenced the two wrought iron drawer handles at the console's base. Doing so was her way of reminding me that it was expensive and to behave. The cost was of little importance to me. My radar was scanning every inch of life within earshot for signs of my transgression on the bridge. My crusty, bloodshot vision wasn't helping, but I couldn't relent, not for a second.

But what's done is done, I told myself. It was 9:00 a.m. now, with no sign of Erika. Strange, because she was an early riser. Usually before six, but never past seven. Unanswered questions churned in my belly. I'd had mornings before when I woke up exhausted, and today was no exception. I was careful not to arouse suspicion, breathing only when necessary because Grandma was awake, pacing between the bedroom and her kitchen. Her floor plan mirrored mine. She had moved into the apartments after Grandpa died and my uncles sold their home on Cedar Lake Avenue in San Diego. It was a Craftsman-style house with a huge backyard that sold to a young Navy family, new in town from Virginia. Grandma enjoyed being close to the shop where her sons carried on with the family business. Uncle Bob was ecstatic to have his mom so close. Whenever time allowed, he would climb the stairs to her apartment, take her in his arms, and swing her around. The higher and faster he spun, the louder she giggled. I loved seeing her happy. It meant the world to me.

Love torn and emotionally bankrupt, I scrambled for energy outside the caffeinated buzz not percolating in the kitchen. Never trusted and often ignored, my gut instincts knew a call to Erika could further scar me with the burn of conditional love. We had this terrible habit of trying to out pain each other. It was a dangerous game of emotional chicken, often leading to regrettable fits of anger. If she went for my jugular, I cried wolf and begged forgiveness. After Sergeant Joe declared her a tyrant, it occurred to me that her affectionate ways were a sad cry for help. Still, I couldn't ignore the impact of her life on mine. My body felt old, drugged, and beaten. I was sober drunk without the stench of hangover fog. Before my entanglements with death, museum-worthy sunrises used to inspire me. I told myself that nothing short of peeing the bed could motivate me to rise and face the day. Nothing except Erika's every last need.

I thought of her walking barefoot on the sand near where the water shrinks down the beach. Oh boy, did I have it bad for her. She loved to tell me that the ocean is more than we can understand. That it loves and heals, wrapping her brine around our lives, asking only for our respect in return. I needed to hear Erika say she loved me one more time. For the first few seconds of each morning, between when I woke up and when I opened my eyes, I was normal and loved. Today, not so much. I wondered, was Sergeant Joe serious when he said suicidal people are also homicidal? Lying face up, staring into the dust particles floating in the Friday morning silence . . . what was the point? As the night before had brought a terrible dream, I saw the monster I envisioned tackling me on the bridge. When she arrived, I played dead, feeling her slither softly under the covers. A deep, cunning snarl stressed her deranged smile. She wasn't alone. I gripped my blanket tight, feeling the heat of their cold firestorm eyes pulling me into a blackened window full of screams. "Fear not," she said, "for I will always be with you." The taste of her torture blistered my throat. I loved her too, but why must I suffer to prove it? I guess because sometimes the most loved starved people often beg for validation in the worst way.

I didn't want to move. I didn't want to get up and out of bed and on with my life. I needed to stay down where I belonged. My show of tears meant nothing to anyone, not even me. Another day of drowning. Another day more dead than alive. I reached into the vortex of my depression only to find more rejection. My heavy eyes drifted around the room; their efforts focused when the phone rang out across the apartment, sending me into a tizzy. Off-kilter, I kicked off the quilt and rolled off the bed onto the floor. The brown shag carpet felt soft against my skin. Though I'd driven straight home from the bridge, I didn't know how far I'd traveled. On my knees now. I crawled into the kitchen, jerked the lengthy phone cord from the wall, and returned to bed until the wee morning hours of Saturday January 19th.

Chapter 17

–

After a full day sleeping off a week of dreary suicidal depression, I awoke dark and early Saturday morning with a half-empty glass of water next to my bed. There were crackers too—saltines. I don't remember getting up, not even to pee, but there they were, crumbs and all. Bless her heart. Maybe Grandma brought them down to check on me. After a cautious stroll through the apartment, I hopped into the tub for a shower to kick off the day fresh and clean. Surprisingly, my spirits were trending towards an all-time high. Oh how Erika loved to bathe with me I thought. And seeing this happy sight would make her so jealous. I wondered if she was thinking about me. She wouldn't just forget me, would she? Conditioned to the world's twisted perception of gays, I allowed its paranoia to contaminate my relationships, perpetually causing Erika and me to fight amongst ourselves just to feel something other than pain. Often, it made me question why God cursed us with a disease that made other people sick with hate.

I enjoyed having both a shower and a tub. Mine were Palmolive Green. Just like the soap. Grandma said the apartment looked good on me. But I hated the way I looked, especially naked. Decadent steam now enveloped me, the kind where the water is hot enough to sting but not burn. The air, opaque and dense, clung to my hair and washed the morning breath out of my mouth. I closed my eyes to dream of better days ahead. The calm of my steamy dreamland was short-lived, interrupted by the shrill of a desperate lover calling. But wait, wasn't my phone unplugged? I thought I'd unplugged it but couldn't be sure. *Grandma*, I thought. *She's to blame. And what's she doing coming in uninvited, what else does she know?* Outside my reach, the phone continued to ring. I knew it was Erika, but it may also have been Karen since I hadn't seen her in weeks.

Whoever it was would call back if reaching me was important. But deep down, I knew it was Erika. When the rings returned a second time, I yanked back the shower curtain and sprang from the tub with a head full of lather. Before I could steady myself, my wet feet slipped sideways in opposite directions, back-pedaling me forward across the mission red Spanish floor tiles, face first towards a lip-splitting door jamb. The white cotton panties crumpled near the toilet supplied just enough traction to avoid a concussion. Once stable, I ran so fast, I made it across the apartment in about five steps, dripping all over before the third ring subsided. It was Erika alright, and she had my undivided attention, even if I seemed a tad aloof.

"Babe? Are you there, babe?"

I can't tell you if Sergeant Joe's Hai Karate was to blame, but the next thing I knew, Wilson Street was looking for a fight.

"You got some nerve calling me," I snapped, chewing my nails, holding back a swarm of deadly intentions.

"Please!" she said in a baby like voice.

Her sleepy intrusion intensified my defenses, leaving me stuck between love and hate. But she sounded sweet, like a tender welcome home kiss from swollen, pouty red lips.

"Come home, lover. I need you, babe. I need you."

Here we go again, I thought—one minute up, one minute down. My eyes welled with tears knowing I was about to jump for the second time. In the past, I would fold to her slightest advance, but not this time around. It was over. My throat clenched its fists. There was no phlegm or spit to swallow, only anger for the beatings I had endured to ease her suffering. My raspy voice searched for traction. I was sick of her intense feelings of relief after treating me so poorly. I began breathing noisily, pounding my fists into my thighs thinking of her emotional baiting.

"Erika, I can't do this anymore."

Ready to strike at a moment's notice, she snapped, "Right on, bro."

"Can you please stop?" I sighed, wanting to cry.

I really hated when she called me bro. She did it intentionally whenever she was mad or ready to smear me. Usually, she called me babe. But you wouldn't believe how little it took to go from babe to bro. Once she accused me of smoking after eating roasted peanuts. Funny thing because I'd never smoked a day in my life. Not so much as a single puff of a candy cigarette. Anyway, Erika had been goofing off, doing cartwheels at the beach, when a clutch of loose sand grabbed her foot and spun her sideways, corkscrewing her into the ground against a canvas of purple sky fire. A recent graduate of a Certified Nursing Assistant program, I knew to triage her with ice and an elevated limb. Afterward, I ran two stop signs, racing to the drugstore for supplies to fashion a splint around her swelled appendage.

Her excuse for blasting me with false accusations was predicated upon her fear that goofing around with me forever marred her with a debilitating limp. That's right, it was my fault. But nothing could have been further from the truth. Besides, I would have loved her with bloody stumps, let alone a hiccup step, my fault or not. Her mania, not my actions, had steeped me in fear, but this did nothing for the resentment I held for the issues she projected onto me. I was back in that place where love lived to hurt. A love that sent me to the bridge in search of healing.

Never again would I be this raw as I was that cloudy Saturday morning on the phone with Erika. Her power died the night I didn't. "Yup. Always my fault," she said. "Don't contact me again," she continued. "Cuz you're fucking with me and I'm tired of it." I was at a loss. "But you called me," I said, fanning the flames of an already out of control narcissistic fire.

"Screw you bitch." The hate in her anger rumbled like a violent tornado.

"That's it, Erika, I'm done!"

I stood in silent disbelief afraid I had somehow gone overboard. No one could have seen this coming. We had double-dipped our topsy-turvy emotions many times before, and enough already as volatility was the most natural element of our ecosystem. Erika's tongue-tied calm was frightening.

"Oh really," she growled before subjecting me to a brutal verbal assault unlike any time before. "You don't quit me bitch; I quit you. You're a drunk ass loser just like that pathetic mother of yours, Bottles."

Erika weaponized my mother's struggle with alcohol whenever she felt backed into a corner. My mom's name was Georgia, not Bottles, but this meant nothing to her kill-or-be-killed mentality. For the second time, I slammed a phone into itself to stop Erika's relentless assault. Only this time, no sooner had the receiver hit the cradle when the phone erupted again.

"What?" I snapped. "Say it again. I dare you."

But Erika had other plans. "Okay, you win. I'm sorry. What's with all the hostility anyway? And really, where were you yesterday?" Before I could answer she cornered me. "Drop whatever you're doing and come home to me right now. I need you, babe. I need you badly. And we can talk about everything when you get here."

What the hell, I thought. *This might be a setup*. I asked about the girls. "No girls," she said. "What about your brothers, are they there with you?" "No, sweetheart, it's only me. Ryle and Scott are visiting Roy in La Jolla and you know how those queens love to gossip." Erika continued apologizing between fits of laughter and tears. "Just come home and let me love you."

And just like that, I was smitten all over again, making plans with the one person you knew would disembowel you in two seconds, just because. I knew better living in constant fear of her cult like power over me. But I still needed her to need me. That and my mind had conditioned me to believe she was the only person alive able to validate my existence. She was more than a good time. She was my entire life.

"You didn't tell anyone about the other night," I asked, fearing she had betrayed me.

"No, babe, no one will ever know you attempted suicide."

Just to be sure, I hit her with an unmistakable warning. "As God is my witness, if you tell anyone, I'll return to the bridge and jump with my blood on your hands."

This sent her over the edge. She cried; deep agonized breaths reserved for the dying, thus sending me over the edge deep into her madness. We were us again, but for how long?

Threatening suicide is never okay, but I felt it essential to cover my liabilities. After a few touch-and-go moments, Erika convinced me I was safe with her. Satisfied she was telling the truth, I hung up and raced off to finish my shower, dripping wet nakedness hot and heavy in love. I couldn't imagine my life without her by my side, angry or not, for she allowed me to be myself when no one else was around. And for me most of the time, that was enough.

But there were more pressing issues at hand. I was now on the clock and had to hurry because Erika's control issues were counting down. Though she never specified an official arrival time, I knew Erika, and keeping her waiting was sometimes painful. A few minutes here or there never resulted in a bloody nose, but close enough. I didn't take it personally because she loved me. I knew she did!

There are few things in life more difficult than pulling snug denim over damp legs in a hurry. A nervous feeling hit me, pulling the stiff jeans past my knees. Sergeant Joe had encouraged me to reconsider climbing back into the lion's den when I got lonely, but I had a love to salvage and could have cared less about anything anyone had to say. Where was this U-turn back to Erika leading me? And how would it be seeing her after our latest tailspin?

Life's uncertainty was my sweet spot. I loved not knowing what was coming next because there was always an outside chance it could be fantastic. I'd flown into this pattern of storms many times with Erika, but this time felt different. Different, because this time, the tail wasn't wagging the dog; I was. My outfit needed to be perfect. After I tore through my closet, a dense pile of shirts, pants, and blouses covered the bed in a heaping pile of colored fabrics. If it were up to me, I'd have picked a T-shirt and jeans. But it wasn't up to me. Like Grandma, Erika demanded I look a certain way or else. Ah, but isn't love swell? Yes, love, the most potent drug of them all. So I chose a maroon sweater with a knitted collar and brown boat shoes Erika bought me the previous summer shopping on Catalina Island with her mom, Linda.

Chapter 18

–

The last time I saw my brothers was at a high school football game. Monte Vista versus El Capitan. Before that, we occasionally crossed paths whenever Dad would stop by for a loan from the grandparents. Of course, the Monarchs were beating the pants off the Vaqueros twenty-eight to zip before Allen split early to cruise for chics. Good ol' Dad. If it wasn't one thing, it was another. He was forever in debt and unemployed because of his temper. His erratic behavior drove Grandpa mad—so much so that he would leave the room whenever Dad walked in complaining about this or that. This scenario played out for years. The last time I was in his care, I accidentally electrocuted myself, playing with a frayed electrical cord. It zapped me into unconsciousness. I was too young to remember, but to hear Karen tell it, my eyes locked, then rolled back into my head. Dad, drunk and passed out, didn't know his baby girl lay critically injured in the back bedroom, close to death. His wife or girlfriend at the time scooped me up and ran with me in her exhausted arms twelve blocks to the emergency room at Grossmont hospital. I never stayed with my dad again after that night. By the eighth grade, a short haircut transformed me into my brother Paul. We were redheaded twins, right down to our happy freckles.

Thinking about it, my slide into despair may have begun one innocent Easter Sunday. It was the first time my three siblings and I had come together in months. After church we gathered around Grandpa's medieval dining table for a family feast. Hand-carved from heavy dark wood with thick square legs and oversized brass nailheads biting the corners, its barbaric stature suggested Count Dracula's mountain-top castle. Grandma, who'd cooked all afternoon, served us mouthwatering honey-baked ham adorned with slices of juicy pineapple, cloves, hand-peeled mashed potatoes, and homemade rolls still warm to the touch.

Allen and Paul were living with Uncle Wes and Aunt Beanie as our dad was somewhere drunk, falling off his stool, telling lies to some broad bellied up to a bar. Karen lived with us, albeit for a short while, and we were beyond ecstatic to share a holiday meal with our brothers, together as one. But destiny had bitter plans for our happy Easter celebration. Dinner had started innocently enough. I was busy behaving like a proper young lady while Allen lumped mounds of mashed potatoes on his plate of delicate china trimmed in gold leaf.

Satisfied with his creamy white tower of mush, he looked in my direction. "Hey, dude, pass the butter already." I paid him no mind because I thought he was talking to Paul, seated next to me. Allen pitched a few more hey dudes our way when I gathered that Pauly wasn't the intended target. Confused, I looked at Grandpa and smiled and he, in a show of appalled force, threw back his chair, jerked Allen out of his, and kicked at him with his gimpy foot. Allen, traumatized by Dad's repeated beatings, lunged forward to avoid Grandpa's hobble and wonky sideways kick. But Grandpa yanked him back hard by his collar, hard enough to choke Allen and leave a red mark below his Adam's apple. As he worked to wrestle himself away, Grandpa cracked him upside his head with a brutal slap.

Grandpa Hank's swift defense of my honor frightened me. Years would pass before I understood the significance of my brother's playful yet incendiary remarks. While he never meant to hurt me, my first experiences with judgment were undoubtedly homegrown. It was, however, the last time anyone joked about my appearance while Grandpa was alive. Later, on summer trips to Idyllwild, boys around town would ask me if my fingers smelled like onions from scratching my swampy balls, thus cementing a foundation of abuse that eventually drove me to the bridge.

The day we lost Grandpa in May 1970 devastated me. It's funny how hearing the word "terminal" affects the living. My experience was typical. First I bellowed sadness, then I got angry. But then something strange happened; I came to accept death and soon learned to embrace its sensibilities. In it I learned pain was only temporary. That I could live free for a hefty price.

Riddled with colon cancer, Grandpa Vogt survived six failed surgeries and a colostomy bag. Days before, the last strokes robbed his ability to speak. Grandpa shared one last gem of wisdom with me from his hospital bed.

"Lori Vogt," he said, reaching out from under his itchy blue blanket and ripping out the lifelines feeding his sick body. "Better to die on your feet than live on your goddamn knees." Instantly, bloody I.V. fluid covered the floor beneath his hospital bed as I stood and screamed for help. I'll never forget the vulgar language spoken by healers in long white coats. They kicked and fought almost as hard as Grandpa as they bound his limbs to the bed with leather restraints.

He died six days later in OR #3 after a blocked surgical drain burst his colon. My grandfather's passing was a pivotal moment. In it, I learned the actual value of family—or lack thereof. Crude and without remorse, Grandpa's lazier offspring attacked his dying wishes with threats of lawsuits and violence the second he became mute. At the end of his deathbed in a private room on the third floor overlooking Mount Helix and the La Mesa valley, while he lay near comatose, my dad, grandmother, and aunt clashed, pushing and shoving for control of his fortune like bloodthirsty wolves. Grandpa's closest allies disregarded him like a decomposing animal carcass saddled with tumbleweeds blown across a deserted highway in the sunset of his life. I thought, *Wow. If the family patriarch gets mistreated in his critical time of need, what will I get in mine?*

Don't get me wrong, my family doesn't bear horns and devilish pitchfork tails. But the phrase blood is thicker than water should come with a warning label. I often wonder how my life might have gone had World War II not stolen Mom's parents. Would being raised by them, away from my father's loathsome influence, have allowed me to grow and prosper as God intended? Or would they have forced me to reject myself too? And to think: I was the lucky one because Grandpa and Grandma Vogt chose me.

Chapter 19

–

I admit I did some second-guessing after my Saturday morning call with Erika. I wanted to be with her so badly, but I didn't. You might think I'm crazy. That I resisted love as madly as Erika. Nope, not a chance for I adore love and happiness. I have wanted it, fought for it, and, yes, cried over it and the least likely to die for it. I mean, who wouldn't crave the one emotion capable of transforming them into a blooming flower. Thanks to broken parents, I chased it all my life.

Outside of loving pillow talk, our life was an imbalance of hot sex and even hotter fights. I needed more. I needed lazy Sunday mornings together and picture books of memories stacked a mile high. While fun, sex is for swinging singles. I craved monogamous lovemaking reserved for a committed relationship. I knew for our connection to thrive, I needed to do my part and come clean to the entire world about who I was and what she meant to me. And Erika needed to be a little less uptight and a lot more understanding.

My spirits, like a phoenix through the ashes, saw hope where there once had been none because we always came back together once the dust settled. I'd had my doubts earlier, but I was ready to take another chance on us. My brush with death was possibly the shot of life our love needed to flourish. Thanks to a handful of dedicated highway patrolmen, I was about to land in the pot of gold at the end of Erika's rainbow. While I waited for who knows what, I plotted my plan of attack, mapping out each second of our next fifty years together. It was exciting times. Perilous, but exciting, nonetheless.

While grateful for my grandparent's love, the vulnerability of intimacy and trust had so far eluded me. As partners, we sometimes lack the patience to communicate our needs. This flaw diminishes equality, leading to bad blood between otherwise compatible lovers. If I knew one thing for sure, it's the need for love in everything we do. Without it, we're nothing. I'm not talking about having a warm sculpted body under the covers to satisfy a sexual need. No, I'm talking about self-love. *Amore per se stessi* as the Italians say. I also came to realize the danger in not loving oneself if we intend to welcome another's love into our lives.

Obviously, I was in way over my head with what I thought I understood, but I believed true love never failed. And I got down on myself when it did. I'm talking way down. Ah, but isn't true love worth the proverbial broken heart? Nothing else compares to someone willing to open themselves to you fully and completely. Love is best in those intimate spaces where each breath becomes one without conscious thought. I craved the type of love willing to get lost in conversation at three in the morning. The one that says we're not close anymore, but I am here if you need me. My sister and I were suckers for all the bells and whistles of new love. And I won't ever apologize for being in love with love. For love has made me strong when I was at my weakest. And love has made me insecure when strength defined me. Love has also made me late. But before I could leave, I needed to check myself in the mirror for flaws one last time.

On my way out of the bathroom, an empowering thought came to mind: If my story had made the news, might it have inspired kindness in someone whose sister, neighbor, or best friend was weighing the odds of life after death? If I could survive, then why couldn't someone else? Feeling appropriately cute, I snatched my purse from atop the kitchen's tiled counter and scrambled out the back door without a jacket, taking louder steps than usual, not thinking my stomps would alert Grandma. I fumbled my keys with excitement, nearly ripping the ignition off the steering column starting the Nova. The distance between Erika and I was now a formality of busy overpasses and red lights. I didn't stop to think about my actions. I just went, dammit. I just went.

Even so, I reversed down the drive, honking a proud golden roar. But as you know, Erika thought I was a cheater. This weighed heavily on my mind. She accused me of it so often, I actually felt like a cheater. But I never did cheat, not once. "Who's the lucky guy this week?" she'd yell when things between us got prickly. Love to me is sacred—a virtue, based on value, care, and respect. A gift to be shared, not tossed about for a fun time. The rest is a bonus. I'm not sure why she felt the way she did, but it could have had something to do with the many relationships torn apart by her own promiscuity. She loved forcing me to explain myself, even when I made perfect sense or had nothing to say. Another projection, perhaps, to keep me guessing. Whenever she got angry, the names of the men I had dated before we met became a flashpoint for her aggressions. I mean, of course, I dated guys when I was younger. And so did she, including every prom and homecoming dance from tenth to twelfth grade—but I couldn't mention her past, ever. She knew boys never sparked my fancy, even though I married one at eighteen. And I never disliked boys. They just never blew my skirt up, if you know what I mean.

While Erika and I were on the phone, an old nemesis had reared its ugly head. She had a terrible problem with self-esteem. No matter how many times I glorified her beauty, she would cut me down to satisfy her insatiable anxiety.

"I'm glad you still like me," she'd said. "But do you think I'm pretty?"

There was no question about it, but I knew where this comment would lead us, and we had enough on our plate already.

"Well, do you?"

What was I going to do, say no?

"I probably shouldn't wear a two-piece anymore, huh?"

I dreaded these moments of narcissistic self-pity. "Wear what makes you happy," I said, tired of going in circles.

"See, I knew it. You think I'm fat. Just six short months ago, I felt beautiful poolside in Cabo, and now you think I'm fat."

I didn't think she was fat, but that's not the point. By now I had learned it was best to let her run out of steam naturally, no matter how accusatory she got.

"Can you please be honest? Am I going to embarrass myself if I keep wearing a bikini?"

"Honestly," I said, "no, you won't embarrass yourself."

"Okay, thanks for the feedback. It's hard to know when I feel people are always making fun of me." She blamed her physical appearance for my refusal to introduce her to Grandma Vogt, telling me, "I went shopping with my mom yesterday and was super self-conscious by the end, feeling like every person looked at me the way you do."

Like I did? What the hell was she talking about? I practically worshiped that girl from the word go. Erika wasn't ugly. She was the most sensational creature I had ever seen. Her beauty stunned me so intensely that I had to walk a half-mile in the other direction to avoid seeing her again. I mean, she was out-of-this-world beautiful. Let no one tell you love at first sight isn't real. Just ask new parents who hold their infants for the first time if love at first sight isn't real.

The day we met was the weekend after graduation from high school. Karen and I were at Mission Beach roller skating the bikini-clad boardwalk packed with perky suntanned curves when out of nowhere comes this blonde bombshell. She stepped out into the tantalizing blue horizon in front of me, and I just about died. Right then, she became my plan A, B, and C. It was a glorious day. But I wasn't the only gawker salivating over Erika's sunbaked butter-soft glow. It fit her high cheekbones like a glove. She floated when she walked, rocking her curvy hips with each gorgeous step. Trust me: there were plenty of dudes lurking about for a piece of her bronze pie. Strangely enough, out of everyone she walked by, I was the one she chose. Whatever it was, we shared an obvious connection across the sandy shore. I don't know how we knew. We just did.

Chapter 20

–

One of the best things about driving is the time it gives you to think. The black roads hugging the land supply a safe place to reflect. I was at my best when behind the wheel. Life could be good, I thought. But something was missing, missing from the start. Deep down, I knew Erika was as anxious as me. She played tough, but she was anything but tough. Her bark was definitely louder than her bite. She was what the kids today call a snowflake.

Now, what about the girls? Were they waiting in the wings to flog me? I didn't know, but I was about to find out. They crossed my mind at every exit I passed. Heading into Mission Valley, I drove farther away from Karen's safety net the closer I got to Erika. I would slow, then speed up, trying to think of an excuse to get out of this hot mess before it was too late. I didn't notice at first, but my nervous gut drenched my back in ulcer-worthy sweat. For all my flaws—and there were many—I couldn't afford to go backward anymore, not after my night on the bridge. Erika sounded sincere, but so had she all the other times we fought to the death.

The unfortunate part is that she could have helped me help her. While her family was more forgiving on the surface, privately they were nastier than mine. Maybe not as abusive, but equally concerned about their social status being impacted by three openly gay children. Plus, we both shared the same social stigma in our circle of straight friends and closed-minded acquaintances. Like so many others institutionalized by fear and violence, I kept coming back to avoid a few of my biggest fears—abandonment, and rejection. Having felt this before, I considered going to Erika's an acceptable risk. Bottom line, everyone has a destiny and I convinced myself time and again that Erika was mine.

A mile from her exit, my gummy hands grew nervous with anticipation. Each stiff knuckle cracked drumming "Wipe-Out" against the wheel. A mile to live, a mile to die.

I wasn't on pins and needles, but close. I was on fire, tearing through the gears. Just past SeaWorld, beyond the Sunset Cliffs and Nimitz intersection was Point Loma Boulevard. From there, a slight left and hard right were the only obstacles separating Erika and me from the first embrace of the rest of our lives. I prayed she was telling me the truth about the girls and her brothers. I wasn't sure I could trust her and knew better than to date someone like my mom. Ignoring my reality, but not the lovely beach community, I slowed for the last sweeping corner on Point Loma Boulevard to find Erika's neighbor Raul, "the freakin' Puerto Rican," backing out of his driveway two houses up from my destination. I could see him waving at me through the rear window of his hand-waxed Volkswagen as he drove away towards Dog Beach, unaware of the magic about to happen. Raul was an avid gardener, and when not waiting tables he relaxed by thinning out the leafy shrubs covering his privacy wall while sipping an iced cocktail. You couldn't miss him if you tried. Or his romantic accent. Rich and buttery, he sounded intoxicatingly prestigious. His suave look rocked feathered black hair and tan shirtless muscles as tight as his shorts. Sometimes he used scissors. But never on his hair. Nothing touched the lion's mane ever.

Would his actions be so friendly if he knew I'd almost killed a cop? We sometimes joked over beers about his beige Beetle's whitewalls being classier than my yellow bomber, so maybe he'd understand. To be honest, the morning's vibe felt peculiar. Too good to be true. My dreams and nightmares were often the same, so I continued rolling cautiously, well below the posted speed limit. Maybe Sergeant Joe was right about climbing back into the lion's den after all. But this was no time to waver. I'd come this far and couldn't afford to lose faith. Yet someone had to pay the price of my free will—but who?

I'd helped Erika pick out her house right after we started dating. The selling point for me had been the cute little arched doorway leading to the backyard. The cozy pad was a late college graduation gift from her parents. Or a tax write-off, depending on who you asked. There it is, on the left, next to the neighbor with the yard full of blueish-green cacti. Doesn't it just feel like home sweet home? Don't you just love how the bronze door and blue window trim accentuate the white stucco and red-orange tile roof? The simplistic interior shares the same rustic Spanish curb appeal as the exterior. With three comfortable bedrooms and a decent outside space for entertaining, every detail of the house suited our active lifestyle perfectly. We shared many tender moments beside the fireplace centering the living room's largest wall. Layered in smooth stucco and curved masonry, it was an absolute masterpiece. Erika didn't like to get dirty, so I stoked the hot, glowing embers and swept the cold pale ashes after each burn. One crackling fire was often enough to warm every square inch of togetherness on those balmy San Diego winter nights chilled to the bone.

At this point, my head was pounding. Our reunion couldn't come soon enough. My gaze, near delusional, blinked uncontrollably, knowing that returning to Erika was possibly the wrong decision. My thoughts raced wildly. I went back and forth arguing with myself, wasting valuable time in the process. Usually Erika watched my arrival from behind her lacy, full-length drapes. But her hourglass silhouette was missing. The ornate glass double doors that opened to the front yard sat between two fifteen-foot royal palms. In the summer months, she opened the doors wide so the gentle ocean breeze could refresh her spirit, although this mostly made the house smell like salty seaweed.

I needed reassurance to see my plan through. Like, from a higher power. Seconds away from the most momentous decision of my life, I clasped my hands together in prayer and laid my head against them on the Nova's steering wheel.

Sometimes I felt foolish after praying because I was asking for help from the same God responsible for the burden of my countless blessings. *Better days ahead*, I thought. *Now, let's get to it*. I had no surge of orgasmic adrenaline to open my door this time but rather eased it open so as not to disturb the tranquility of passers-by. Suspicious of my intent, and with everything to lose, I slammed it shut and strolled across the street to the cobblestone walkway leading to the home's terra-cotta-tiled front porch. Sabino, Erika's Mexican gardener, was a magician. He kept the small yard up to country club standards. He seriously used a sharpened metal ruler to edge the grass near the sidewalk. Oh, and the flowers. There were red ones, yellow ones, and purple pansies, too. No matter the season, Erika's yard was the sharpest on the block.

Once I cleared the last step onto the porch, my heavy heart thudded feverishly out of control counting every last blemish on the brass mail slot. I was scared so shitless, I wanted to piss my pants. Reality isn't reality until it is.

I worried love wasn't waiting on the other side. Plus, there was a problem. A big one. Too big to ignore. Why hadn't my Erika met me with the full force of her love? In good times and bad, her response to my arrival was equally passionate. The silence behind the door compelled me to wait. But for how long? I pressed my hand against the door's smooth walnut surface and softly turned the antique-styled knob. It creaked open. Something was amiss. In the corner, a shadow flickered. I froze, dissecting the danger shiver by shiver. My mind screamed *run away* while my body pressed on. Erika never left her front door unlocked for any reason whatsoever. Inside was nothing but tense calm. I felt it everywhere, pushing back, saying not welcome, leave now. From the Brazilian cherrywood floors to the clouds obscuring the walls with gray sunshine, everything said *escape while you still can*. The silence breathed into the dust floating in the flecks of daylight. I focused on the arched bedroom door ten paces straight ahead. I moved ever-so slowly.

"Erika," I whispered. "It's me."

I stepped cautiously so as not to wake her if she were

sleeping. It had been a long few days, after all, and lord knows she loved her sleep.

There was no answer. The quiet seemed to reveal movement in the walls. My eyes darted around the room, looking for signs of life. Again, nothing. Cautiously, I stepped into the room to find an empty bed. It was oddly undisturbed. A flood of worry rained down upon me. I searched high, then low, under the bed and in the closet, only to find Erika missing. A sinking feeling of anguish crawled inside me. The horror reminded me of my true feelings. "*Be careful what you wish for*!" I couldn't fathom what was happening. I had gone from one nightmare to another. My love wouldn't leave me alone with death in my heart, would she? What had I done?

I'm not proud to admit that I sometimes wished for Erika's demise. I hated knowing that I was capable of being my dad when pushed. What would I do If I found her dead? Had she called my bluff and raised me a death? Was my broken heart to blame for her motivation? Memories of silent cars and desert sands took me back to that place where suffocating news robs your ability to breathe. Fearing the worst, I threw my keys to the floor near the braided sandstone rug beneath the living room's teak coffee table and sprinted towards the back door facing her detached garage, where her parents stored boxes of old fishing invoices.

With all my strength, I shoved my shoulder against the door's warped edges and thrust myself inside to find more of the same. Her silence was no longer a virtue. My search of the garage yielded nothing. No running car. No exhaust fumes. No invisible host. But her scent was everywhere. The bold freshness of her Tide laundry detergent momentarily fooled me into believing I'd found her. Disappointed, I hung my head and walked back into the empty house towards the bedroom, more distraught than ever. Maybe she had gone to the store—but how? Erika walked nowhere without a crowd. The frenzied thud in my chest urged me to keep searching. In a moment of clarity, a glaring oversight struck me. I hadn't checked everywhere. The bathroom was hiding a secret. I executed an about-face to find time had stopped. It was no longer abstract; it was alive, a physical presence with weight and energy. I found peace in the realization that every obstacle in life had prepared me for this crucial moment and whatever awaited on the other side. Now, standing squarely before the door, I reached out to test the fluted doorknob as if my life were at stake. Locked tight, it refused to turn. But I'd found Erika. I begged for a response. "Please, baby, open the door." Desperately, I cried out her name over and over.

While she pouted in silence, I knocked softly to show my concern. Each thump proof of my undying devotion to her. As she continued to ignore me, I kicked at the bottom of the door, hard enough for a crack of light to show. Suddenly the door exploded in my face, ending my morbid concentration. In a flash, screaming fissured eyes smeared with black mascara grabbed me around the neck and squeezed tightly until her fingers crushed my windpipe, cutting off my airway. The force of her attack shoved me against a wall and held me there until her hands trembled as my eyes bulged with fear. Revenge or regret, the choice was mine. I didn't want to hurt her. Never ever. She already hurt enough for both of us. I had hit back weeks before, but not this time. The heavens must have heard my plea for leniency because she dropped her hands and simply walked away, sobbing uncontrollably, pulling at the ends of her hair. Now I was in control. Whenever she hit rock bottom, I was there to pull her out, and today was no exception. She could turn on a dime and did so often. Once she got us banned for life from a car wash over some tiny water spots on the bumper. One second we were enjoying a beautiful day at the car wash together, and the next, we were fleeing a violent scene before the cops arrived.

I followed her into the kitchen. As angry as Erika was, she looked good. I knew in that moment God had made her to run through my veins. Yet I still doubted her. I grabbed hold of her shoulders and pulled her close. This marked the first step in our ritualistic recovery. The dense mood between us was now a high-wire act of do as I say, not as I do. We were us again, but for how long? I spun her around to face her, heart to beating heart. She offered no resistance. My hands came together in the small of her back, pulling her hips into mine.

"Why do you want to die?" she asked, trembling.

I couldn't tell her. The scritch of branches outside clawed the side of the house. A clash of biblical damnation raged inside with no one to blame but me. But Erika was none the wiser.

Amongst the cozy candelabras lending old-world warmth to the dining room, I broke the ice and silenced her with a kiss. In times like this I wished the world could see how naturally our chemistry flows when life is all about us. At that moment, every wall that had ever existed between us crashed to the ground. She whispered in my ear. "Kiss me, again!" We couldn't help what was happening, nor did we want it to end. I leaned forward into her and felt her breath fill my mouth with passionate forgiveness; no tongue—only beautiful surrender. Erika breathed her love into me, asking for nothing in return. After the most intense experience of our lives, she withdrew from me, dripping with gratitude. Her dilated pupils were misty and content. She looked angelic. Her crying eyes radiated soft, swooping arcs of light. Never had we shared such an expression of vulnerability. This time I devoured the bait—hook, line, and sinker.

"Please never leave me," she cried. "I need you forever."

How could I ever leave her after such a tender revelation? I did my best to assure her my suicidal night was a me issue and in no way tied to recent problems in our relationship, leaving her snagged, hook, line, and sinker.

We wound down over the next three hours, arguing love, blame, and innocence from one room to another. The heated passion we shared in the kitchen cooled when Erika flipped me off, seated on the toilet with her pink floral-print panties stretched around her bony ankles. I found the duration of our squabbles lessened if I took the blame. However, every apology inspired a fresh round of verbal humiliation meant to break me. The harder I tried to soften her, the worse it hurt me. Erika was no dummy. She knew right where to hit me. You could see the intelligence in her eyes, like when a hooded king cobra looks at you before striking.

This was the first time I feared Erika had killed herself. She physically needed to claim the victorious last word over me, which made her suicide less likely than mine, but still. Erika felt couples without conflict lacked the stamina needed to grow beyond themselves. Clashes between us were commonplace and used to measure our level of dedication to one another—her idea, not mine.

Before she'd allow a peaceful end to the morning's fiasco, I would have to swear allegiance to her supremacy. Knowing what I had to do, I drew her attention away from my face to the damp shoulder of my maroon sweater. Thank God she couldn't feel the chill in my brain. "Look what you did, silly."

Her smile said *take me, I'm yours*. Ignoring my own tears, I softly wiped Erika's away. First the left cheek, then the right, before painting an arrow pierced heart across the center of her chest with grains of mushy eyelash goop. She tugged at the belt loops around my waist, signaling a truce. Next came the final apology. A glint of poetic romance serenaded by the charm of imaginary fireflies. Followed by a relaxing foot massage, compliments of yours truly. The pièce de resistance if you will. Running both defense and offense, another chapter in the book of our tumultuous love ended with me safely in the arms of acceptance, after nearly dying. But for how long?

Chapter 21

–

Just between you and me, I knew better than to cower to Erika, but I couldn't help myself. I knew she wasn't good. She wasn't inherently bad, but she wasn't good either. Yet I didn't care one way or the other. Our connection gave me an identity complete with emotional support and a social outlet. But I felt empty. I guess because I was good at giving love but sucked at receiving it. Still, I worried about losing my support structure and the social network that came with being in love with Erika. Over time the abuse I endured seemed a small price to pay for sharing in her life, only I didn't realize it made me depressed, confused, and lost. Not lost in love. Just lost.

I know you understand how it feels when you think you love someone more than life itself. It's a pain we all endure at one point in our lives. Some have it worse than others, but just like death and taxes are certain, so is giving second chances to that one heartbreaker who lives to suck the very life from our essence. So why did I keep going back to Erika when I knew better, you ask? Simple. Because I was hooked on our potential and the fake façade she had shown me at the onset of our relationship. And over time I became a slave to the abuse because I understood it to be my fault. I considered myself a slave because from my perspective, only Erika held the power to set me free.

Now for whatever reason, my allergies were unbearable the morning of our explosive post suicidal reunion. Dr. Converse told me winter mold spores were to blame. I swear my nostrils had been superglued shut. After such a hard morning, Erika fought to stay awake. Too much booze might also have been to blame; I'd noted empty wine bottles tipped over in the sink when I'd arrived earlier. Erika was one of those lucky types who could sleep anywhere, anytime—especially when she drank. She snored too, and this morning was no exception.

The deeper she snored, the more plugged I became. Allergies aside, I worried about the inquisition to come. What would it be today, I wondered? And could I survive it? I hung my face off the side of the bed to escape the sound but repositioned when her body shifted. If I were anywhere but spooned beside her when she awoke, there would be trouble. Nothing I tried helped quiet her sleepy snorts. Neither a pillow over my head nor jammed fingers in my ears eased the pain. I don't know how something so cute and cuddly held the power of a Mack truck in her pointy snout. Normally I sawed logs right through her noise after making sweet passionate love, but she was especially loud this morning. I didn't mind, though. Being awake while she slept allowed me to watch her dream, and nothing in the world was more precious. The merlot-colored silk between us accentuated the rise and fall of her chest with each peaceful breath.

Her beauty was striking. Neither fame nor shame could ever besmirch her cover girl looks. But she was hard to look at, too, as there is no pleasure without pain. If she didn't feel pretty, things got ugly fast. Just then the covers shifted. I readied myself, taking care to smile wide. "Aww, pumpkin," she moaned, waking to face me with disoriented eyes, half tangled in the grips of a fuzzy pink comforter. "You look so happy," she said, looking around the room as if she were dreaming. It pains me to think how she hurt so good. I reached for her, letting the covers fall from my nakedness. She welcomed me with a soft kiss from her juicy red lips. Erika was the first to introduce me to the wonders of the female body. Unlike a man, a woman purrs and sings when touched in the most intimate ways. At first I was nervous and clumsy, but she showed me how to make her silky warmth moan with pleasure. Mine too.

We dated occasionally for about six months before our first naked sleepover. It was a night of many welcomed firsts. Before then, I had slept in shorts and a tank top kept in a small dresser in her spare bedroom closet. Having a place of my own in her house meant I was special. Erika refused to allow the other girls to clutter her space with their junk. This leg-up gave me a spark of royalty. While I slept in the nude now, old habits proved hard to break as who doesn't enjoy being comfortable? I was for sure more comfortable dressed than naked. Though I was shy, when Erika and I started rolling, my inhibitions freed me to love wildly, without care or concern.

Coincidently, I went through this phase where I'd cover myself with a pillow for no good reason, regardless of whether or not I was naked. I know what you're thinking. How does this girl expose her most intimate areas to her lover's five senses, then cover up like a bashful introvert? It could have been a life spent hiding my misunderstood guilt. I believe my struggle with nudity and being with another woman resulted from years spent hounded by society's forced morality and decency standards. Every aspect of who I'd become contradicted the lessons learned as a child. I didn't see a boy when I saw myself because I wasn't a boy. If my love was so wrong, why did it feel so right? I guarantee turning a blind eye to such bigotry was the reason lying next to my lover's nakedness was so freeing.

Erika could read me like a book. There was no hiding from her trust issues. She couldn't have cared less about my insecurities. And what she wanted, she got. "Drop that pillow, you square." Her soft, pedicured hands clawed at me. She kept at it for an hour, stopping only long enough to readjust back to her good side. Like she had a bad one. Our playfulness turned serious when she dragged her nails down to the creaminess of my inner thigh.

Only Erika could give my goosebumps the chills. For the next hour, we satisfied each other in mouth-watering passion, leaving us spent atop her tender silk sheets.

Flush faced after an orgasmic connection. "So why a butterfly?" she asked, tracing the colorful lines tattooed over my heart. Little did she know Karen had the exact same tattoo. I wanted a reminder of her even when we were apart. "Did it hurt?" she asked, flicking at it with her finger.

Erika didn't wear press-on nails; she got them done at a fancy salon in La Jolla with the other socialites. Her favorite polish color was wild rose. I kept my nails natural. I found the clean look suited me better. But don't think she didn't try to indoctrinate me into her cult of glamour and excess. Erika's next move had little to do with magic hands. Disgusted by the nasty habit she abhorred, she gave my knuckles a vicious slap. "Stop biting your nails, loser."

I didn't all that often, and mostly when she was around. But this was for me to know and for her to never find out. "It's cheaper and healthier than smoking cigarettes," I told her, inviting another playful slap. "Now tell me the truth about this tattoo," she demanded, pushing me with both hands against her gold-velvet tufted headboard, which radiated gilded exuberance against the room's stark-white walls. "You're not leaving this bed until you tell me." Erika wanted facts, details, and evidence because she felt something sinister inspired my painted lady's gorgeous wings. *What a psycho*, I thought. *How can there be anything sinister behind a butterfly?* "Because it's your butterfly," she said, poking at my chest with her index finger as if to fight. Erika was smart and knew the truth lay somewhere in the middle between her and me. She was right to feel the way she did. Occasionally I had a flair for the extreme when pushed. It's a hard truth to ignore when our last two serious breakups had inspired me to marry a man, then jump off a bridge. I never saw myself as reckless. But then again, who does?

Chapter 22

–

Erika's bedroom felt cozy now from the silver pearls of sunshine pushing out the slow cloudy cold. "Now that we're back together," I said, "let's talk about everything we've never said." I wanted to know what kept her up at night. And how me almost dying had affected her.

"Baby, I was inches from death, and if not for this cop, you'd have a memory on your hands. He hit me like a freight train," I said, "WHACK!" Slapping my hands together to mimic what could have been my last living step. Her eyes welled with tears. They were genuine, I'm sure of it.

"Oh, babe, I didn't know you were hurting so badly. I wanted to drive to you yesterday morning. I promise!"

Like so many times before, I wanted to believe her. I needed to trust that we still enjoyed the same things and were moving forward together.

"You and I both know what would have happened if I showed up in La Mesa frantically searching for you. Your crazy grandmother would have chopped my balls off man, and I didn't want to expose us on the heels of you attempting suicide."

Truthfully or not, Erika was right about Grandma Vogt.

"Babe," she said, "I'm not sure how much longer I can

sneak around your family. I don't want to pretend anymore. This is our life, dammit, not theirs."

Her sincerity danced in my imagination. *Finally*, I thought. *She loves me with all her heart.* But I always knew it, I truly did.

"It's not just destroying you; it's destroying me through you," she said.

Erika was right. Fear of my family's scorn was destroying our lives. Every painful word she spoke revealed a thousand truths. Coming out to my entire family was the only way. I could deal with the outside world, including Dad because he was too embarrassed to admit anything. Most people minded their business, anyway. We didn't flaunt our relationship or even kiss in public. Society, for all its shortcomings, allowed us to exist to some degree if we behaved. My family was another story.

That Erika wanted to claim us publicly after I'd tried to commit suicide made me fall in love all over again. But an open dialogue would be critical to our survival. Especially since I'd always feared my family would disenfranchise me for our alternative lifestyle. I didn't care about their money or clout; I could make my own. Their acceptance is what I yearned for most. The past could no longer be our future. But there was much danger in disgracing my pedigree.

Sure, Erika and I had broken up many times before, but salvaging our love indefinitely was possible. To be fair, Erika and I had created many beautiful memories over the years. She had this way of celebrating me like no other. On holidays and special occasions, she spared no expense to create thoughtful experiences not sold in stores.

There was less sunshine now and more clouds. The broken rays of warmth had all but gone away. Being so close to the ocean, the overcast sky appeared less dreary and more natural when stormy. I noticed from an early age that if the sky was sunny blue, so was the water. Same if the sky was gray. At night, the blue-gray surf turned a desperate shade of black—the kind with no end and no beginning. I needed Erika to understand how fragile my tender heart had become, how I could hear and see things in the dark not meant for the living. Outside, sheets of rain now battered the windows.

The quenching droplets splashed and puddled, blurring our usual sunny view.

"I'm worried about you, my love. Does Karen know about the other night?" she asked, wiping her nose with a tissue crumpled in her hand. I looked away in shame. "Well, if you won't answer me about Karen, at least tell me how you wound up with this godawful tattoo."

Before today, Erika hadn't wanted to talk about my tattoo because she thought it low class. More than once she commented about it being trailer trashy. Pulling a shirt over my immodesty, I walked Erika through my diary of ink.

"It was more spontaneous than planned," I said, watching her focus grow more intense. "Between you and me, the shop I selected wasn't exactly in the best part of town."

"Sounds about right," she said, almost cavalierly.

"Well, the moment Karen saw me that day, she knew there was something up my sleeve. I believe it was a Friday because work paid me the day before . . ."

I didn't need to work. Grandma Vogt would have let me exist on her payroll forever, but I sought the freedom of nine-to-five employment instead.

When I got to Karen's front door that morning, I hurried inside, like always, without a ding from the doorbell. Before young Grego caught sight of me, I hit his mama with the news. "Pack your bags, Sis, you've just won yourself an all-expense-paid trip to tattoo town courtesy of Pepsi-Cola and the MoonPie motor company; some restrictions may apply, see Old Doc Webb for details." She shook her head and blew me off. "MoonPie Motor company?" she smirked. "God help us all." Grego chimed in, his energy wound tight, ready to explode. "Yahoo!" he chirped. "Moo pies, Moo pies, Moo pies!" He made the biggest mess when he ate their gooey goodness in the backseat of my car. There would be chocolate marshmallow crumbs everywhere but on him.

Not one to waste an opportunity, I joined his merry dance and swung myself closer to his mom. She was hesitant at first. "Are you out of your mind?" It didn't matter to me that she was a mother. She was my sister first. And a devoted partner to the very end. Besides, some extra color would make her pale pallet better, not worse. She knew not to disappoint me when I was hot after something. Thankfully, she trusted the wild child at the center of my sentimental heart. We were always doing fun stuff together. Where she went, I went. We were close—maybe too close. But I couldn't imagine my life without her or the pop songs we sang to the annoyed people in cars at red lights.

I intended to hit downtown about noon, but the snares of sister gossip held us longer than expected. We debated whether to take Grego, and ultimately decided he should come along for the ride. Karen smoked two cigarettes, one after the other, suffocating me with the claustrophobic clouds of her nervous energy. I, for one, was juiced. The black-sheep sisters had never looked so grown-up. A tattoo, I thought. What an adult thing to do. We were mere miles away at this point. I got so wrapped up in the excitement of it all, I forgot about my dreaded fear of needles.

We took Interstate 8 to the 163 and made our way onto Tenth Street in downtown San Diego, while the Coronado bridge floated in the distance ahead between a canyon of multistory buildings representing industry and commerce. The warm sunshine felt good. But it would set in a few hours, so we hurried. The concrete jungle, shaded by its dense population, welcomed the night sooner than the rest of the city. My watch read 3:45 p.m., but already hustlers were working the streets near the dingy pool halls where more than eight-balls got shot.

To say we were out of our element would be an under-statement. We circled the grand fountain at Horton Plaza three times before finding an unsafe place to park. In 1960, six days before the presidential election, Senator John F. Kennedy had spoken there in a last-minute appeal for votes. We didn't see any presidents or senators shaking hands or kissing babies, but we saw a skinny pimp hard at work supervising his ladies chatting up parked cars across the street. Grego spotted him first. "Momma," he said, "who's that sparkly chocolate man?" The dark, beady-eyed stranger wore a large afro and custom-fit turquoise suit with crisp white alligator shoes. The look his greedy eyes gave us said *Fresh meat*. Mine said *Holy shit*. Crowding a red fire lane, I stepped over a grungy ghost with five days' worth of beard passed out on the sidewalk next to my car door.

It broke my heart to see a once-vibrant person reduced to an alcoholic speed bump. So far, my rebellious march into adulthood had done nothing but fill me with raunchy regret.

Trouble was everywhere, littering the sidewalks with spent cigarettes smoked to the filter's edge. These transients, some more troubled than the city's arthritic alcoves, frequented the pawnshops and two-buck hotels when not solving the world's problems swimming at the bottom of a bottle. I remember passing the scariest liquor store I'd ever seen. Inside, leaning against a dilapidated wood counter stocked with jugs of cheap muscatel and an oversized antique cash register, stood this unshaven ogre with a black patch over his left eye. His butchered smile flashed missing teeth full of decay. With his hairy hands held wide, he rocked back and forth, pretending to masturbate for our pleasure. "Oh my God!" I screamed while a flock of young sailors coming up behind us laughed hysterically, mimicking his kinky actions pump for pump.

The dereliction of life worsened, approaching Old Doc Webb's Fourth Avenue spot. A faint smell of urine wafted in the crevasses between the X-rated bookstores and suspect card rooms poised to swindle a gambler out of easy money. My desire to flee grew more profound with each step. But so did my resolve. In the crowd ahead of us, surrounded by brick and boarded-up windows, a raspy voice conversed with himself. "*Arriba, Arriba, Arriba!*" he shouted into the air. "Two for the price of one, but not one without the other." This dude looked more dazed than confused. "Shake and bake, please. Shines two for one. Get 'em while they're hot, but don't blame the gringo when he calls bingo."

Karen drew back. "Let's get outta here, Sis," she said, tugging at the back of my shirt. "Like, now, Lori, before someone kidnaps us or something."

But we stayed for a while, watching and learning. Or so said the shoeshine man spinning about like a circus pinwheel. I think he did more than polish shoes but couldn't be certain. No matter, he was funny as hell. Even if crazy. If disbelief were dollars, I would have bought the whole sidewalk a round of drinks from the deviant liquor store we passed earlier. I had to meet this bald man of mystery half dressed as Davy Crockett, with dirty feet clad in sandals with toenails to match snapping out shoeshines from his pile of soiled rags. When he smiled, his mouth stretched wide. "Nice ta meet ya! Myself, I'm donkey free since sixty-three but thank you for asking." Karen, now close beside me, couldn't help but laugh.

"Howdy, the name's Ratatat Pat," he said, spitting machine gun sounds to drive home his message. Short with cartoon-like features, he was everyone's best friend. A bystander smoking a Lucky Strike affectionately referred to him as the unofficial mayor of Fourth Avenue. His colorful presence lent safety to the anything-goes kind of world we found ourselves deep within.

I asked about his accent. It carried a slow pace, born of home-cooked meals and Sunday get-togethers. He said the wrong bus going the wrong direction had taken him from western Kentucky to Hollywood, where he hitchhiked to San Diego in search of the perfect Mexican skunk. Before we adjourned inside the tattoo parlor I heard about through Ronnie's sailor buddies, a husky Marine with his reddish hair, cut high and tight, thought it might be fun to challenge "da mayor" to a drunken debate. Big mistake.

You knew something profound was about to crack off when Ratatat's glassy eyes appeared to change color. Completely off-balance, with his left foot firmly planted on the sidewalk, he raised his right leg Bruce Lee style and offered the overgrown bag of wind a wobbly kung foo kick. My head nearly spun off its axis when he karate chopped at him, saying, "You picked the wrong cracker, Esse." For those who don't know, Esse is Spanish slang for homie or bro. The funniest part is that the Marine was whiter than Ratatat, and neither one could fight. A second later Ratatat was flat on his back laughing hysterically rolling back and forth on the dirty concrete.

Inside Doc's world, order prevailed. Follow the rules, or don't. It was simple as that. Any disrespect would get you bounced, but quick. Right away, you could smell the rubbing alcohol pinch the inside of your nose. There was bleach too. Lots of it. But mostly musky spice from the sweaty men crammed around us.

We were both pleasantly surprised to find such a clean space compared to the trampy world outside the tattoo parlor's cramped walls. Sailors from every fleet stood nuts to butts, awaiting their turn in the master's chair. We drew curious stares from the crowd of sea dogs looking for a night or two of transient love. Though surrounded by horny boys of all ages, Doc thankfully forbade all forms of hanky-panky. A sign above the door made that clear. It also declared: No children and no swearing, ladies present.

This was obviously of little comfort to us. Maybe Doc

would make an exception for Grego since we drove so far from our comfort zones specifically to see him . . . fat chance.

Along with kicking Grego out, he refused me for not having proper identification. Doc was a stickler for the rules if ever there was one. To me, this was a sign to retreat, but not to Karen. Tough as nails, she respectfully cornered Doc and explained in great detail the many particulars about my vital statistics. Like a computer, she fired off dates, ages, numbers, and graduations without flubbing her lines.

"Okay, fine," he said, half beaten into submission. "Pick your poison, ladies, then get in line, but the baby stays outside." Karen went first. After a snippety ten-second powwow about second thoughts, I rolled Grego outside to where Ratatat was holding court and counted the black spots of fossilized gum stuck to the sidewalk. Inside, Karen examined the countless drawings framed in rows along the walls in Doc's reception area. I told myself there would be no discount for buyer's remorse should either of us have a terrible outcome. A former sign painter and show card letterer for movie theater marquis, Doc freehanded his art. He worked behind a chain stretched across the room to keep bystanders from shading his light. Feeding my voyeuristic tendencies, I stood on my tiptoes for a peek of him bent over a strapping young buck. Underneath the zap of Doc's tattoo needle, an eight-legged octopus was coming to life. The realism was striking. Doc was better than good; he was terrific and worth every penny of the ten dollars he charged us.

Wild excitement filled Karen's eyes as she traded places with me so I could make my selection. "Sis, check out the Monarch butterfly, frame seven, bottom row, center. Oh, and all the autographed pictures of movie stars too. He has 'em all over the place along with some ball players and boxers." From swastikas to serpents, Doc's offerings seemed endless. The orange butterfly was just as she described. Doc said the name Monarch was somehow related to a past King of England, adding more mystique to an already life-changing excursion.

"Hmm," I wondered aloud, "is this the one?" A sweet voice answered from behind a desk in the corner. "Honey, you can have anything your little heart desires." The grandmotherly voice belonged to Doc's wife, Carol. A busybody at heart, her job was to keep the boys in line so Doc could work in peace. How did I know? The look on her face said so when one squatty sailor in the opposite corner got a little loud boasting about his pain tolerance. Carol and Doc's place was more than a shop. It was a parlor of the highest regard. World-famous and proud.

While I waited with Grego, Karen made her way to the back where Doc worked his magic, and the rubbernecking stopped when Carol smiled and closed the door to the room's fondling eyes. About thirty minutes later, Karen appeared with a satisfied grin.

"How was it?" I asked nervously.

"Not bad. It really only hurts when the skin vibrates."

I wasn't sure if she was joking. "What? Are you kidding me? Gross! You know how much I hate needles."

"Come on, loudmouth." She laughed. "Get in there and take your medicine."

I was never so scared in all my life. Sitting down, I made a promise to myself not to wuss out. Getting tattooed was my idea after all so I'd look like a fool if I quit now.

"So, you gettin' the same black widow as your sister?" asked the jokey artist. Art, it seemed, wasn't his only gift. His gray hair didn't match his dark eyebrows, worn above his thick prescription lenses. Nor did they help him see I was about to die in his pseudo electric chair.

"Black widow?" I winced, wiggling about nervously to the point of sheer panic.

"Relax," said Doc with a tip of his black-billed captain's hat. "Okay," he said after a few quick test zaps. "Here we go." Carol held my sweaty hand and stayed with me the entire time while I was under the gun. Her presence was a great comfort. Initially, the pain was overwhelmingly intense. Like a million bee stings at once. I bled a little, too. Not as much as Karen, thank God. But enough to consider this a medal-worthy war wound. Thankfully, Doc took his time working the small square of exposed skin with great care. A few drinks might have helped ease the pain, but soon he was wiping away smeared blood and ink from my fluttering wings with a sponge he tossed into a sink that smelled like wet chickens clucking in Mississippi mud. Once Doc sanitized and bandaged my new tattoo, I was ready to let my ego make some serious noise. My legendary hypochondria had survived the prick of a thousand needles.

After we paid, adding a monumental two-dollar tip, Karen and I hugged on the sidewalk beneath blinky lights to the cheers of our many adoring fans. What a feeling. Through my tattoo, I had conquered the world and had Karen to show for it. With Grego fast asleep in his stroller, we twirled and skipped down the street, growing cockier with each jovial step.

Karen was so proud, popping off to every Tom, Dick, and Harry we passed, telling them her scaredy-cat sister survived a whale of a tattoo session gnarlier than getting a tooth pulled without Novocain. Hooting and hollering ourselves, we heard Ratatat's husky tobacco-cured voice celebrating from at least two city blocks away.

He must have been a megaphone in a former life because this dude had some serious pipes for a chain smoker. Even the winos near the Golden West Hotel took notice. They stood teetering at the end of their drunken lives, sloshing about in approval of my achievement. Welcome to the best day of my life.

Upon hearing the complete saga of my infamous tattoo, Erika smiled and fell backward into her sea of silk half covered by the fuzzy pink comforter, knowing the happiness I felt was neither sinister nor irrational. There were no more blank spaces between us, except for one.

Chapter 23

–

The rain was still coming down, but only in drops now, not sheets. Perfect weather for a cozy Saturday morning. Erika's vulnerability was irresistible. Cheeky yet profound. I was proud of how far we'd come in such a brief time, all things considered. Still, lingering doubts chipped away at my heartbroken soul. I couldn't shake them, no matter how much I replayed our reel of fun times together. But there was no way I could show weakness of any kind. I worried Erika would at some point use my suicidal status as a sympathetic tool to gain favor with her butch friends, who claimed her as their token lipstick lesbian. I needed to strike first to prevent this from happening. I wouldn't let this ruin our day, however. There would be plenty of time to deal with the girls. I was sure of it.

Things were falling into place. Easy comes to mind. Almost too easy. Soon this latest tragically predictable outcome would be nothing more than another lesson learned. Time to keep the faith and move on. But then something curious happened. After some light conversation about nothing in particular, Erika climbed out of bed and wandered into the bathroom to shower alone, without so much as a word. I sat there awaiting an invitation, but it never came. She was such a priss—large and in charge of her ivory tower, no bigger than mine. "There are used cars, and there are exotics," she would say. Sometimes she loved me the way I was, sometimes not. Slightly perturbed, I got out of bed and teased my hair into a presentable state. I thought it strange how it actually felt like a winter's day. In San Diego, there's no white Christmas or fall harvest to rely on for a change. For the most part, spring looks like summer, and fall like winter, and so on. There's no separation. No changing of the guard. The more the seasons change, the more they look the same.

While Erika showered, I made a fire. In the corner beside the fireplace sat an aged Spanish guitar. Erika was one of those fortunate kids whose parents forced her into every imaginable lesson possible. From music to language, Erika and her brothers were more diverse in their knowledge than anyone I had ever known. When the mood struck, she would light candles and play her Spanish guitar for me in the dark. The expressive instrument moved me every time she strummed it to life. Her vaulted ceiling's acoustics gave the long melodies a rich and flavorful tone. When the candlelight's wispy release teased the romantic air between us, climax felt possible through her sensuous music alone.

On either side of her fireplace were two matching leather couches. They added substance to the pastel watercolor flamingo hung over the mantel. The fire, now burning through the gnarled bark, worked its way across the log's charred surface to the red-hot coals cracking and popping below the smoke's black fizz. Against the heat, a childlike voice startled me. I gasped. A sudden rush of icy dread stiffened my muscles, prickling my tiniest hairs. "Where'd you go, love?

Are you okay?" asked Erika, cluelessly chomping her pink bubblegum, combing out the wet knots from her tangled hair.

"Jesus," I said. "You scared the crap outta me."

"Sorry, old man. You need to be on your toes if you're gonna hang with me."

There was a long pause.

"Gee thanks."

"What's with you?" she asked, rolling her eyes. "I said I was sorry."

She wasn't though. But I wasn't about to start trouble. I had something else in mind.

"The girls," I said. "Will you help bring us together? You know, get them to like me a bit more."

Surprised, Erika looked away from me and at the aqua surfboard in the corner. "You mean like friends kinda together?"

"Yes," I said, smiling wide enough for the both of us.

"Like for real?" she asked cautiously, suspicious of my motives.

"For real," I muttered.

"Why the sudden change of heart?"

"Because I love you?" That should have been enough. But it wasn't.

Erika's answer to my request came with a condition that I never saw coming but committed to nonetheless: I was to apologize to the girls both as a group and individually or die alone.

"Take it or leave it," she said, "because my friends aren't negotiable."

"Of course," I said. "Never expected them to be." But

everything with Erika was negotiable. Especially people. She saw them as nothing more than an object. A supply to feed her narcissistic tendencies. "Do you know what this means to me?" she gushed, obviously not thinking about how her threats affected me. But I knew, which is why I disregarded myself in trying to please her. The spiritual capitol I invested in her supplied just enough peace to see us through troubled times over and over again. And it worked every time, her being so predictable and all. With a healthy fire still burning, Erika latched onto me and spilled us onto the couch. It didn't matter that we were about to open Pandora's box. What mattered was our love and this seemingly monumental step forward.

"God, I love you," she said, pulling me deeper into her embrace. While she squeezed me, I imagined my father smashing me in the face with a frying pan. I was dead to him and felt useless without Erika or the girls there to prop me up. I could taste the iron-rich blood running down my chin as our hug turned into a kiss. Morbid, I know, but that's seriously how I felt.

My sin was no longer lukewarm on the back burner. It was boiling hot. Fire red with no means of extinguishment. I thought of the crosses that flanked Wilson Street. Though they rose mightily into the air, offering forgiveness, I saw them as matchsticks with a headdress of sulfur ready to incinerate me. This could have been my nervousness talking, or the truth. The problem was, I didn't know anymore.

Just then the phone rang. I knew who it was, but Erika told me not to worry.

"Let it go," I said as she pulled away to answer it, tripping over the coffee table and stubbing her toe. This gave us a laugh. Mine nervous, hers excited. What might this midday interruption bring? Something good, I hoped. When she answered, Erika's furtive movements said the caller's identity were none of my business. With her back turned to me, she confirmed my fears. I knew it could be only one person. Marsella.

"Who was that?"

A surprise," she giggled, charging towards me to snuggle her nose into my neck. She took me down like a championship wrestler in heat.

"Love me, babe."

My brain fogged up with clear visions of being tackled on the bridge. A suicidal flash back reared its ugly head, ransacking my musings. I realized memories of her shouting had the same effect on my psyche as war upon a soldier.

Not a safe place to be a day after attempting suicide. Erika was on top of me now, smothering me into the couch, tickling my sides with reckless abandon.

"*Stop!*" I screamed, wiggling violently under the playful nature of her happy intent. "Don't, you're hurting me."

The flow of screaming tears that followed took her by surprise.

"Oh my God, Lori, what the hell's wrong with you?"

The emotions encompassing me were violently unfocused. I felt electrocuted, void of optimism and courage. I longed to be alone without needing her to trash me. This time, however, Erika backpedaled to absorb my pain. Her emotional rescue sprang into action to comfort me after belittling my sentimental heart. As I exposed my vulnerability,

Erika cradled my head against her bosom and dumped her emotions into my growing puddle of sorrow. There was no holding back. Years of pent-up fear flooded out, asking for the return of my innocence. She held me tight, kissing my head softly for an hour until my shivering tremors subsided.

"How about a drinky poo, pumpkin?"

It wasn't uncommon for Erika to cheer me up with a cocktail. The last time something this serious went down she dragged me to Hollywood where, in the days after Ronnie and I split, we lived lavishly from one end of the City of Angels to the next. Including Beverly Hills, where Erika booked a suite at the most exquisite hotel. For all its wonder, the Beverly Hills Hotel couldn't compare to the most iconic dive bar of them all, the Frolic Room. This historic watering hole was the place to be seen when no one was looking. Its cozy mysteriousness was the perfect setting for a post-divorce party beneath dim rose-colored lighting. On Hollywood Boulevard, I tripped over a fellow bent down in white knee-high gym socks kissing Marilyn Monroe's star on the Walk of Fame. Ronnie also understood my cinematic passions; for our honeymoon he took me to the Lake Tahoe location where NBC filmed *Bonanza*. My all-time favorite show. He snapped a picture of me hugging a life-sized cardboard cutout of Little Joe, played by Michael Landon. My baggy white T-shirt didn't match the hunky cowpoke's rugged look, but the fresh mountain pines were a welcome change to the congestion clogging the freeways back home. Unlike with Erika, my connection with Ronnie was never lustful. We enjoyed our time together, exploring and sharing deep conversations. Devastating him hurt badly. I revisited the memory of our honeymoon in the mountains daily. From the moment we met he treated me like a star when I deserved nothing. The same is true well past the bitter end.

The day I met Ronnie he was sweating bullets trying to kick-start a cold-blooded chopper. Custom curved and stretched. The red metal flake gas tank between his long skinny legs glittered in the sun against the sweltering black-top. His frustration trickled down his forehead like warm chicken soup. When the uncooperative chopper coughed and backfired, he would just smile and laugh to himself. His gentle approach hugged my soul. Tall, about six feet with a thin but muscular build, he wore short brown hair and a neatly trimmed beard. He looked cool though even with the heat pressing down on him. Sunglasses aren't required kind of cool. But he was not too cool to call his mom every day. She was the apple of his eye.

Being mechanically inclined didn't hurt, either. He was just what I needed in more ways than one. But falling for him was a surprise. On the morning we met outside my sister's place, I had just driven the twenty-two miles from Ocean Beach after Erika had wished me bon voyage by throwing my green hard-shell travel case into the street. It was small, round with a flat bottom like a hat box and a flexible handle I could wrap around my hand for safekeeping.

Leave it to me to get busted for chatting up three blonde surfer chicks in bikinis smoking a marijuana cigarette walk-ing to the beach. It was an innocent exchange. I was taking out the trash when they cruised by offering peace signs and a hit of their burning weed, which I refused because smoke makes me gag. The next thing I knew, a jealous rage sent my travel case soaring, scattering jeans, undies, and tops across the boulevard. After tossing my belongings into the street, Erika locked me out. I spent the next two hours squatting against the house below her bedroom window, begging forgiveness, until my feet fell asleep. Once I'd lost feeling in my hips, I limped away, heartsick, without saying a word.

The night before we'd made sensual love in a sea of erotic purple-black light that caressed our natural delicacies. Erika was anything but silent then. Thinking about being lost in her lust made a broken travel bag seem well worth the pain. When Erika surrendered herself to me, I swear the angels sang. But while beautiful, our love often crucified me with passionate mistrust. On the other hand, there was never any worry about being wronged by Ronnie. He was a gentleman's gentleman who never struck a foul blow upon anyone.

The sand-colored house he frequented across from Karen's second-story apartment on Claydelle in El Cajon belonged to a close friend from the Navy. I had seen him before on walks with Karen and Grego to the bodega down the block but never paid much attention because my relationship with Erika was already a full-time job. Karen and Ronnie were friendly, but not close friends you might say. Erika was more than I could handle most days so the idea of adding a handsome man to the mix was never in the cards. But there was something about him. Believe it or not, there was sexual tension between us right away. It was comfortable though, not dirty or forced.

Without thinking, I walked towards him searching for something to say.

"Hi. Nice bike ya got there."

"Thanks, but it belongs to that dude over there," he said, pointing to a long-haired fellow kicked back in a lawn chair wearing a red bandana tied around his head. "But he's about as good with tools as he is with women." Initially, I thought Ronnie was crazy for wearing a black leather vest warmer than the thermal haze baking the street. Like Erika, he had these eyes that sparkled like the Vegas strip whenever he smiled. "This one's mine," he said. Pointing to a brown chopper next to him with a tall sissy bar and swept back handlebars with black grips.

"Is she flooded?"

"Yeah." He smiled. "How did you know?"

"How about a ride first? Then I'll tell ya," I said, forgetting all about Erika's drama.

"What color brown is that?" I continued, taking charge of the conversation.

"It's pearlescent camel brown with two coats of wax."

Such class, I thought. His style was second to none.

"I don't normally take strangers for rides," he said. "But for you I'll make an exception."

I was beyond excited. As he extended his bashful hand, I blurted out my name.

"I'm Ronnie," he smiled back nervously. His calloused palms were as clammy as mine.

My first impression was that his loyalty was beyond reproach. I asked about the black Ford I'd seen him drive on several occasions. "Yup," he said. "I built her from the ground up just like my bike."

"So do you live around here?" I asked, thinking I already knew.

"Sorta. I live in Lemon Grove with my mom. I'm fresh off the boat from Vietnam and trying to piece my life back together, if you know what I mean."

I didn't know what he meant, but I was eager to learn what made him tick.

"You aren't a pilot by chance, are you?"

"No," he laughed. "But I can be if you want me to."

It turned out he served several tours in Vietnam as a Navy Seabee. He told me Seabees build infrastructure in combat zones requiring their specialized construction skills. "Sometimes we fight too," he said. *This guy's a walking, talking war hero*, I thought, taking note of his modesty.

I fell harder with each word he spoke. I was bursting inside, wanting to rush into something I didn't understand with my obvious twin flame standing before me.

"Now how about that ride?" he asked, leaning his buddy's bike on it's chrome kickstand.

With two mighty kicks, his shimmering golden brown chopper roared to life filling the morning air with exhaust filled anticipation. Each twist of the throttle vibrated my insides against themselves. Vroom, vroom, vroom. The raw power shook wildly in his hands. After he centered the bike in a comfortable upright position, I climbed on the back and we were off, thundering down Claydelle with the wind whipping through my helmetless hair.

Soon we were inseparable, hanging out whenever possible. Where he went, I went. Our combined worlds just made sense together considering our shared love of the custom car and bike culture. The intense kindness we showed each other manifested itself so beautifully leading to hours of deep conversation. In him I was home. It's like we were mirrors staring back at each other. On paper we truly were a match made in heaven. But then the real me showed up.

I had the best of intentions when we walked down the grassy aisle in his mother's backyard, August 6, 1972, about ninety days after we first met. A month later we split. Our surprise engagement lasted longer than the marriage. Shortly after the ceremony after we moved in together, Ronnie went away on military maneuvers and returned home to find Erika and her pals shooting pool in our living room. The devastation on his friendly face was indescribable. This should have been my rock bottom, not his. But mine had a way to go. I remember him standing at the door; the color drained from his face asking, Why Lori? Why?

Karen was there too and looked mortified. Worse than Ronnies look of heartbroken horror. She was sick right away, knowing she had to choose sides. She loved us both, but I was her sister. After a few choice words, mostly from Erika, Ronnie begrudgingly packed his belongings on the spot and tore out the door. The black burn out marks he left peeling out of the driveway lasted an entire year before they faded. I know because I drove by our love shack to remember our good times together more often than I'm proud to admit. Our humble one-bedroom duplex was close to his mom's house in Lemon Grove, so thankfully he didn't have far to travel after I sent him away. He was better off without me anyway. At the end of the month, I left as well, leaving the pool table behind to cover the rent.

I always felt Ronnie deserved better. Falling for him had been a shock. And because of me, our fresh start together ended before it began. We hadn't yet signed our marriage license when I realized my mistake. By then, it was too late. I felt legally bound to a man who could never have me. At times I felt trapped between two opposing sides unwilling to share me. I wanted to love him forever. And I did, in my way. I still do, in fact. But I had constructed our explosive romance on a foundation of lies. My lies. A series of legal maneuvers dissolved the marriage within a year, but never our connection. It's rock solid with or without papers.

It was later in the afternoon now, about three-thirtyish, when Erika revealed my surprise with giddy childlike eyes.

"I'm sorry your family are such assholes, but hey," she said, still chomping her gum, "Look on the bright side, you still have me and the girls so let's throw caution to the wind and have some fun tonight, you old fuddy-duddy."

Sure, I had her, but my family was only part of our problem. The lingering suicidal anguish surging inside me should have been enough to stop me from accepting her invitation that could possibly include the girls. I needed to regroup. I needed us to be alone with ourselves together for a while longer without any outside influences to complicate our progression.

But "Okay," I said, flashing a reluctant smile. "Let's have a drink."

The second biggest mistake of my life.

Chapter 24

–

To ease the tension building inside me, I continued feeding Erika's rebellious ego.

"I feel so safe with you right now," I said, looking deep into her ocean blue eyes. Like, hop in the Nova and drive all over town yelling, "I love Erika!" kinda safe.

"Tell me again," she said, so full of herself her head couldn't help but swell. She was who she was, but I loved her all the same. Judgement was something I passed only on myself.

"What if we go out? Like to the Chee-Chee Club to celebrate," she asked innocently, drawing me in.

I knew it. "Is that what the phone call was about earlier?" I asked.

"Yeah, Marsella wanted to know if we were free for a few rounds of fun tonight, but I said I'd have to check and call her back."

"Gotcha," I answered nervously, knowing she was lying straight to my face.

"Hey party-pooper," she said, sensing my hesitation. "It might do you some good to get out. You know, cut a rug, let loose, kinda thang." She was a social butterfly and needed her nightlife fix every couple of days regardless of whether

I went along. Her hips were rocking with the waves in her eyes attempting to bribe me with her sexy moves. Boy, was she hard to resist. With each seductive twist, she drew my soul deeper into hers. However, leaving the comfort of our cozy fire made for two seemed senseless. But this outing was for Erika, not me. Besides, what could a few drinks hurt? On the other hand, it felt wildly inappropriate to be heading to a bar when the last thing I needed was something to cloud my judgement further. But I had committed myself to change, and I wasn't about to disappoint Erika again.

It's easy to miss the Chee-Chee Club if you're not looking. Located on Broadway in downtown San Diego, its dark, modern façade allows it to drift unnoticed, save for the pink neon Chee-Chee spelled out in cursive light above the front door. Inside the main entrance's diamond-shaped window stands a bar wrapped in burgundy tile and oak trim with a curving black base that shapes the dimly lit room. Filled with welcoming, friendly conversation, from the wooden wall bench I sang along more than once to the sounds of the bellowing jukebox with the fun-loving bartenders and friendly crowds in the smokey dugout. The public squalor between the Chee and waterfront couldn't tarnish the welcoming history of this landmark establishment serving up companionship since 1941. Thinking of the Chee awakened memories of my trip to Los Angeles with Erika. I fantasized about the room we had shared at the Beverly Hills Hotel, where I practiced my Oscar speech in the bathroom mirror, with a plastic bottle of shampoo standing in for the coveted award. We spent the entire weekend in bungalow 5A. Erika argued that its stucco exterior was salmon, but everyone knows it's pink.

Our room had BIGSHOT written all over it. I could have slept in the deep ivory tub surrounded by emerald-green marble, it was so huge. The lush patio amused my senses with succulent, pointy-tipped blooms, keeping the honeybees busy with sweet nectar. The rest of our romantic hideaway reveled in eccentric woods, magnificent dark stones, and stormy colors. Masculine and robust, each room made a unique statement—the exquisite linens, soft like clouds, balanced the suite's rugged appeal. I melted, wrapping myself in the creamy white bath towels. Oh, and the bathmats—like stepping on warm snowflakes.

Los Angeles, I thought. Los Angeles will make me happy. I was there often enough, so why not? Moving there made perfect sense. Still close enough to visit Karen and Grego at a moment's notice, but worlds away from my troubles back home in San Diego. Erika had to come with me. She just had to. And I wouldn't take no for an answer. This was the perfect opportunity for us to start a new life together. I wanted forever with her more than anything. I believe she did too.

Across town, Officer Johnson was on his date with his wife. He had mentioned something in passing the morning we met about taking Saturday off to celebrate her birthday. Here he was ready to sacrifice his life for me on Friday, then spoil his wife on Saturday while I was thinking of every excuse not to share time with the one person I said mattered most to me. The guilt I felt for being so self-centered hurt deeply. Officer Johnson's wife was a lucky woman. Erika, not so much.

"Hey babe, I need to shower," I said, staring out the window at the deepening puddle of water about to float my Nova down the street to the Pacific. "This dang rain," I shrugged. "My extra stuff's still out there in the car babe about to drown."

"Wear something of mine," she said, watching me slide my toes into her cork flip-flops discolored by dirty feet.

"Okay, you've got yourself a deal. But nothing too tight."

I felt reborn, seeing her look at me with accepting eyes. For the first time in months, a flood of true happiness lifted my spirits. Suddenly I didn't mind going the extra mile for Erika. Suddenly heading to the bar for drinks sounded like a great idea. Marsella and Renee weren't all bad, I told myself. While crude at times, they were also battling their own demons.

Seeing them stumbling drunk weekend after weekend saddened me. They were more than the empty booze bottles they lost themselves in. I hated knowing other people suffered. Together they were the lesbian version of my father, and underneath my dislike for them was the innocence of my pain, wanting to fix their brokenness. Yeah, they hit me and locked me in the closet here and there, but Marsella's perfect smile and Renee's hysterical laugh needed a friend almost as badly as I did.

The last time Marsella had attacked, I'd fought back, swinging wildly at her thick eyebrows, which enraged her enough to snap my glasses in half before slamming me head-first into a closet wall. She and the other girls kept me locked down for at least two hours. Water under the bridge at this point. They were drunk and out of their minds, so how could I blame them when I might have done the same? Besides, it was time to live and learn. Maybe now they would respect my decision to come out of the closet and publicly claim Erika like I did Ronnie. Perhaps I wouldn't need her to run defense any longer if the girls would give me a chance to prove myself worthy of their friendship. I would know by the end of the night, but it was imperative for Erika not to utter a word about me being fired last week or attempting suicide.

Together in the bathroom, the clock was now ticking. Erika's haunted rusty pipes sometimes banged and rattled for no reason. Other times the shower ran cold if the toilet were flushed. Her house, while aesthetically pleasing, needed some serious internal upgrades including a new water heater not so quick to leave you cold. After chatting me up for a few more minutes, she left me to shower alone because she was afraid the steam would ruin her hair and makeup. I was sure she was making her rounds on the phone, assembling her crew for what was sure to be an epic night, celebrating my switch to the dark side. The girls were not casual drinkers.

As alcoholics in training, they could have unionized with the amount of booze they killed off nightly. Erika overindulged when pushed but was otherwise a light social drinker, preferring fruity drinks sweetened with colorful liqueurs and cherries, not the sour mashes known to crank the other girls' volume. I kept it simple with cold beer and the occasional margarita. Drinking just to drink was never my thing. But who doesn't like a good buzz now and again, right?

Erika's bathroom was obnoxiously white except for the black grout between the wall tiles and the gorgeous soft cherrywood planks under her iconic ruby clawfoot tub with raised sides. It took several minutes for the shower's intoxicating steam to erase the goosebumps sprouting on me since stripping down to brave the short-lived hot water supply. And as expected, I was in and out, half-washed in less than five minutes. Afterwards, I ran down the hall to the stone fireplace to curb my winter chill. Only to find Erika had done the impossible, placing two small logs on the fire while I was showering.

"Look what I did, babe," she said, broadcasting a cheesy grin, pointing to the angry flames popping and sparking behind the chain skirt, keeping the fiery beast inside its cavernous playground. Amazed, words escaped me. Instead, I slid my wrinkled, waterlogged hand underneath her mauve turtleneck, causing her to lurch forward and trip over the couch, trying to escape the cold shock of my sneaky touch. "Oh my god," she shouted with a look of unsettling misery. The distressing rings of her busy phone interrupted our playful confrontation. Louder than most, and possibly defective, Erika's phone rang longer and faster than most other phones. Its obnoxious cry signaled a coming storm I'd all but begged for but deep down wasn't prepared to face. Still, I believed going out for drinks was the right decision.

Outside, parting clouds teased us with blocks of late afternoon sunlight, bringing a kaleidoscope of color to the wet gray shading the dark sky above. A fast-moving storm building in the distance offshore offered only temporary relief to the rain-soaked ground, struggling to absorb the earlier downpour. I opened the front door to find the ambient temperature had dropped, meaning another torrential down-pour was imminent. Opposing storms seemed to be on a collision course and no one could predict the outcome.

Wearing Erika's favorite pair of shorts, I looked flirtier

than usual. But not quite as sexy as the blue velvet wallpaper in the spare bedroom down the hall she turned into a fashion boutique. Seeing me in them really turned Erika on. She wanted me. I could see the sexual fire in her eyes as she burned the shape of my backside into her memory bank. As she drew closer, wrapping me in her arms, she whispered CHA CHA CHA into my ear before wiggling down my body. I was dripping. Though not my everyday style, I admit, those shorts were beyond cute—a little snug, but cute. Purchased in Hawaii and crocheted from mustard-colored yarn, they were perfect for running around the house without panties. An intricate pattern of revealing circles stitched together allowed my buns to feel the heat of Erika's Ocean Beach wildfire like never before. Soon burned fibers released an acrid vinegar-like odor telling me to back away. But another fire was raging inside.

I loved the heat but could do without a blistered behind. Wearing the shorts was a conscious decision. Feeling slightly uncomfortable, I wanted to show Erika her sense of style and fashion was important to me. What we needed most was mutual acceptance and mercy between us, not more push and shove. If I were truly going to capture her imagination for all time, I would have to humble myself even further and embrace her passions over mine. So far, I was off to a good start, considering I was still walking about the house smiling, knowing a reunion with the bane of my existence was hours away.

Chapter 25

—

If you know anything about Southern California, then you know the local swap meets are a big deal. Being Saturday, I reflected on the good times spent with Karen roaming through the endless piles of junk lined in perfect formation on drive-in theatre movie lots from Riverside to Yuma, Arizona. Sometimes we'd pretend the sticky blacktop was a Mediterranean market surrounded by beautiful Italian architecture. Oh, the fun we had together. The best part was never knowing what you might find browsing the lost treasures waiting for a new home. Everything from black velvet renditions of Elvis and Donald Duck to used rubber swim fins or copper antiques covered in heavy patina can be yours if the price is right. Poor Grego would lose his mind at swap meets. All the colorful toys, trinkets, and old bicycles for sale drove him nuts with excitement. More so than Disneyland, which like Jack in the Box tacos, is a staple of any Southern Californian's existence.

Once I saw a shrunken head hanging in the back of a decrepit Winnebago camper van selling musty incense and curtains strung together with beads and seashells. Its face looked like a dried-up apple with no wrinkles, floppy earlobes, leather ties binding its lips. There were also no clumps of glue or stitches holding the tiny head's wiry hair in place, so it must have been real. Yet I couldn't tell if it was male or female or what animal the bone in the nose came from. Talk about creepy. It was beyond that and then some.

"Karen," I said with a straight face. "Look, he's smiling at you."

"Eww, gross," she said, shaking her head in disgust. Grego joined in, giggling his approval. Standing next to me, a shirtless know-it-all covered in gray back hair corrected me with his deep manly voice, "It's fake you know."

I mumbled a sarcastic reply under my breath hoping someone else would shut him up first for ruining the moment. It was close to Halloween after all, and nothing says "Boo" like a shrunken head. While the self-proclaimed expert wearing hand-me-down jean shorts continued schooling the crowd in the ways of black magic, we split before he planted some voodoo curse on us.

Besides my Christmas cowboy boots from Dad, my greatest gift ever came from the El Cajon swap meet. One Saturday, Karen had grabbed me by the hand and walked us to a small booth on the backside of the action, where a middle-aged Mexican man named Jaime (pronounced hi-me) made monogrammed jewelry fashioned from fourteen-karat gold wire. His broken English was about as good as our Spanish, but together we connected the dots. After the help of a passing interpreter to iron out the details, Jaime went to work. After a few bends, tweaks, and snips, Karen presented me with the coolest ring in the shape of a golden L. My heart stopped when she slid it on my finger. Her thoughtfulness overwhelmed me. I was never so happy. Right there in front of everyone, I bounced on my toes as tears of joy streamed down my face.

"It's genuine gold," she said proudly. It was too. Beside my grandfather's watch, it was the only jewelry I felt comfortable wearing. Sure, I wore the ring Ronnie gave me while we were married, but to me it symbolized lies we would all live to regret, although saying so fills me with panicked thoughts. A month later, I returned the favor, getting her a monogrammed gold ring of her own. We cried and hugged. "Always and forever," she said, squeezing me tightly in her arms.

There was never a dull moment between my sister and me. Including the time Ronnie came home to find his marital home overrun by drunken lesbians in heat. Not my proudest moment, that's for sure. And that's my point. See, I was always screwing things up. I tried not to, but just couldn't seem to help myself. I needed to be with Karen. I needed her to hold me in her arms and tell me everything would be okay. That none of this confused suicidal heartache would matter in two, five, or ten years. But at this point, I couldn't burden her any longer. She had her life, and I had mine. We were apart as much as we were together. Besides, she would put Grego to bed soon and needed this time to wind down her day.

"Go to her?" said my still small voice. But I resisted, choosing Marsella and her gang of bullies and thieves instead. After Erika's champagne mouth announced she had "shit, showered and shaved," we headed out the door to my awaiting Nova. I unlocked Erika's door first, then took my place behind the wheel and said a silent prayer while blabbering about having just got my car washed.

At the end of her street lived Dr. Franklin, a retired neuroscientist who'd recently lost his wife to cancer. As we rolled by, not saying a word to each other, I watched him wasting away before my very eyes, swinging on his front porch alone. He was waiting to die. I recognized the look behind his dark-framed bifocals. You could tell he missed his wife. You could tell he missed his life's work studying the mysteries of the brain. And with his kids grown and living happy adult lives on the East Coast, what else was left for him to do but die? I couldn't ignore how seeing him made me feel. Never mind the happy red and yellow hibiscus-covered Hawaiian shirt he was wearing. This was a man without a purpose. His frail presence spoke to me in a way Sergeant Joe could never understand.

Heading east on Interstate 8, we drove between the San Diego Sports Arena on the right and SeaWorld on the left. I couldn't shake the worry beating inside my heart, which unknowingly slowed my freeway pace to about forty miles per hour. A friendly reminder from a fellow commuter honking in my rearview mirror sped me up to sixty, past SeaWorld's 320-foot sky tower needling into the atmosphere. The rotating capsule's six-minute ride gives sightseers an unob-structed view of the ocean shore converging on downtown's mighty footprint. To my left, directly across Interstate 8's four lanes of traffic, was the Midway district and home of the 12,000-seat Sports Arena, looking like a concrete bunker turned inside out. It stands forcefully atop thousands of yards of smooth blacktop lined with yellow parking stripes.

Each weekend, the arena hosts a swap meet of its own where everything, including the kitchen sink, is for sale.

Along with basketball games, the arena also holds concerts. Karen and I saw Led Zeppelin there in 1973. It was the first time either of us got high. Sitting in the nosebleed section put us in the worst possible place to avoid the clouds of self-rolled smokes passing between friends two sections below. The mind-altering haze looked psychedelic, twisting about in the green, yellow, and red stage lights beckoning the audience tuned in to a wall of sound playing to their rock-and-roll fantasies. We, too, danced away our worries with the eclectic, mostly long-haired crowd, leaving rejuvenated in the wake of amplified creativity. Only we waited for hours to leave afterwards because I was in no shape to drive being so high and all.

Now I worried about Karen and Grego at home, sitting around their hulking coffee table, wondering where I was, since it wasn't uncommon for me to swing by uninvited every other day. I hadn't seen either of them in the weeks since our harbor cruise past the naval shipyard and the imposing concrete towers supporting the Coronado Bridge, whose foundations dug one hundred feet below the bay. A trip to the swap meet could get us back in the swing of things, I thought, making a mental note to call or stop by Monday or Tuesday afternoon.

My defenses were on high alert. I wanted to believe with all my heart that Erika loved me. What I can tell you for sure is how incredibly needy I felt coming off that suicide attempt. Sitting beside me with her hand on my leg, Erika was probably studying my every thought from behind her judgmental eyes. She would have turned my internal dialogue into a swinging barroom brawl if she knew what I was thinking. It was clear I was serving two masters. While Erika fed my wildest physical desires and occasional deep thought, she also fueled the darkness I feared most. She was my grandmother as much as she wasn't.

Making our way onto Broadway, I watched her undress me with her lustful eyes. If you could have seen the way she looked at me with her pouty lips, you would understand the intensity warming my insides. Whatever that thing is people talk about having, we had it for sure. Maybe a good night awaited after all. Swinging open the Chee's door after sneaking the Nova into the Travelodge parking lot at Ninth and A streets, the girls' gleeful banter coming from a back booth was loud enough to override the glitzy flash of a dinging pinball machine counting my nervous steps. Upon seeing me, they stood, singing my praises; they cooed; they gushed, welcoming me with open arms. I nudged Erika, hinting she needed to pace herself against the seasoned drinkers ready to egg her on. But it was on the moment we walked inside.

I saw Marsella first. Her intense stare burned a hole right through me. She was looking at me with an I-know-your-secret kind of smirk. Erika had talked. I looked into her eyes. I was angry but undeterred. *Who did Erika tell first?* I wondered. *What to do?* I asked myself. With Erika, you never knew, so everyone was suspect.

Then, for whatever reason, I buried my worries, realizing my judgment was condemning the entire group without cause or evidence. And from there forward it was on for me too. I couldn't have been more excited, buying the gals rounds of tequila with hugs and smiles for all. My second hurdle to stability was almost behind me. Happy girls meant a happy Erika which meant peace for me. I decided not to drink more than a beer or two to keep things in perspective because tonight was about balance. Well, that and making sure everyone made it home safely after last call.

For the next hour or so, I watched Erika hunt for admiration frolicking between tables of festive patrons scattered about the floor. They toasted her suggestive behavior, causing my jealousy to rage. By now Erika's eyes were glazed over. The sting of coconut piña coladas wobbling her drunken legs let me know she had lost sight of us. I was devastated. Nibbling my nails, I nervously watched the love of my life practically get naked. Remember when I said her parents accepted her sexuality? Publicly they did, but I'm not sure if the gloves came off behind closed doors. Erika didn't learn that strike-first mentality from me. So it almost felt acceptable to let her deflect those deep-rooted feelings of inadequacy in peace.

Not because it was okay to harm me, but maybe by allowing her to vent, I was keeping her safe from those all too familiar insecurities. Was saving others my purpose? Perhaps I could become a place of refuge for those struggling in silence. A safe harbor if you will. After all, most of society suffers from the same issues. Only some are packaged differently than others. As for Erika and me, both of us were young all-American girls from wealthy families who shared a love of the ocean and forbidden passions.

As the drinks continued to flow, I distanced myself from the party. The vibe from Marsella was getting hostile and no longer therapeutic for me. Nothing about the way Marsella started behaving said welcome. Every time I caught her stare, my insides tumbled. From the start, I wanted this night to be about Erika and me, not the whole darn group. After several glasses of water, I headed to the bathroom for some fresh air. This was no time for complacency, so I grunted out a quick pee and hustled back to the table in search of secrets told from Erika's loose lips.

The drinks were coming faster now. I was trying my best to have fun—like, really, really trying. Needless to say, the rest of the gang was having a blast. Even Marsella. "Put her in reverse grumpy," laughed Renee, shooting shots of tequila minus the lime. She sensed the tension and wanted no part of it, for once. What came next was a downright dirty shock, but no surprise.

"So," said Marsella, gloating, with her arm around my girl, "I hear you've taken up diving."

A blast of fear rocked my fragile anxiety. Her words sliced through me. My ashen face sunk. The bug-eyed stares from across the room could see there was no equalizing the pressure building inside my embarrassment. How could Erika turn on me so suddenly after all we had been through? Stupid question, I thought, remembering she'd promised to love me forever. But Erika talked badly about everyone, including her treasured Marsella and Renee, who she had secretly dated for over a year in high school. This was the final straw. Never again would they use my yellow taxi service as a punching bag. Verbal or otherwise.

Holding my head high was paramount. I couldn't let them see me cry again.

"Thanks for nothing," I growled, wanting to bleed from my eyes.

"Ah, go back to your precious family, you bowlegged twat. You probably piss standing up, anyway," she laughed, holding her index finger out like a half flaccid penis.

Not surprisingly, I blew a gasket. If looks could kill, mine would have claimed two, maybe three lives. Without warning, I balled my hands up and struck the table, centering the girls, with a mighty blow. Cubes of cocktail ice exploded into the air. I was beyond angry—inconsolable and blistered. That's when time stopped for me. The last thing I remember was calling Erika a liar. Not a fucking liar, mind you, just a regular plain old liar. She was boiling over, but I didn't hear a sound. Sometimes I drifted away when Erika blew up at me. I'd daydream about being a song comforting the forgotten. Not an everyday ordinary kind of song. An Elton John song of course. I loved him.

"Say what you will, Erika!" I shouted over the group's stunned silence, "But I deserve better." She fired back before I could finish.

"Same here, skank. Besides, I'm tired of tasting men anyway, you pathetic fraud." I knew she was just projecting her sadness onto me, but still.

"No man has ever come between us," I said, thinking of my sweet Ronnie.

"Yeah, well, my parents have three gay kids' crybaby, so save your sob story about poor Grandma Vogt and the rest of those racist, homophobic, murdering bastards you love more than me. Screw you and screw them!"

There was nothing more to say. Fake and self-absorbed, the girls had finally won. Erika was now theirs to do with as they pleased. I felt grateful knowing my ride on Erika's roller-coaster was over. Pushing my way towards the door, the nuisance I left behind taunted me all the way to the sidewalk outside. Halfway across the street, I turned to look for anyone to call me back inside, but there was no one. I was completely and utterly alone. How did I ever get so low?

Overlooking downtown is Balboa Park. Its storied architecture and stunning floral gardens attract thousands of visitors per year. Karen and I spent many days here people watching in the summer sun when gas money was in short supply. Grandma liked to keep my pockets light on occasion to keep me in check. By the grace of God, I arrived safely at the park's west entrance after peeling away from the Travelodge parking lot at Ninth and A, without yielding to any red lights or stop signs. Thankfully, I was smart enough not to drink much while at the Chee, otherwise I might be stuck between Erika's thumb and wishy-washy friends.

Without the love I counted on for validation, I wept uncontrollably. Now that my secret was out, what was I to do? Surely this was a night I would soon live to regret. And for this I broke my easy rider's heart. To let off some steam, I circled the parking lot, driving in slow circles over the painted lines beneath me. The only witness to my despair was acres of freshly cut grass. Out of options, I picked up the pace. My childish antics caught the attention of a nearby neighbor who called the police. Seems everyone is not a fan of the Saturday night blues. Shortly after I stopped spinning my maddening circles, a white San Diego Police car appeared, blocking the paved exit to freedom. First he blasted me with his spotlight, but not before turning on the blue flashing light centered on his Gran Torino's rooftop. The annoyed officer wasn't the least bit impressed by my delinquent behavior.

"You, there. What in the Sam Hill do you think you're doing?"

"Who me?"

"Yeah, you." He was one tough customer, Texas accent and all. He must have been ex-military. Most cops were, according to Sergeant Joe. I couldn't see much against the blinding spotlight pointed in my direction, but he was clearly in no mood for playing games.

"Please," I said, trying not to cry. "I'll leave right now, sir."

"What's your name?" he snarled.

"Mine?"

"Yeah, yours?"

Here we go again, I thought. "Well, Miss who me," he commanded. "I suggest you take this little show of yours someplace else. I don't care where, just go. Got it?"

"Loud and clear," I said, ready to red line the engine's RPMs on the tachometer mounted atop the steering wheels column. The rebel without a cause in me wanted the last word, so I took it and eased past him as he backed away from the exit, imaging myself dropping the hammer to an unknown destination.

Chapter 26

–

By the time I hit Interstate 5, my angry mind couldn't see the forest for the trees. Only there were no trees. Just black sky, pavement, speeding cars, and tears. From all directions, streaks of light rushed by. It was hard to know what to trust. I had become a slave to my lover's wicked ways. Such an impracticable existence should be easy to correct. I struggled to compute, changing lanes recklessly without reason. I couldn't take it anymore. I inhaled deeply before screaming until the wind completely sucked itself out of my body. The last thing anyone needed was me at this point. Especially my trail of intimate victims. I had spoken the love that dare not speak its name, not once, but twice, and failed miserably, breaking Karen, Ronnie, and Erika's hearts in the process. But what about my broken heart? Echoes of my past indiscretions awaited me where love went to die. The bridge was calling me home.

"No," I said. "I won't go. I can't. Not now. Never again."

It was clear, Erika and I were no more.

"She's the home wrecker," I told myself. "Not me."

It was high time she and the girls learned a hard life lesson. Dad too, but his time would come later. This was my time, not theirs, and I was in control, not them. Across, in the northbound lanes of the freeway, the flashing red and blue lights of a speeding police car were exiting towards Nineteenth Street. On the officer's radio, a life-or-death saga was unfolding.

Unbeknownst to me, I was the life-or-death situation broadcasting across the San Diego police department's main radio frequency. The SDPD officer from the park, steadfast in his duties, had followed me thinking something might be amiss.

With his round blue light flashing in sync with the blaring siren, screaming behind me, I continued on about my business thinking only of myself. The speed limit sign for exit 14A reads forty miles per hour—a comfortable pace for those driving safely. One can never be too careful when crossing a bridge twenty-four stories above the water. For the second time in a day, I forcefully gripped the steering wheel for control. And with my eyes wide shut, blindly cut across three lanes of traffic without looking. Nothing's the matter, I thought. Everything's fine. And everything will be better once I'm gone for good. I was pushing seventy miles per hour now. This time I wouldn't fail. I was betting my life on it.

Showtime! As I thundered to a stop in the evening haze of downtown's broad shoulders, death felt certain. I had again made it to the bridge's summit without a scratch to show for my wounds. The dark horizon gusted in the distance. I felt it on my face searching for the edge. Death was happy. But I wasn't. I scrambled not to make the same mistake twice. There were cars to dodge this time, but nothing I couldn't handle. Running for my life, a white blur pushed past, spinning me sideways onto my knees. Losing valuable time, I clawed at the road for traction to right myself and carry on. A few feet from where I landed, the car that skimmed alongside me squealed to a full stop. But he was too late. Time: 6:58 p.m.

They say you see it coming, the flash of light where space and time come together where life can no longer exist. There is no pain or worry. My yellow brick road had indeed become a street of gold. This time was different, this time I didn't fail. The transcendent light of heaven, clear as crystal and garnished with many precious stones, opened the gates of glory and welcomed me home. As a disobedient believer, it was more beautiful than I imagined.

In life, I struggled with man's interpretation of God and his presence because it often lacked the courage to inspire unconditional love. This reality seeks only to serve one purpose. To the church, I was the filthiest kind of sinner. Forgive me? Heavens no, but in the end, the joke wouldn't be on me, for I was home. I was dead now. Before tonight's tragic ending there was a time nearly a year ago when I had looked to quell the evil within. It was Easter Sunday 1973. The Reverend G. Arthur Hammons was at the pulpit of the Christ Church Unity in El Cajon, around the corner from where I first met Ronnie. Inside the chapel a rainbow reflected across the floor from a massive stained-glass window, showering the room with reflections of light—red, green, and blue.

Here I wasn't a freak. I was just a girl. A welcome visitor amongst other sinners willing to forgive a stranger. The pastor spoke of God's eternal Easter promise. He declared the meaning of Easter as eternal life with a God who suffered and died for us. This same God who also rose and triumphed over death. In my irrevocable act, the essence of time no longer mattered, for I too would rise. All that remained was for Erika to claim her just due. But it was not meant to be. The struggle that began with my father and ended in the throes of drunken, abusive love again thwarted by a dutiful police officer in the exact spot as before. Another face-plant. Another failure. Another near-death experience. The white flash that brushed up alongside me was the passenger-side front fender of a pursuing police car. America's finest, as they call themselves. But this time was different. This time I was handcuffed. The officer who cuffed me was so aggressive he bruised my petite wrist bones locking me up tight. But then again, I know shackles aren't built for comfort, so who am I to complain when I'm the one who drug him to the point of no return.

Chapter 27

–

The red-over-white ambulance powered through the city, its flashing lights ablaze. All I had ever hoped for and dreamed of died minutes before on that godforsaken bridge, so why did I feel so alive? Each hint of acceleration tilted the swerving tube around corners and over bumps, jostling my anxiety to dangerous levels. My kidneys felt bruised and disrespected from being kneed in the back repeatedly. The unapologetic ambulance driver slammed me into the rails of the aluminum cot in his race to save no one.

I could see in the eyes of the bashful attendant tending to me that chatting up the walking dead was harder than he imagined. He was out of his league, but so was I. Perhaps he was new. Perhaps his inexperience was ill-prepared for the fragile killers of the world like me. Perhaps I would be his first and his last. His silence repeated itself over and again. We rode the entire five-minute ride without a word spoken between us. Thankfully, we had the screaming siren to keep us company.

Act naturally, I said to myself upon arrival at the hospital. *What they don't know won't hurt them.*

After taking me into custody, the inner-city officers had identified themselves as San Diego police and shoved me handcuffed into the cramped back seat of a white cop car against a black metal cage. This was about twenty-five minutes before the ambulance raced off with me in fear of my life. From a crouched position, I watched the officers search my Nova with reckless abandon. They were hunting for a bust. Though they had saved my life, the circumstances felt markedly different from before with the CHP.

San Diego police operated from a different playbook than the Highway Patrol. These were cops. Tough guys who signed up for the dirty work. They had me on full display for anyone who cared to look. I could see headlights backed up in both directions. Casually dressed onlookers stood outside their cars acting out my despair with their flailing arms as busy officers armed with flashlights and black batons lay flares to keep the curious gawkers away from the action.

Unlike Officer Johnson, the San Diego officer who cuffed me, had a long black holster that swiveled when he walked. He looked about thirty. And was super tall too with an athletic build and a clean shaven face to compliment his big blue eyes. In his mind, he had saved the day. Little did he know my criminal intent was dead on arrival. He introduced himself as Officer Kevin Patrick. A strong Irish lad if ever there was one.

"So why did you run?" he asked, looking at me firmly with his hands gripping the front sides of gun belt. He wouldn't have believed me if I told him, so I kept my mouth shut. But he demanded an answer. So I bulldozed him with the truth. This left him with a helpless look about his masculine face. Hell, he could have been a college all-star, for all I knew. The way he pulled me back over the edge as I dangled staring into nothingness, continues to impress.

But don't think I didn't give him a run for his money. There was a moment when I thought I had him beat. The freedom I'd felt was incredible. It reminded me of carefree days as a child flying my hand out the window of Grandpa's purple Chevelle station wagon on road trips to the Grand Canyon's steep-sided iron-red walls. My last thoughts breathed a sigh of relief, falling away from my troubles. That is, until the scrappy officer Patrick dug his hands into my back, lifting me away from the edge practically over his head, somersaulting me in the air onto my side, which didn't hurt nearly as much as you might think. At the time it didn't, anyway. A knee in my back later locked me down tight. It all happened so fast neither of us had time to think.

"Car's clean," came a frustrated voice directing a fire engine to a stop near where Officer Patrick tried to box me in with his speeding car. "Alright boys, let's wrap this up and get the traffic moving," barked an impatient officer in the crowd. Sitting on the edge of the cruiser's backseat with my feet planted firmly on the ground, I told Officer Patrick my issues weren't criminal. I think he believed me. But like Officer Johnson, he also had a boss to answer to. After waiting for the police to search me for a second time, the firefighter tasked with checking me for injuries was satisfied I required no rescue. With all ten fingers and toes accounted for and no blood loss to report, what other conclusion could he make?

"I apologize," he said, "I wish there were more I could do. But everything seems to check out okay so the PD will take it from here." It was all so impersonal. After gathering his medical bag, he wished me good luck, then walked his infectious smile back to the fire engine parked beside my

Nova and removed the canvas overcoat and black helmet he had donned in preparation for anything.

"Lori?" asked Officer Patrick, standing between two scowling sergeants who looked nothing like Joe Zafuto. "We understand this is your second visit to the bridge. Is that true?"

I slumped over, dropping my head below their knees. "Yes."

Suddenly, an ambulance ride to the hospital didn't sound like such a bad idea. "Can you please just get me out of here?" I cried. "Before someone I know sees me?" Once at the hospital, I'd call Karen. She'd know what to do. Better from the hospital than the jail, I thought. Anything but jail; being in a police station once before was bad enough. "Just please get me out of here," I begged again, longing for the attention I so desperately felt I deserved.

The khaki uniforms worn by San Diego police and the CHP were similar but different. One wore gold eagle-crested shields and no arm insignias, while the other had stars for badges and blue and gold shoulder patches. The two sides seemed at odds discussing the inevitable end of my night. But there was no sign of Sergeant Joe or Officer Johnson. I never expected to see them again so soon, but a friendly face about then would have been nice.

The full impact of my wrinkled life was once again front and center in another shocking display of disorienting lights sworn to serve and protect. I felt no peace held safe against my will. The same tears and tension I fought, kicked, and ignored carried over from Friday. Thanks to me, backed-up traffic in both directions shut down the bridge for over an hour. Only cars full of families this time watched my life unravel before their very eyes. Some looked on in horror, while others cried at the sight of me. Many of the officers behaved as if opening the bridge was more important than protecting and serving. They saw me as a crazy, disobedient criminal. Someone who endangered their lives. This was true, but only to a point. Still, a little more compassion would have gone a long way. Was a simple apology from anyone for the extra tight handcuffs too much to ask? And where the hell was Erika when I needed her most? Oh yeah, getting drunk with her sordid affairs. But I had learned my lesson once and for all and just wanted to go home.

My options at this point were simple, and all included some form of custody. A far different experience than my night with Sergeant Joe and his crew. One, face a handful of felonies, including assault on a police officer. Or two, take a slow ride in the meat wagon to a semi-voluntary psyche evaluation to help me see just how troubled I was. The San Diego officers were showing me compassion after all. For this I was grateful, as jail would have been a tough pill to swallow. I chose option two, thinking the food might be better. But that didn't mean the district attorney couldn't bring charges later, as Officer Kevin Patrick explained it. He was careful not to say too much. "But to answer your question, madam, about going home tonight," he said, "There is no way in hell you are walking off this bridge scot-free without answering for what you've done." Little did he know I intended to do just that when the time was right.

Chapter 28

–

When I arrived at the hospital, I was pinched and bleary. Oh, my car. What was going to happen to my car, I worried? Here I was, a grown woman requiring cops, fire engines, and a stretched Cadillac ambulance to sort out her relationship troubles. All of life's troubles, really, but you get the point. *I won't think about this moment when I'm older*, I thought.

Flat on my back, strapped in across my waist, the Emergency Departments automatic doors swished open for my gurney to an unfolding drama, making way for another siren shattering the distant air with its precious cargo. A life hung in the balance. A life more important than mine. There are no get-well flowers in the emergency department. Only the metallic tang of cold bed rails and crisp bleached sheets wafting amongst the smells of greasy meat and lemon-pine cleaners. It was dinner time and, on the wards above, bland food from the cafeteria was being served on trays used more than a hundred and one times before.

My hip hurt from being sacked twice in as many days, and I wanted to go home. Biding my time, my gaze swiveled around the bustling corners for an open room to claim. Like I had a choice. But a girl can dream, can't she? A private room would do, away from the hacking coughs, shivering in their wheelchairs near the nurses' station. Noisy intercoms cried out above me. Hisses of pain sandwiched between lonely moans from other patients reminded me I was somewhere I didn't want to be. A longshoreman type wearing steel toe boots and a black beanie cap getting stitches in his hand momentarily distracted my worries as I rolled past his room.

"Put her in five," came a frustrated voice, older than dirt, holding a clipboard in her busy liver-spotted hands. "We'll be with you in a minute," she suggested before speeding away to the ambulance entrance doors whooshing open with an incoming critical patient.

An overdose? Maybe a heart attack, or a car crash possibly. It was hard to tell. *Nice*, I thought. *Someone worse off than me*. I was amazed watching orderlies and nurses race to their predetermined positions, swarming the oncoming patient like a colony of bees protecting their queen. My emotional wounds for the moment were safe and found themselves relaxed to the point of sleepy exhaustion. An hour or so passed before I awoke to find the green privacy curtain around my hospital bed pulled tight to better shield the intrusive overhead lights. My tired eyes struggled to reacquaint themselves with reality when a smiling burst of brunette energy about my height threw open the curtain to introduce herself.

"Knock, knock," she smiled.

Her positivity was infectious.

"Hi. My name's Molly, and I'm going to be your nurse tonight."

She spoke with swooping hand gestures. A touch of crimson jumped off her nails as she read over my chart. She worked the three to eleven shift and would go home in a few hours. But for now, she was all mine. "So, what's cracking?" she smiled, knowing I needed a good laugh.

Talk about a loaded question. Where did I start, and did she have an extra twenty years to spare? "Lay it on me," she said, listening intently while taking my vitals, not missing a word of my sad story. No doctor had ever made me feel as important as she did. She was personable, not clinical. I could see for the time being I made the right choice in not choosing jail.

Molly's crisp white uniform reminded me of the one I had worn training to be a CNA right after high school. However, mine lacked the starched intellect of a college nursing degree. My medical career, like many of my successes, was short-lived. It was all fun and games until I had to work with actual sick people.

I hated being a failure which is why I didn't like talking about the medical field very much. With such dedication, I asked Molly why she was a nurse instead of a doctor.

"Simple," she said. "I wanted to be a soldier, not a general."

The longer we talked, the further behind she got in her duties. I counted two new admissions while she checked me over. What I admired most about Molly was how she appeared comfortable in uncomfortable situations like mine.

"The doctor will be in to see you soon," she said, waving goodbye. "But don't you worry," she smiled bouncing away, "I'll be back before you know it." And with that, she pulled my curtain shut and disappeared.

Somewhere close by, intertwined with the medical

chatter floating about, came the abrupt, halting sounds of a seasoned police officer. There was an urgency in his voice. Instantly I knew who it was. There was no mistaking the accent demanding to see me. The harder I listened, the closer the stern voice came to my corner of the emergency ward. From the opposite side of where I was looking, a hand gently appeared, and grabbed hold of the weighted privacy curtain before sliding it back just enough to see me. It was Sergeant Joe. Time: 8:58 p.m. "Hey, kid. How ya doing?"

Ashamed, I stared into the bottom half of an elegant chrome fire extinguisher peeking through where Sergeant Joe came through my curtain. The polished exterior, long and round, turned my thin expression into a chubby fun-house caricature. *Fighting fires must be cool*, I thought. *Who doesn't love firefighters? Jealous Cops, I guess.*

"Earth ta Lori, earth ta Lori, is anyone home? Earth ta Lori."

"Huh? Whoa, I'm awake, I'm awake," I said, dodging a large knuckled hand waving in my face.

"Boy, am I glad ta see you. I got here as fast as I could."

"Thanks." I whimpered, pretending not to cry.

"Hey now," he said. "Everything's going to be okay. I promise."

I wanted to believe him. Seeing the sadness crying in his eyes showed me just how much he cared. But I worried I had upset him. That he would have me prosecuted to the fullest extent of the law for making him look stupid after releasing me a day ago. But I didn't want him to leave me alone.

"Apparently SDPD is on the way, but don't worry," he said. "I think they just have some follow-up questions for you, or so I heard."

This upset me all over again. Suddenly, the curtain ripped open.

"Sorry to keep you waiting," said a charming Ivy League voice. My heartbeat spiked, seeing the God of every straight woman's idolatry. "Hello, I'm Dr. Cushman, but you can call me Bruce. Now let's have a look at those eyes," he said, shining his penlight into each pupil for signs of intoxication. Of course, nothing illicit was on board, as I'd planned to ferry the girls home between midnight and last call.

Dr. Cushman was young, toned, and attractive. He was dressed in tailored trousers and a fitted shirt that smelled heavenly, like a fine cognac dipped in success. I closed my eyes as his cold stethoscope listened to my broken heart. With short parted brown hair and simmering green eyes, I could have fallen in love under different circumstances.

"Everything sounds great," he said, jotting notes in my chart. I barely winced out a grin from the pull of self-inflicted nausea. The thin gold lines dominating his navy blue tie gave him credibility beyond his years. My heart was bouncing off my ribs with each look into his eyes.

Not because I was sexually attracted to this mental stud. Heavens no. It's because I could tell he cared so much for people like me. He could have been anywhere in the world doing anything his heart desired, but he was here, and I was grateful.

After assessing my vitals, Dr. Cushman asked Nurse Molly for a CBC (blood panel) and two aspirin.

"I hear we've had a bit of a rough night," he said.

"Yeah, you could say that," I cringed feeling like a complete and utter loser not worthy of anything.

"Well then, let's talk about what brought you in tonight."

"I'd rather not," I whispered numb and embarrassed.

"I see. Now, let's have a look at those wrists. Then the good doctor raised his hands above his head and asked me to do the same. "Can you wiggle your fingers for me? Good. Now, how about a couple of powerful fists? Excellent! I can see you're a little shaken, but medically you're fine. The red marks on your wrist should go away in a day or two, so don't worry. But I'm a little more concerned about the wounds I can't see, if you know what I mean." I did, but it was none of his business. I wanted to lie and tell him this was all a massive misunderstanding.

"You look like someone who knows how to enjoy herself," he said. "So why the sad face?" The doctor's remark caught me off guard. But I answered him the best I could.

"I don't know. I'm just a little mixed up tonight, I guess."

"Are you still wanting to hurt yourself?"

"No! No, I don't, not anymore."

"Good. But I'll be honest, I'm really concerned, and recommend you visit with a trusted colleague of mine before any discussion of going home."

Though I never said a word, the doctor knew exactly what I was thinking. "Questions or concerns?" he asked watching my body language with a heavy look.

He could see I was wavering.

"Now try not to worry and remember, we're going to get through this together. I'll be back in to check on you in a few minutes. In the meantime, can we get you a cup of water or something?"

"Water would be great."

Alone again with Sergeant Joe, there were more questions sure to come.

"Look, kiddo," he said, standing beside me, "I know you want this Erika to love you, but she doesn't, and the sooner you realize that fact the better."

This was the last thing I needed to hear. But he was right.

Sensing I needed to rest, Sergeant Joe excused himself to grab some coffee. In the meantime, Nurse Molly popped back in with a small paper cup filled with lukewarm water.

"Hey," she said, watching me down the water in a single gulp. "Is there anyone I can call for you before the night gets any crazier?"

"No, I'm okay. But how about a shot of Demerol and maybe a one-way ticket to anywhere but here?"

"I'll see what I can do," she laughed. "And hey, keep the positivity going. Because a good sense of humor will go a long way with the doctors."

"Thank you," I said, relieved that hope was on the horizon.

"Say, I know I've only been here a little while, but do you have any idea when I can go home?" She knew this was coming by the speed in which she answered me. "Sorry, Charlie, but that's above my pay grade. Seeing how you're not disruptive and lack extreme hygiene, I think you have an excellent shot at getting out of here at some point."

My curiosity got the best of me. "What's extreme hygiene?" I asked, wrinkling my nose.

"Think stink on stink," she laughed pinching her nose with her fingers. While by my side, Molly confided in me after hearing my story, she had called her mom just to say hi. "Almost as good as a hug," she said, "But not quite. Now try and relax until the doctor can see you again. We're kind of busy, but we will squeeze you in between chest pains in room one and a first period down the hall in eight. Now can I get you anything else before I go?" A switch flipped.

"Yeah, you can help me get out of here."

"Sorry, can't help you there," she smiled tossing back the curtain.

"Yeah, but I don't think the doctors can keep me because I overheard the highway patrolman the other night complaining about being unable to detain me for being depressed. And if they can't, you can't, right?" Her concern for me was palpable. "I'm sorry, but I have to go, Molly. The cops made a mistake and I'm not supposed to be here."

"Hold on, Ms. Lori, please don't do anything you'll regret until I come back." Near panicked, she ran off to get Dr. Cushman. As she scuttled off, Sergeant Joe returned. "Hey what's going on?" he asked.

"Nothing."

Not satisfied with my answer, he took a quick sip of his coffee before speaking.

"Lori, I can see you're torn, but you said it yourself da night before last. Enough is enough."

My tears pushed back against him. "But how will I ever replace Erika when no one else loves me?"

"Says who?" he growled.

I attempted to remind him this wasn't a life-or-death situation, but the fury of his throbbing jugular veins met my self-justification head-on, halting my reckless denial with a series of angry gestures. In two sentences, Sergeant Joe went from a mild-mannered conversationalist to a Shakespearian inner-city weapon of war. I feared for my world. In my moment of self-pity, Sergeant Joe's anger stepped forward, inviting me to picture him knocking on Officer Johnson's front door at 1:00 a.m. to inform his twenty-three-year-old widow that I had murdered her husband. There was no fooling this streetwise guardian. His years of gut-wrenching experience pleaded for my attention. But the desire for love, even if tainted, had gained the upper hand over the decorated officer.

"She doesn't mean the horrible things she says to me."

The disbelief on his face was unsettling. His pupils were fixed and dilated. The soft fluorescent glow above now burned white hot. I felt the disorienting float of my nausea return, tilting my senses, when Sergeant Joe called me out again.

"Young lady, please tell me you don't believe this nonsense you're telling yourself."

I knew Sergeant Joe was right. Still, I pleaded for understanding as his approval meant everything. I needed him to believe in me and to tell me again I was worthy of love, but instead he forcefully called me out again.

"Have ya forgotten ya tried to kill yourself twice now from my beautiful bridge?"

"No, I haven't forgotten."

"I know you'd take a bullet for this Erika but its time you realize she's da one behind the trigger. I'm sorry for being so blunt, but I don't want to lose you. Not like this."

Sniveling, with my arms folded, "Thank you," was all I could muster.

"I know you can't lean on your dad, but is mom a possibility?"

"No!"

"I'd be happy to give her a call."

"No, that's okay. We haven't talked in over two years anyway, so what's the use."

"Hey you never know."

"Trust me, Sergeant Joe. I know."

"OK, well da offer's on da table if you change your mind. Now I have to run, duty calls, but I'll be back ta check on you later. And fer da love of God, please let these people help you before it's too late."

Before walking away, he rubbed the top of my head, smiled, and waved goodbye. It was good to see him too, but this was no time to reminisce. Psyching myself up, I waited five minutes before making my move. Not ten steps into my escape, a familiar voice stopped me in my tracks. It was Dr. Cushman. Fearing he would notify security, I stared down at my feet, fingers knotted together in prayer that he would leave if I ignored him. Fat chance.

"Not so fast, Ms. Vogt."

"Doctor, please. I just want to go home."

He could see by my conviction that persuading me to stay wasn't going to happen without a fight. Like with Sergeant Joe the night before, I wanted to stay, but I had to go.

"Well, if you intend on leaving against medical advice, the lawyers tell me I need you to sign yourself out. But I implore you to stay and let us help you."

"And what about my purse?" I asked out loud to anyone crowding around the nurses' station who'd listen. Below our shoes were streaks of dried disinfecting mop water masking a cesspool of invisible germs. "Can someone please get Ms. Vogt her belongings so we can all get back to work?" The doctor knew I intended to learn my lesson the hard way, but he couldn't have been more wrong. With my purse in hand thanks to Nurse Molly, I signed the treatment-refusal form, smiled and said goodbye, but not without some regrets. I knew Dr. Cushman and Nurse Molly only wanted to help. But I just wasn't ready for that type of commitment. Especially since I'd planned on leaving before I arrived. And just like that I was on the run again, not caring a bit about the bloody Highway Patrol, San Diego Police or their follow up questions.

My hampster wheel of doom was spinning out of control, racing towards an unknown future. Knowing there is no light without darkness, I swallowed my shame and spun around to face the automatic entrance's wide glass doors and walked out of the hospital of my own accord thinking it was time for Mom and me to bury the hatchet. She was close by, but first I had to find my car. Time: 10:05 p.m.

Chapter 29

–

With two fresh suicide attempts to atone for, I strolled away from the hospital's stagnant, barely breathable air looking for answers. Free from the bleachy, green-tiled walls of hospital life, I headed towards an incoming taxicab dropping off a grandmotherly gal limping slowly with the aid of a brown wooden cane. I offered to help but, like me, this elderly fire-cracker cherished her independence more than anything. Inside the cab, I blurted out, "A to Z Towing, please, and step on it." It was common knowledge among the car clubs at the time that if the cops impounded your car near downtown, A to Z Towing was the first place you looked. The infamous tow yard was five minutes from the hospital, so the mystery of my beloved Nova's whereabouts would quickly be revealed.

Bingo. Not five minutes later, crossing Boston Avenue from Thirty-Second Street I saw my yellow beauty sitting just inside the gates, still waiting to be processed. Before another second passed, I jumped out of the cab, tossing the fare on the front seat, and raced inside to free her before another grubby hand smudged the paint. After paying the tow fee and impound charge, I made a quick inspection for scratches, slid behind the wheel, and eased my way back onto Thirty-Second Street east towards Thirty-Sixth Street for a long-awaited mother-daughter reunion. There was no time to waste. I needed to hurry before I changed my mind. Facing me head-on was a screaming ambulance shattering the night's collective hush. Having just left the emergency room, I couldn't help but feel part of the drama unfolding before me.

I read an interesting quote once that said: *One must part with the past to advance the future.* After years of hanging on to several unhealthy relationships, tonight was about clearing space for the impossible to happen. First stop, Mom's place. Time: 10:45 p.m.

Easing off the clutch between second and third gears, I had a monumental decision at hand. Approaching Thirtieth Street, free will demanded I choose a lane. Peace versus chaos. Right for Ronnie. Left for Mommy.

Nothing about visiting a graveyard at night feels natural. The best thing about Mom being dead was she could no longer leave me. For two years now, Mom lay trapped beneath six feet of dirt and rock. I felt her still clinging to the life she let slip from her grasp. This was the first time I'd visited her grave since she died that fateful Friday night, December 1, 1972. I even missed her funeral I was so distraught.

The wrought-iron fence bordering Greenwood cemetery looks as scary as it sounds. Stone faced, with fingers clenched, I cautiously wound my way towards Mom's headstone. Driving with the window down, I breathed in the smell of dirt from newly turned soil. Another grave. Another death. Haunting Mom's graveyard after hours reminded me of the power that comes with dying. But if this were true, then why was everyone so sad when it happened?

In order to keep family close we'd buried Mom at the cemetery across the street from where Grandpa Vogt was entombed. I warned myself not to trespass at such a late hour, but I had to make my peace with Mom. The engravers carved her headstone from a slab of dark marble with silver-gray swirls highlighting its message reading: Beloved Wife and Mother. She died in the days between Thanksgiving and Christmas. While Mom's desert home and preoccupation with alcohol kept us apart for years, I couldn't deny the need for her mother's intuition. Knowing how much she suffered only intensified my secret cravings for her.

For a mother's practical sensibilities are never lost on those they carry in the womb. I loved my mom, Georgia, before I was born, and I love her to this day. No matter her faults, she was worthy of love and its redeeming qualities. Suddenly, death wasn't so inviting. Each flutter in the dark startled me. All around me, dormant tears cried out for companionship. I knelt down. The feel of chalky dust on moms headstone gripped my fingers tracing the outline of her name. In the shadows beyond her grave, some headstones, weathered by time, leaned away from their upright positions. Some were covered in dead leaves, while others bore the scars of wilted flowers. The ageless souls unbound by mortality's rules walked with me amongst the gnarled trees, buffering the whispering winds blowing about. *Take care*, they warned.

The day Mom died, my music stopped forever. I barely understood the soul-crushing finality of natural death, let alone the landslide of suicidal self-destruction. The coroner's report listed Mom's untimely end as SUICIDAL DEATH by CARBON MONOXIDE POISONING. Learning the truth about Mom's violent life with her husband, Neal, made her death an impossible burden to bear. Gone two years by then, I could feel her cries for forgiveness bleed from deep within the afterlife. In the days after she died, a clear picture of her living hell emerged through the authorities' investigation. I first heard of her lonely end about a day after she died. I wish I could describe for you the feeling of hearing that the mother you longed to know better took her life without saying goodbye. In the hours after receiving news of her death, while still reeling from losing my Grandpa, I yearned for anything to believe in other than sadness. Details of Mom's last days made the grieving process a horrific challenge. A sheriff's investigator by the name of Deputy John McDonnell called me the morning of Dec 2, 1972, with questions regarding Mom and Neal's relationship.

There wasn't much to tell since I didn't know, but I gave him all I knew about her troubled life. He said, "The Kern County Sheriff's Office responded to a possible death call on Bowman Road about one mile west of the county dump in Ridgecrest, California." Apparently, two young lovers in a camper discovered Mom while they were searching for the perfect spot to love the night away. "In their search for secluded privacy in the open desert, they came across your Mom's white two-door Ford Falcon sitting quietly in the dark. On closer inspection, they found the engine was cold, with a fifty-foot black garden hose running from the tailpipe to the decedent's lap. Next to her was her brown dog, also deceased."

The official tone in which he spoke lacked all manner of warmth. This made his crime-scene description even more chilling than he described. Georgia wasn't a decedent; she was my Mom for God's sake. Understandably shaken, the kids who found her high-tailed it outta there and drove 166 miles south without stopping to Costa Mesa where they contacted a trusted friend who called the sheriff's sub-station in Ridgecrest at 12:07 a.m. on December 1, 1972. Responding deputies did indeed find Mom's white Ford Falcon cold to the touch with an empty gas gauge and ignition key in the on position. Besides her and Tinker Bell, the only other items found inside were an empty quart bottle of vodka along with a paper sack holding three unopened cans of beer and a full pint of vodka. That night Mom's body was transported to Kern County General Hospital in a white van for an autopsy. Thinking of my mom as the victim of an intrusive autopsy kept me awake more nights than I care to admit. Television has a way of making them look painless, but I know better because what they don't show you is what hurts the most. Of course, my analytical mind searched for the obvious needle in the haystack. Where were Mom's purse, cigarettes, and suicide note?

If she killed herself, where was her good-bye note? Several people in the family pressed the investigators for more answers, but the deputies investigating Mom's death refused to speculate on anything not matching their initial findings. Meanwhile Neal told the cops that the last time he saw Mom was the Monday before her death driving past the house. He claimed Mom called him late Wednesday night and begged him not to hang up on her because she wanted to talk things out. The next day Mom was found dead.

Neal identified the black hose as having come from their

house's front yard. He first noticed it was missing on the thirtieth, after coming home late from work. Can you believe the sick maniac asked for his precious hose be returned after the investigation concluded? Talk about heartless. And I thought Erika was bad. I don't know about you, but the last thing I would want hanging around the house was a hose used to kill someone I loved. On the day of her autopsy, the coroner submitted a blood sample from Mom to the crime laboratory of the Kern County Sheriff's office. They found the sample contained .188 milligrams percent alcohol along with a contained concentration of 62 percent carbon monoxide. Now I don't know what that means per se, but I do know that whatever it means, it was enough to kill my mother dead. The only question being, by whose hand, Mom's, or Neal's?

Now, sitting Indian style on the damp grass over her grave, I shared everything I was feeling inside. I knew Mom wouldn't judge me because we were one and the same. Both in death and life. In a world of death surrounded by the living, I opened my heart wide to her. In the hour we spent together, I spoke about life, dying, and the happiness found in the middle. For my own sake, I recited the Lord's Prayer to ward off any demons lurking behind the stone angels standing guard over us.

> **Our Father, who art in heaven,**
> **hallowed be thy name;**
> **thy kingdom come;**
> **thy will be done;**
> **On earth, as it is in heaven.**
> **Give us this day our daily bread.**

And forgive us our trespasses,
As we forgive those who trespass against us.
And lead us not into temptation;
But deliver us from evil.
Amen.

Chapter 30

–

For the first time in ages, my troubled mind was truly at ease. After visiting my dead mother, it was clear the finality of death wasn't for me, but how did I continue to live having come so close? I was lucky to be alive, and I knew it, even though the idea of being a survivor was unsettling. What now? And what would my dark angel think of my sudden desire to live? Well, I was about to find out. For some reason, Idyllwild was on my mind again. Rolling past streets clogged with cars and filtered light, I heard the call of an eagle echoing off canyon walls from high above their nests in the tree line. I dreamed of the sappy sweet pine smell giving the wilderness its treasured signature. I would have given anything to trade my polluted life of concrete and steel for the abundant kindness of the forest and the trees. Being in the mountains, surrounded by nature, had a way of righting all the world's wrongs. Don't ask me why, but life made sense to me the higher I climbed away from the inhumanity of sea level. A hawk with blood on its talons was beautiful to me, not traumatizing. It spoke of life feeding life, much different from the opportunistic vultures who prey upon weakness for pleasure, not survival.

But the forested dreams of Idyllwild were too far away,

considering my limited means after bailing out my car. With nowhere to go, I exited at Spring Street and headed straight towards Karen's upstairs apartment, praying for the best while preparing for the worst. A few blocks away now. The memory of a rainy-day fund stashed in a Hush Puppies shoe-box behind an old green sleeping bag in my bedroom closet caused me to drift towards a telephone pole dreaming of the escape sixty bucks could provide.

Thanks to Andrew Jackson and a forgotten Christmas bonus from Grandma, I now had options. Sixty of them. With cash on the brain, I revisited the ridge tops above Strawberry Creek, forgetting that Grandma sold the family home there a year after Grandpa died. It was set among tall cedar trees and mountains of rocks bigger than the sky, and just thinking about it made me smile. Idyllwild was a small town with an authentic community atmosphere, and Karen and I spent every childhood penny we found on candy from the local sundries shop each and every visit. To us, it was a magical place. Part of the charm I found in mountain life was the ability to get tired, relaxing from doing nothing.

Well past midnight now, parked outside Karen's apart-ment, I felt like a juvenile delinquent skipping school. Sitting there alone, I wept for our dad because he couldn't see the life he'd lost to his bigoted principals. Never would he know the joy of teaching his grandson to fish a tumbling stream with orange and yellow leaves covering its banks. Or the warm embrace of a loved one after making a cherished memory. A sad situation not likely to correct itself anytime soon. By now my eyes were heavy. So heavy, I couldn't move, think, or even dream.

But I did dream in the worst way imaginable. As exhaustion began to unfold me, I heard Officer Johnson call out to me. He was in pain and needed help, but my drowsy lashes fluttered him away as sleep swallowed me whole. Tossing and turning, sprawled out across the Nova's front seat, I heard him again. "Lori, two days have passed since I tackled you on the bridge. You're probably asleep, tucked in safely, while I'm alone, stranded at the end of your life, feeling you slip from my grasp. And because of this, my perfect world quit spinning at 12:35 a.m. the Friday we met. I battled the grim reaper on your behalf and won. But at what cost?

"Being a cop isn't easy, you know. It's a zero-fail mission. People think we're robots unable to empathize. That we live to search and destroy. It's not true. Sacrifice and service are not words to me. They're a way of life. Our encounter reminds me of something I heard in the academy as a recruit. 'Men,' the drill sergeant yelled, 'forget everything television, and the movies taught you about being a cop.' This job I've chosen is hours of boredom followed by seconds of sheer terror. In four months on, I've seen everything from vehicle pursuits to decapitations. Most shifts burn slow with mounds of endless paperwork. Often I'm a roadside counselor balancing a world of love and hate for less than a garbageman's wage. But I wouldn't have it any other way. And the terror I spoke of finally found me the night you gave up on yourself, which is why I'm now forever haunted by you. But I wonder if you're okay. I cringe thinking of you being snatched away by death's unforgiving hand. Why do you want to die so badly? Please tell me because I need to understand. Because I keep seeing you in the water. I'm unable to let you go. I guess it's my way of keeping you safe. I'm tired now. I think I'll sleep."

He felt so real. Like he was actually talking to me in real life. But he wasn't. He was a dream reminding me of just how far I hadn't come. An hour later I awoke drenched in sweat, shivering at the sound of a descending airliner turning west over La Mesa towards San Diego. For the first time, I didn't feel safe in my Nova.

Miles to the south, Sergeant Joe was thinking of ways to break the news to Officer Johnson about my second attempt at suicide. I imagined their conversation going something like this:

"Tom? Hey, buddy, it's Joe."

"Oh, hey Sarge! Can ya hang on a sec; I gotta turn down my music."

"Sorry ta bother ya so early, but I come bearing bad news, my friend. Remember, Lori?"

"Of course, Sarge, how could I forget?"

"Well, she made another run at da bridge last night."

"What?"

"Easy, big guy, she's alive! San Diego Police sacked her at about 1900 hours, from what I understand. I came in four hours early, was working an 11-80 in the South Bay when she went Code-3 up da bridge. She checked herself outta da hospital against doctor's orders before I could get back ta her. Rumor has it she got half-way over da edge this time around."

"Jesus, boss! Is there anything we can do?"

"I dunno, kid. Maybe say a prayer or sumthin. I mean, you know da drill. It's a medical issue, remember. Besides, I heard da quacks chalked it up to a ditzy girl with wounded pride and let her walk. I saw her briefly, but she was pretty defensive with me. You two bonded, and hearing from you might help. Gotta hand it to her though, pal! It takes some big balls to make a run for the border two days in a row. I'd call, but she needs a sensitive college guy dis time around, not Brooklyn Joey. You reach out! And help her find a reason to live. Capeesh!?"

Properly freaked out. My entire body dripped nervous sweat. And my hair, I looked like someone had backed over me with a lawn mower. Frazzled, it was time to leave, but University Avenue was foggy and dangerous. I was hungry, craving pancakes, sausage, and hash browns. But was too tired to eat. Yet I felt okay considering I was 0 for two with the bridge. A mile from my apartment, I began thinking of places I could park and sneak in without getting caught. After deciding on a space out front of Grandpa's shop, I walked around the corner to Wilson Street concocting a series of outlandish maneuvers sure to get me inside.

My first thought was to crouch and lower my exposure along the path to my apartment in the back-right corner below Grandma's single-pane watchtower. Of course, anyone awake with open blinds would have spotted my hunched approach from their bedroom windows, but I had to try something, even if I looked foolish. My efforts paid dividends, netting me a safe place to rest my eyes. Time seemed complacent in my one-bedroom sanctuary. The outside world drifted along cloaked in morbid black. Not your typical cover of darkness, it was the kind of pitch-black that cries for your emotional history to re-create the past. I felt like a pawn in the game of life, standing in white sand on the bottom of the ocean surrounded by blinding, ice-cold water. This ability to see where no light shines comes when death is near, breathing reminders of eternal damnation.

I reminded myself the silhouette on the wall wasn't following me, but I didn't trust myself to believe it. A minute past midnight, I thought again of Mom's autopsy. A man had literally held her heart in his hands. He weighed and measured it against her conflicted mind before passing his judgement. I promised myself then and there I would not suffer the same defeat. Nor would I force Karen to go on without me. I decided life was going to be lived, in spite of death, not because of it. The new morning sunrise couldn't come soon enough. But I feared to sleep alone, worried about what my dreams might reveal. Dreading sleep over my insomnia, I plopped into my soft bed, fully dressed, and prayed for sleep to rejuvenate me. Snug as a bug under my quilt, I reflected how praying sometimes made me feel childlike.

Five hours later, I awoke in a state of panic, thinking I heard pounding on my front door as deep-rooted terror set in. I needed normalcy to untangle me. I was close but worried I might fall again without someone to catch me before the clock ran out.

Feeling the stiff ache of sleepy exhaustion, I sprang from bed in slow motion to feel the shaggy carpet grip my toes as I gazed upon my queen-size fortress with the taste of morning breath on my lips. Night after night, she held me. No prejudice, just acceptance. For a few brief seconds, each morning, between when I awoke and opened my eyes, I usually felt normal and loved before reality set in. But not this morning. I was up and moving because my life depended on it, not because I wanted to be. With nature calling, crippling bladder pains intensified walking the ten sleepy steps down my narrow hall to the bathroom. Salvation seemed a flush away so long as I survived the toilet seat's cold grip. How had self-destruction become a priority at age twenty, and why was Officer Johnson visiting my dreams? Did the disappointment staring back at me have the answer? I worried because I went to bed so sure of myself. And was now so full of doubt? After a deep breath, I stared into the mirror to expose myself.

Standing there without a soul to blame but me, I flexed my lips into happy frowns. The more I practiced, the sadder I got. I had again circled back to before the beginning and knew I was running out of time. I needed another reality check to gauge my intent. But why did the girls have to call me a boy when my curves were all woman? Wide awake, I stepped into my tub, hoping a hot shower would breathe some life into me. There, between the sparkly atomic star-burst shower curtain and green-tiled walls, I revisited the past with a handful of reasons to carry on.

Chapter 31

—

Freshly showered with dry, tired eyes and a slight anxious cramp in my belly, I stood in the darkened living room and made a mental note of simpler days gone by. After years of layering on the illusions, I was ready to surrender my ego and live my best life regardless of what death had in mind. Grandma, fast asleep not ten feet above me, would soon awaken, so I had to get moving before she arose for her morning rounds. While the sun had yet to rise, there was no mistaking the sound of morning birds chirping in harmony alongside the rusty pre-dawn creak of my kitchen's screen door hinges. I knew God's universe would never accept my pledge of honest happiness without prayer, but I had to hurry. Time was of the essence in more ways than one. Never again would my secrets tell lies. From this moment forward, I told myself, brutal honesty would rule the days and years to come.

Lazily wandering around the corner of the apartments, clunky sleep-deprived steps said my tank was empty and needed a boost. I was full of gratitude but needed coffee, and lots of it, for whatever awaited me in the unknown beyond the veil of self-discovery. I paused for a moment under the eerie void of Grandma's bedroom window draped in sheer curtains and pondered the morning I first mentioned Ronnie to her.

"Oh dear," she said. "Courting has become so iffy these days. So hands up, eyes up and absolutely no hanky-panky." But she was happy for me. Afterwards, she was practically shoving me out the door. "Hurry and eat," she ordered. "We have a date to plan for, sweetheart." I didn't want this to be a big deal, but I allowed her to take me shopping for a new outfit later that day.

After hours spent rifling through racks of evening wear at Marston's department store, I settled on a blue vest with decorative gold buttons and matching slacks along with a yellow blouse with oversized lapels and long sleeves that hung past my wrists. For shoes, I went with an open-toed sling, black with an adjustable strap and two-inch heel. But dinner wasn't happening without Grandma first trying to disguise me with blush and eye shadow. I refused, reminding her Ronnie was a man's man and not into face paint. Besides, he liked my rosy Irish cheeks just the way they were, young and fresh.

Grandma's place lacked the modern touch. Her stone cherubs and opulent mahogany mirrors gave the impression of stepping back in time where the only electricity available thundered down from the sky. The precision *bong* of her vintage grandfather clock synchronized every hour on the hour, like a watchman sounding a gold-plated alarm. When Ronnie's confident knock struck the front door around six-thirty, Grandma hurried to greet him. This surprised me. She practically tackled the front door without her usual grandmotherly waddle to welcome him inside. She gushed when he bent down and kissed her hand.

"My oh my," she said, with a gracious smile. "Isn't he just handsome?"

He was, and I was in trouble. Big trouble.

After ten solid minutes answering, "Yes ma'am, no ma'am," Ronald got permission to take me out for Chinese food until no later than ten-thirty. He was a true gentleman in every sense of the word. I could tell he was nervous and wanted to make a good impression. Some men would have balked at Grandma's interrogation regarding career goals and financial status, but not Ronnie. He answered every question like a trained professional. After clearing the first hurdle, Grandma remarked how our "outfits complemented each other."

His green-and-white checkered shirt and brown trousers softened my leisurely sophistication with simplistic blue-collar style. Never in the history of Chinese food were two people more appropriately overdressed to eat chop-suey. We were off to a good start and I appreciated Grandma helping me bring a surprised smile to Ronnie's face.

After being seated for dinner, it was game on. Throughout the night, our conversation comfortably wandered between the importance of family and custom hot-rod paint jobs. This went on for hours. In the end, it was the perfect date. With Ronnie, there was no pressure to be anything other than myself. There's immense value in that, though I couldn't see it at the time.

Truth be told, I don't think Grandma ever forgave me for divorcing Ronnie. And I never forgave myself for marrying him. But not because of him, because of me. No use crying over spilled milk, though. In Ronnie, I made an incredible forever friend who has loved me beyond infidelity, and a mountain of lies, without turning his back on me when I needed him most. It's just too bad I turned mine on him.

Chapter 32

–

Standing next to the Nova, I faced the ultimate gut check. It was Sunday morning now, and the darkest part of me struggled to accept that I needed to matter most to heal properly. Nonetheless, I truly was committed to change this time. I had to be; my life depended on it. After a gulp of fresh morning air, I slid behind the wheel without a plan or destination in mind. Wow, I thought. Progress. Honestly, I didn't know what I was doing or where life would drag me next. I just knew I didn't want to hurt anymore. As I backed away from the curb reading my Grandfather's proud name written in bright lights above his shop's front door, I reflected how proud he would be that I wished to face my demons alone, without the aid of an emotional crutch. Don't ask me why, but this was the day I felt worthy enough to call myself a Vogt. And also hungry. So hungry my stomach might have out-growled my car. Cranking the steering wheel left onto La Mesa Boulevard, past streets lined with palm trees, I saw the eastbound freeway and headed towards the shadowy sunrise racing me to the peak of the Laguna summit thirty-three miles away. With my arm out the window and the wind blowing through my hair, I flew without so much as a feather or wing to carry me. I was off, rocketing towards the sunburnt desert and for what, I didn't know. And that was okay, because I was gaining positive momentum, just like Sergeant Joe said I would once I changed my mindset. I wasn't out of the woods yet, but I could taste the freedom about to change me. Today was going to be a momentous day. I was sure of it. When the opulent glow of warm sunshine began radiating skyward from behind the mountains east of me, I felt the tender side of Erika beckoning me from afar. She needed me. But I couldn't let her in. I needed to keep going, as far and as fast away from her as I could.

It was then that I realized my life was a collection of events circling back on themselves. I assumed this meant I wasn't a square peg and could fit anywhere, even where I felt I didn't belong. It was true, after all. Everywhere I went, there I was. And that was a good thing if I allowed it to be. Boy, talk about a gut check. "No more circles," I repeated out loud to the hum of eight cylinders chugging along well above the posted speed limit. No more circles, indeed. It was time to go where I hadn't been before. It was time to be who God created me to be. And it was high time I stopped lying to myself and everyone else for no other reason than pointless validation.

Hard on the gas, I crested the summit and freed myself from the cloudy valley below me. The change in temperature was immediate. Warmth was all around, hugging every fiber of my being. And the voice of death was long gone, nowhere to be found. Hopefully never to be heard from again. Maybe she had moved on. Maybe I had outgrown her in the hours since she last tried to kill me. While the sudden changes in me seemed, well, sudden, I welcomed the self-respect pouring into me, from where, I didn't know. But its origins didn't matter, for I was loving the way it made me feel. The best part was that Erika would love seeing me this way, too. "Happy and balanced," she would say. "We need to be happy and balanced."

I needed to call her and share the good news. Life was about to get fantastic. I just knew it. Powering down the grade, I passed the stacks of rounded boulders, some big, some small, towering over the bone-dry stretches of sandy dirt covering the desert floor deep in the Jacumba Mountains. Some stood larger than a house; they looked to have survived a Martian invasion and had surely outlived the dinosaurs and cave dwellers known to roam these parts millions of years ago.

An early explorer named Padre Pedro Font dubbed the skyward thrusting rocks "sweepings of the earth." They seem fragile, but I learned in school that their cracks and erosions would last tens of thousands of years to come, and more rock would rise to replace them alongside the undulating highway swinging east to west. It's also where I shot my first gun. An old .38 caliber snub-nosed pistol. Grandpa said it was his Saturday night special, but it was a Tuesday, and I was afraid it might backfire and shoot my eye out.

I was near the bottom of the grade now. The last sharp bend in the road on my journey down the mountain revealed the glare of heat waves rising above the long, lonely stretch of highway to the California-Arizona border.

About twenty or so miles ahead on the left sat Naval Air Field El Centro. I was hungry and needed a break, but without Ronnie, the base was off-limits to me. Jesus, I thought. Here I was, running from Erika on my way to who knows where, thinking of Ronnie while looking for a phone booth to call Karen. I was in deeper than I thought, but that's what happens when you think for yourself, when you're your own worst enemy.

While small and used mainly for training, NAF El Centro was always special to me because it's the winter home of the Blue Angels and the place where new pilots became one with the team. Oh, how I longed to be part of a team. Any team, really. But the Blues would have been out of this world to me. The news reported they had flown into town a few days before my drive over the pass, but the skies were quiet that morning. I could hear not so much as a crop duster flying low over the onion and watermelon fields lining the Imperial Valley. There was nothing but dry Sunday-morning silence to pique my curiosity.

Since I had nowhere to be, I figured I'd grab some breakfast at a roadside spot sure to serve the greasiest bacon around. You know, the kind truckers and late-night drinkers crave. I also wanted some eggs and a stack of golden, buttery pancakes. Maybe a full belly would satisfy my hunger. It was early, after all. Besides, maybe there would be a phone booth nearby where I could dial my sister. I'd have to call collect, but we could keep things short and sweet until we met up in the coming days. And maybe call Erika too, if she would accept the charges. I mean, what could it hurt? Right? She had to be wondering about me. Surely my absence was weighing heavily on her mind, wondering if I was dead or alive. And even if she was mad, it's not like she could harm me since I was virtually in another state. Once again, I prayed for peace but prepared for war. But I wasn't a fighter. I hated fighting.

I wanted things to be different between me and everyone I knew. I wanted to change for those who doubted me. I wanted to be celebrated, not tolerated. And even if I was never going to see Erica again, I needed to hear her voice and share my newfound perspective. To tell her that she was wrong. This would clear up everything, I thought, and let me step into myself with a clear conscience. This foolish way of thinking had me walking a troubled path fraught with danger, but in my mind, I was safe, even from myself. Now all that was left to do was eat.

Chapter 33

–

The next few miles hummed along in quiet solitude. Breakfast would require me to backtrack a mile or so from the desolate Interstate to old Highway 80, but Miller's Café was worth the trip. The stone cottage with the low-pitched roof sat at the edge of the concrete highway beside a row of telephone poles opposite the stand-alone repair shop with three service bays. Miller's spread took up roughly three acres, and some maps listed the cluster of four buildings as if it were a town. Including a Texaco fueling station out front for empty tanks like mine. Thanks to the Christmas money from Grandma Vogt, I had just enough to drive to hell and back. But today death knew better than to mess with me.

Some travelers found the detour off the interstate to Miller's outpost inconvenient, but I loved how the highway beside it appeared never-ending. After swooping into the parking lot towards the wooden awning between the café stone façade and repair shop, I rolled down the window to inhale the crispy flavors from the hot griddle floating in the air. Watching the dust settle, I realized the endlessness I felt might only live in my imagination. The universe was screaming for me to make my own luck. So, I did. A calmness walked me past the front door and into the modest diner. My anxiety was so low I no longer felt the need to burn myself to keep others warm. There were two open tables sitting side-by-side in the middle of the room, their wooden tops draped in red-and-white checkered tablecloths hanging almost halfway to the floor.

"Take your pick, sweetie," said a middle-aged voice identical in every way to my mother's. Her brunette beehive rose above her friendly smile waiting for me to pick a table. And when I did, she quickly poured me a cup of coffee while spelling out the mornings breakfast specials.

"Where you from, darling?" She asked, watching me peruse the menu. She knew right away I wasn't a drifter by my polite response.

"San Diego," I said, watching her smile back at me.

"Me too."

"Really?"

"Yup, Been out here in the sand box six years now." I waited to hear the reason why she chose to settle in the middle of nowhere, but it never came. I guess some things are better left unsaid. She spoke as if we'd been friends forever. "The name's Rosie," she said. Her skin, like Grandpa Vogt, had matured in the sun like fine Italian leather. It was soft and wrinkled to perfection. I could see she loved the desert. Her relaxed facial expressions said she was living life on her own terms and loving every minute of it. Though she never said, it was obvious the ever-present rush of city life wasn't for her. She liked to take her time. To serve her customers more than they asked for. I envied her style and noted how it mirrored the little girl in me who loved to climb trees and have silly conversations with strangers about the most random things.

The table I chose was furthest from the door, but closest to the kitchen. While moved by the waitress's carefree spirit, serving food was not for me. I might have adored her zest for life, but not her job. The idea of my clumsy hands serving food is almost frightening. But I was happy to be the center of her attention. She kept the coffee hot and the conversation enlightening. And before I knew it breakfast was served. We were laughing so hard when the cook first rang the bell signaling my order was up, that he sarcastically repeated himself two more times before she told the old bird to "Hush." It was a magical moment. Simplistic and unscripted. There was no doubt about it, today was going to be a great day.

Listening to the regulars slurping their morning joe amongst the gossip and swiveling stools, it occurred to me that time might just have been on my side for once. There was no need to rush anything. Life inside the packed diner made sense on every level. There was a reason for everything. And there was no reason life on the outside couldn't work the same. The change I sought truly was in my hands after all. When my breakfast came, I shelved the deep thoughts and focused all my energy on the buttery pancakes before me about to drown in maple syrup. With each bite I fell deeper in love with the idea of living.

I kept my eyes trained on the small glass domes atop the counter packed full of freshly baked goods wondering if I should treat myself. I had succeeded in my intended mission, so why not. My goal that morning was to arise before Grandma found me half dead with nothing but lies to explain my distance over the past few weeks. But I'd done much more than expected in the two hours since the lights of La Mesa faded to black in my rearview mirror. I had lived, and it felt good. I was well on my way to victory when twenty paces in front of me, I heard the diner's creaky front door open, dinging a small brass bell screwed to the top left-hand corner. I looked up and backed away without moving. A rush of anxiety clutched my throat. Followed by a volcanic explosion of fear erupting deep inside me. I gasped for air, my knees ruffling the red checkered tablecloth hiding my terror. I looked away before bending over to snug up my already tight shoelaces. When I sat up, my intense gaze shifted from the dusty tile floor to the khaki roadblock looking in my direction. Standing at the door near the Formica counter displaying those pies and cakes under the glass domes was not one, but two California Highway Patrol officers. The long arm of the law had found me. From the moment I checked out of the hospital, I feared this moment might come even though I pretended not to care.

And I was about to pay for that mistake big time. I felt their cruel energy strip search me. Why here? I thought. The older one with wavy gray hair took his mirrored sunglasses off, watching the last sip of coffee coat my chapped lips. This can't be happening, I told myself. I cursed God. The taste of his slow, cold revenge grew more damning with each breath. There was nowhere to turn. I was theirs for the taking. Rosie the waitress pointed, then smiled. It was now or never. I needed to make my move, and fast. But there was nowhere to go without a fight.

I grew smaller, shrinking in my seat with each step they took towards me. *Go*, I said to myself. *Run for your life until you can't run anymore.* On the brink, my harried, wild expression spoke for me. The stench of unbridled fear soured the morning's tasty vibes. Like on the bridge that first night, sweat from my pulse popped. I grabbed onto my trembling legs, hoping the officers wouldn't notice my angst. They were practically on top of me now. Neither one of them said a word. Not so much as a cough. I could feel their eyes burn a hole right through me. *Just make it quick,* I thought. Third time's the charm, right?

"Good morning, ma'am," said the stockier officer wearing long sleeves. "Does the Nova outside belong to you?" Why was he asking what he already knew to be true? I wanted to lash out but couldn't. The two men interrogating me were strangers, but I couldn't help but see Sergeant Joe and Officer Johnson in their commanding presence. "Because if it is," he continued, "Wow! I'd like one myself, but with a wife, two kids and another on the way, I can barely afford to hitchhike to work"—he chuckled—"let alone drive something that stylish." I couldn't believe my ears. The highway patrol officers I thought San Diego police sent to bag me and tag me were just a couple of hungry guys looking to start their day on a full stomach just like me.

But in the back of my mind, I knew things could change without warning, and the last thing I needed was someone hanging a wanted poster of me on the bulletin board behind the cash register while two of California's finest dined not ten feet away. When they took their seats, I hurried towards the front without the check to pay my bill. But I moved with no sense of urgency so as not to arouse any suspicion. I just needed to go from there as far and as fast as I could without stopping. Outside, I exhaled a giant sigh of relief. I don't re-member getting in the Nova or driving away. But I remember how I felt seeing that black-and-white CHP cruiser parked behind my hot rod like it had something to prove. This was a sight I never wanted to see repeated ever again in this lifetime or the next.

I had planned to fill up after breakfast but split with an almost empty tank not thinking the nearest service station outside of Miller's Texaco was fifty miles east, in El Centro. Let me just tell you, my heart never beat so fast driving so slow. Visions of the unimaginable overwhelmed me, watch-ing the orange gas needle drop with each passing mile. A fright I wouldn't wish on my worst enemy. Every sputter felt catastrophic. Driving. at half the speed, it took me twice as long. But in doing so, I avoided another opportunity for the CHP to serve and protect me should I have run out of gas alongside the highway. After finding a spot to fuel up in town, I drove across the street to a motel and called it a day. This sanctuary in the desert was the answer to all my unspoken prayers. Here I could rest and regroup worry-free that I might disappoint someone else. Plus, the room would have a phone. And from this phone, I could dial anyone in the whole wide world, even Erika if she'd accept the charges. While El Centro might not have been known for its five-star accommodations in those days, the Holiday Inn where I land-ed had every amenity required for me to come out swinging Monday morning. For now, I needed to rest and forget my troubles because they weren't really mine. They belonged to someone else. Someone else indeed.

Chapter 34

—

I couldn't look at the silent phone staring at me from between the two queen-sized beds absorbing the morning's abundant sunlight shining through the windows. The warm comfort reminded me of my favorite person's laugh. The sound of her happiness gave me the same cozy feelings as a tender song played on the radio. She colored my world, and I needed her. But did she feel the same? After pending all of Sunday afternoon glued to the television, I splashed some cold water on my face and headed out for some cheese enchiladas two blocks way before falling asleep to a rerun of Gunsmoke, one of my all-time favorite shows.

The next morning I awoke still sorta hungry, but not enough to leave the comfortable confines of my lair two stories up. Besides, my stomach was kinda bubbling, probably because of the emotion-heavy calls, I couldn't make, turning me inside out. Anxious and needy, I nosed around the wood box nightstand beside the bed. Inside the cubby were a black rotary phone, a phone book, and a bible. Overhead a pair of bronze lamps illuminated my search between the sunflower-colored walls.

After shaking off the morning rust, I twisted my tired body into a lengthy stretch and snuggled back into the warm covers for a few extra minutes of sleep. I felt good. Nervous, but good. Nervous, I guess, because I'd never thought for myself before, and that morning, I was thinking a lot about where I would go and what I would do now that I was free to be me. I still worried about being arrested, but what's done is done, I told myself. I kicked around the room for about thirty more minutes, pacing from one end to the other, stopping only to gaze out the window at passing cars going to and from their final destinations. Cars made me happy. And they had been since I was a little girl dreaming of the many wonderful places they could take me.

Being without Erika was hard. But not as hard as being with her. As I sat there thinking about the last time we spoke and how sweet her affection tasted, visions of her laughing about my death incensed me until the hell in my rosy cheeks burned hot. I needed closure. Either she was in or she was out. It was time to set the record straight. The phone across from me held the answer. It sat silent waiting for me to decide. The choice unfortunately was mine. The roof of my mouth became dry thinking of the potential awaiting me on the other end and what might come next. *Bullcrap*, I thought. Karen and Ronnie would flat kick my butt if they knew I was considering calling Erika after what I'd been through.

I knew then I needed out, but wanted back in oh so badly, and because of this, I was more confused than ever. But boy, did I feel alive. Very alive.

The comfy motel room was brighter now, with light beaming from the east. I could still drive that way if the idea of home proved too dangerous, I thought. Erika couldn't physically stop me, although mentally, she already had. The warm desert air between us, flat and gusty, reminded me anything was possible. Why, I don't know. Maybe because I could actually feel change in the air. An old wives' tale perhaps and corny to some. But I liked corny.

After showering for a third time, I put on yesterday's clothes and brushed my teeth with the tip of my finger. I hated wearing dirty clothes, but I could change when I got home.

After checking out, I let fate take the wheel. On the highway now, chasing the Monday morning sun west. I motored along with my neck bent skyward, watching for signs of the Blue Angels practicing for the upcoming airshow season, but no luck. With each passing second, the odds of seeing them vanished. Maybe another day, I thought, and refocused on the task at hand. Yet the angels and demons were all around me. I felt their love. And their hate. Mile after flat, boring mile, the weight of Karen, Grego, Mom, Dad, Erika, and the girls gave me hope that nothing was about to change. But this forced me to think for myself, and think I did. Hard. Very hard. The ride back was a complete blur after reaching the bottom of the grade heading towards San Diego. Driving with blinders on, I missed the colossal rock fields tumbled for miles alongside the steep grade climbing my way out of the Imperial Valley. Profound because some of my best memories exploring with Grandpa Vogt lived there. We were always on the hunt for an adventure together. The kind that happened organically without a specific goal in mind. I sure missed that old buzzard. Racing to possibly confront Erika was shaping up to be a lesson requiring all my inner-most thoughts. But not one I actually thought about, considering every past reunion of ours ended with the same life-threatening regret.

Chapter 35

—

The Nova bogged and sputtered, climbing out of Coyote Wells through Meyers and Devil's Canyon to the top of the Mountain Springs grade. The tractor-trailer trucks delivering their goods to San Diego and beyond inching along in the slow lane crept ahead with their hazards flashing to signal their slow pace. Summer months proved worse with temperatures often topping 110 degrees.

Nowadays, modern cars fly up at seventy miles an hour without missing a beat. But the marginal cooling systems in the seventies were no match for Interstate 8's vertical wall paved with blistering heat. In fact, one big rig, a silver tanker truck if memory serves, parked on the side of the highway had steam billowing from its overheated radiator. In the southbound lanes, a runaway truck ramp sat at the mouth of the winding road leading eastbound into Meyers Canyon. I often thought about driving into it at high speed, but fear of destroying my beloved yellow Nova crushed me.

My plan heading up the dreaded grade that morning was to hurry home, but by now you know how well me and making plans get along. At one point I stopped along the twisty canyon highway to clear my head. Walking alone in a dried-up old creek bed, I was careful not to step on any buzz tail rattlers slithering about, but to my surprise, I saw not one. A good thing, since I hated snakes. A similar walk about in Idyllwild nearly cost Grego his life when a grumpy old diamondback napping behind a pile of rocks did not appreciate his curious nature. Later nature hikes found me packing a big stick should our paths cross again. Thankfully, they never did. But there were other snakes to worry about that didn't rattle but struck when treated with care.

Chapter 36

–

At the top of the grade near Jacumba stands the Desert View Tower. Built over several years in the early 1920s, this oasis for curious travelers rises from atop three thousand feet above sea level, in the In-Ko-Pah Mountains. Grandpa and I stopped here many times over the years on our travels to and from his love affair with the Anza-Borrego Desert. From the top of the stone tower, you can see all the way to Arizona roughly one hundred miles away. When I arrived, the first thing I did was climb the dusty seventy-foot-high fortress via the spiral wood-plank staircase to the observation deck looking out over the moonlike terrain of the arid valley floor. Even here, outside the gift shop and eccentric museum that's whatever hangs on the wall at the moment, one has to be careful of critters.

Reflecting on my journey from hell to El Centro and back, it occurred to me that my problems weren't insurmountable and that I was possibly my own worst enemy. I felt bad for the pain caused by my inability to deal with life. I felt bad for shutting out Karen when I needed her the most. But nothing compared to the gut-wrenching remorse that accompanies nearly killing two young married police officers. Already I was missing the recycled refrigerated air used to cool the smoky room at the El Centro holiday inn. It felt good to feel something other than nothing. This mindset was an enormous step forward for me. So big, I couldn't help but have a good time that morning.

By knocking on death's door and surviving, I recognized my wretched life had a purpose other than being a disregarded punching bag. Dammit, I was a sister and best friend. A good friend and the greatest aunt ever. Sure, I was still scared to death of how Erika might behave in person after everything, but I was on a mission replace not chase and nothing was going to stop me.

Switching perspectives, I glimpsed the right rear quarter panel of my Nova. Seeing her made me happy. Staring down at her, I wondered if I deserved the happiness daydreaming inside me. Spoiled or not, I knew the value of coming from money and the leg up it gave me. But if that were true, then why did I feel so poor and ostracized? In being blessed with opportunity, inexcusably I used my privilege to run and hide instead of standing tall in the face of danger. Thinking of the Kumeyaay people who inhabited these lands for over ten thousand years before today, a goal came to mind. Not sure why, but it did. One that included the strength of self-love over pleasing the temptations of depression.

I understood reconciliation with my reality might be on the horizon, should I choose honesty over calculated deception. Things had gotten so bad, I believed those who told the biggest lies held all the truths. Sounds like something a shadowy spy figure might say, right? Certainly not the musings of a punk kid afraid of her own freckled shadow. But something was happening. Something positive and gloriously terrifying.

The hand of God was upon me. I felt it everywhere, paralyzing my fear with hope.

After a few more minutes to myself, I closed and then opened my eyes before climbing down the stairs and saying goodbye to the tower's caretaker, who wished me well. Back on the road, I huddled up and made the perfect game plan to slay my demons one by one. But first I had to make it down the road without alerting the highway patrol. A passing border patrol Jeep brought about some pucker power, but nothing worthy of a full-scale meltdown like with the uniformed scare at the café back in Ocotillo. I laughed, thinking how the patrol Jeep's seafoam green paint stood out like a sore thumb against the thirsty badlands surrounding us.

No matter. The solitary border cop motored by like neither of us existed before disappearing onto a dirt road, leaving a trail of dust for anyone curious to follow. I considered doing just that but figured another time, another place.

I was busy making plans for the days and years to come when the interstate's curves winding into El Cajon dumped me onto the East Main off-ramp at the edge of the city.

I didn't mean to exit there, but nothing wrong, I guess, in a little civilization to smile back at me.

I was still thirsty. The kind of thirst only a day in the harsh, dehydrated desert can cause. In years past, when hunting Indian artifacts with Grandpa, he would allow me to sip from his metal canteen. The water inside would be warm and flat, leaving a yucky copper taste in my mouth. Nothing tasted better, though, when heatstroke seemed certain.

I was feeling empowered, but this was no time doddle as the airport parking lot was calling my name. I needed to be sure I was making the right decision in canceling Erika, and I did my best thinking to the sounds of rumbling jet exhaust. As I crawled down Main towards El Cajon Boulevard and the freeway heading towards downtown San Diego, the Pussycat Theater greeted me with her name spelled out in fancy yellow light on red block letters. I went there as a kid when it was a family friendly theatre called The El Cajon, but I'd never been to the Pussycat. I might have been a train wreck, but I was at least a classy one. A few doors down from the Pussycat was Mama's Mink. Mama's was a little neighborhood bar where you could hear all kinds of live music, including country and western. The ultraviolet haze glooming outside couldn't help but disappear amongst the cramped tavern's dark walls covered in felt football pennants. The old jukebox sounded like a car radio passing through the middle of nowhere alongside a herd of restless cattle. Over it hung a classic golden Tijuana nude painting on black velvet. I know because more than once I snuck in pretending to be someone older than I was.

But today the truth was going to set me free.

Chapter 37

–

The alluring sky in the distance blossomed into a brilliant iridescent blue. Scattered about the dreamy, wild blue yonder were patches of fluffy gray clouds. Some welcoming. And some shaded with a dense feeling of hopelessness. For the moment I was content, living as if death didn't exist. But my thoughts were running wild. I was up, then down because I had allowed myself to become trapped between two opposing worlds. One blood, one not, but both equally important to me. To everyone else, I looked boring. A dull stranger with a story no one cared to know. But I was anything but boring and soon Erika and her cronies would know the same.

It had only been a day since she last wished me dead. Not a month. A single solitary day. But our connection was still a valid threat because I hadn't yet shut my eyes for the final time. I missed her though. I missed her badly. Like hard-to-breathe badly. Maybe she felt the same. Maybe not. But the truth was just a few miles away at this point. I worried seeing Karen would be equally difficult because I had no excuse for ghosting her. She knew of my troubles and would be heartbroken to hear of my recent struggles from being emotionally sucker-punched by love. But mostly, I was too afraid to face the truth.

Approaching West Laurel Street from Kettner Boulevard, I could feel the darkness coming for me. But I was ready to defend myself. In the rearview mirror, darting glances shot back at me. My eyes were empty and bloodshot. A right turn later, just past the railroad tracks, a shadow rumbled overhead, teasing my senses with the refined sweet scent of jet exhaust. I was almost home. Cars from all directions zoomed back and forth as I slowed to a crawl dead center with the runway. But all I could hear was silence. Before me, beyond the giant white anchor perched on a patch of grass, across from the Coast Guard hangers, a cruise ship floated in the nearly landlocked San Diego Bay. It looked haunted. A reminder perhaps that I wasn't out of the woods yet. Certain about nothing, I pulled into the airport observation lot off North Harbor Drive once again and sat with my head down for several minutes before climbing out of the Nova to feel the shivering ground beneath my feet.

To my left, the Coronado bridge taunted me from across the bay. With each gust of wind, it breathed down my neck with visions of the not-so-distant past. Still not ready to surrender, the piercing cold rolling in with the tide prepared itself for the night's calm as I weighed my options, yet I couldn't feel a thing. Sure, it was sunny, but the standoffish chill consuming me thirsted for blood. Yet all I could think about was writing "I need you" on a rock and throwing it at Erika's face so she'd know how much it hurt to need her. I was in a bad spot. Standing without a jacket, my teeth should have chattered against the testy air blowing off the water. Rows of goosebumps sharper than pins and needles should have sprung up all across my freckled skin. But they ignored me like everyone else. I was all alone with nothing to show for my efforts. And not wanting to burden anyone, I continued punishing myself. It was then that time took control. At that moment, I convinced myself I had given life my very best and was ready to face its final wrath, consequences be damned. This was a feeling like no other before. And as the minutes turned into hours, I stood forsaken, watching winged silhouettes disappear into a bone-chilling sunset four miles from the dreaded confrontation that would truly define the rest of my life.

Chapter 38

–

As the tangerine horizon faded to black, I knew I couldn't wait any longer to confront Erika face to face and end this madness once and for all.

The airport beacon flashed in the distance, rotating between green and white. It illuminated the scattered clouds seemingly within arm's reach. By now I had the observation lot to myself. A lifelong dream you might say. Hostile arctic winds and all. But I couldn't stay. The longer I stood there by myself thinking of everyone living their lives but me, the madder I got. I could be home right now if not for Erika. But I could also be at home with her if not for my family and her friends. A climax or a showdown awaited if I were brave enough to choose.

There could be no more false starts. At my wit's end, a turn of the key shifted me into reverse and then into a northbound lane. The sparsely lit cruise ship floating behind me thought nothing of my melodramatic exit, while I thought of everything that could go wrong making my way to Erika. My city looked beautiful though. Her glow filled the evening sky with colorful waves of light. Everywhere you looked, life was living for the moment. I was tired of driving. It's all I ever did. Not because I hated it. Heavens no. But because it had become an element of my destruction. I could see it so clearly. It's the place I ran to when life became troublesome. And for the past few years, business was booming. All that mattered to me now was peace. Nothing more. Nothing less. And tonight, one way or another, it would be mine.

Me and the Nova had a score to settle. Her eight cylinders purred running down the miles to Erika. She never failed me, not once. Well, unless you count the time I got a blowout in the desert outside Borrego Springs. And like so many times before, Ronnie to the rescue. I was eastbound towards magnificent Palm Springs to meet Erika and the girls when this explosion blasted a dense cloud of dust and debris into the wind behind me.

The violent failure shook my steering wheel until the shoulder grabbed hold and dragged me into the sand. Luckily, I didn't damage anything or, worse yet, roll across the desert floor at highway speeds. It was terrible; the steering wheel's brutal shutter vibrated my knuckles white with fear. A passing motor home full of Mormon kids on their way to SeaWorld gave me a ride in the opposite direction to a family-run service station fifteen miles from where I slid off the road. My shredded rubber carcass cost Ronnie a 171-mile round trip at the expense of my missing spare tire. Still, he didn't care. He was happy to help. Like when we first came together and broke apart, nothing tempered his desire to be good for me.

I look back on those times with nothing but disappointment. I was rotten, a scoundrel. Yet, there was no excuse for the torment I handed Ronnie. Erika didn't care, telling me good riddance because men weren't supposed to be soft. She was happiest whenever I was under her thumb. I thought I knew what I wanted. The truth is, I didn't even know who I was, let alone what I wanted. Unfortunately, our hot-blooded passion tricked my vulnerability into falling for her again and again. She was a charlatan adept at playing my predictability, and she knew it.

Rounding the slow, easygoing curve before her house, my fret was at an all-time high. But I was pissed and ready to settle the score. The days of being what Erika needed were over. "Stay strong," I told myself, driving past her house, making every excuse not to stop. It was oddly dark with a curious wine bottle on the front porch. After a few nervous laps around the block, I drove to the corner store down the street and made a U-turn before parking dead center in front of her charmed cobblestone walkway. With the wind to my back, I stepped out to a frightful surge of adrenaline, sending shock waves deep into my ever-loving soul.

Sickening memories of our brutal past slowed me walking towards Erika's porch and the heavy door she routinely slammed in my face. It was time to stop being cautious. "Consequences be damned," I told myself, unlocking the deadbolt with an old key I found rummaging through my secret stash of cash Sunday morning. The foyer stood pitch black. The bulb above the porch was burnt-out, making seeing nearly impossible. The entire street seemed darker than usual. Along the wall, a shadow appeared, searching for the light switch. When I found it, the intense light hit my sensitive eyes, blinding me for a split second. There was no sign of Erika—but where had she gone? I cut the lights, flicking them off and on to acclimate myself to the room's thick energy.

A strange smell permeated the air. Its pungent strength fostered an unusual sense of danger walking down the hall to what I considered ground zero. This time, something truly was amiss. I forwent searching the house, as it was obvious no one was home. Perhaps I should have because on the kitchen counter were Marsella's car keys. As I stopped short of entering the bathroom, memories of being slammed and choked against the wall hit me. Two doors down, a sharp, cutting smell coming from inside the darkened chamber stung the inside of my nose. It smelled of rotting peaches and warm piss. I reached into the room, twisting my arm sideways to reach the light switch tucked in the corner beside the mirrored medicine cabinet. Presto. The light bar over the large vanity mirror sparked to life. What I saw destroyed me. My blood froze. Right then and there, I died with my eyes open. On the floor was an air freshener can with a cracked pinkish-orange cap. In the tub, floating in a mix of urine, water, and tomato-red marinara sauce were open packages of half-thawed old-ass meat. Along with shards of broken record vinyl, were my clothes, toothbrush, and favorite stuffed Snoopy doll.

The room stunk to high heaven. Above the tub on the starch-white tiled wall, someone had written I FUCKING HATE YOU in dark lipstick. The message was clear. I wanted to move but couldn't. My knees, locked in place. Everything around me became a blur. My past, present, and future were before me, drowning in a soiled vat of hate. The kind of hate that lives forever and never lets you forget its damning effects. The soft light illuminating my desecrated belongings were but an afterthought in a story that begins with an ending. After the initial shock, I broke free from my trance, stumbling backward into the sharp edge of the countertop. I turned, stepping on the empty peach air freshener can used to cover the urine smell rising from the hellish-looking swamp marinating in the tub. I ran without breathing. I was being consumed by evil. The open front door, my only escape, seemed a million miles away.

I couldn't get out fast enough. Seconds later, the open doorway released me from this nightmarish scene. There was no stopping to think. Our love had died without me knowing Erika was this angry—angry enough to deface her own property. Her displeasure manifested itself in the most traumatic way. A grown woman squatting over a tub full of stinky meat to pee on some clothes is for sure another level of fury. Why couldn't she have just been honest and told me the truth? Why couldn't she have saved me the humiliation of knowing the end had come and gone in a way meant to destroy me? I knew she was cruel, but not this cruel. Outside, I walked with purpose telling myself to keep calm and keep moving. It was then I realized time was running out, but I was strong and could survive this. However, the ghosts of my mistakes were descending upon me, and fast. I was overflowing with regret. Regret for abandoning Karen. Regret for misleading Ronnie. Maybe this was karma coming to collect a debt. Perhaps I had broken my final heart.

But dammit, Erika swore she would always welcome me home with open arms no matter what. So why desecrate our love with such pleasure? I didn't understand how she could want to hurt me so badly knowing how deeply I cared for her. I was at a total loss. Still in shock, I had to get to Karen. She would know how to fix this.

I knew in my heart there was no going back to Erika after such a disgusting display of evil hatred. She had written our demise in simulated

blood on her precious white walls, leaving me no doubt I was dead to her. But where had she gone? And why would she betray me knowing the pain I carried in my heart? Sure, I went there to end the madness and leave single, strong, and in love with myself, but secretly I was hoping she would take me in her arms forever and love me as only she could.

Chapter 39

—

After locking myself in my car, I breathed in deeply, taking a big gulp of air. Without thinking, I did what I do best and drove in circles, crisscrossing the heart of the city many times over before coming face to face with the phone booth meant to save my life. Barrio Logan never felt so inhospitable. Illegally parked, I searched for a pen and began to write grandma a letter crying my eyes out before curling up like a baby praying for forgiveness. After exhausting myself, I knew it was time to make my move. As soon as the damp, bitterly cold air filled my nervous lungs, I coughed hard enough to convince myself I had asthma. The sidewalk beneath my feet felt unstable as I thought about what lay ahead. My heart skipped a beat. Then another as I gripped the telephone, staring blankly off into the distance at the shipyard cranes working high in the sky. A cold rain, dark as blood, felt inevitable. Defeated, I dialed Karen's number and braced for impact.

"Hi, Sis," I said, waiting for her to explode.

"Hey, brat. Where have you been?" Her gentle voice took me in her arms, cradling my cares away.

"Oh, you know, busy. How about you?" I'm sure she could tell something was wrong by the limp distress in my voice. "I just finished up at work and thought I'd see what you guys are doing tonight." Karen didn't know I'd been fired, and it killed me to continue lying to her.

"That's great," she said. "But where are you?" A lifetime of memories weighed in the balance.

"You sound sad."

"Honest, I'm fine. I've just had a tickle in my throat the past few days, but nothing serious."

While she continued to grill me, I cleared my throat, coughing a handful of times for dramatic effect. But this was no laughing matter. Heavy tears fell from my eyes listening to her concern build on the other end. Again she asked, "Where are you?"

I cupped the phone to hide the sound of the occasional passing car. The temperature continued to fall. My jaw clenched trying to preserve what little heat remained inside me. But I was too cold to shiver. My soul hurt. My heart hurt. Everything inside me hurt.

"Come on now," she said. "I'm worried. I've been calling you for days, but you don't answer, and we haven't seen you in weeks." In the background, I heard Grego laughing my name out loud. I could see his infectious smile blurting out *Aunty Loyo, Aunty Loyo.* I delighted hearing him speak my name with such affection. He missed me and I missed him. He was practically mine, and I loved him more than life itself. As the silence between us intensified, a silver-haired woman passed by. She smiled at me with her wrinkled eyes. The air between us smelled bittersweet. My heart skipped another beat. I began counting the ways one can be executed. Erika had gone too far this time, and someone had to pay. Karen felt my despair growing deeper and more dangerous. There was so much to say, but so little time.

"Okay, quit playing around, Sis. I need to know where you are, like, right now."

I wanted so badly to tell her. She continued to plead while I continued to stall. She deserved to know, but all I could muster was strangled sounds. This dragged on for a solid minute before I came to my senses.

"So where are you?" she asked frantically, praying my stubbornness was about to cave. "Just stay where you are, and we'll come to get you." The more excited she got, the calmer I became.

"No, it's okay," I said. "It's too cold for all of that. I'll come to you."

But she insisted, begging me to reveal my location so she, Vinny, and Grego could swing by and pick me up, along with a few pizzas. I needed to be with my family, but I couldn't let her know that. "You're scaring me," she said. "Why won't you let us pick you up?"

"Because I can drive myself, that's why."

"Lori, I need you to be straight with me. Is everything okay tonight? Because you sound funny."

"I promise, Sis, everything's okay."

"Then why won't you tell me where you are?"

The words she wanted to hear were on the tip of my tongue. I tried to force them out. The unconditional surrender I sought was mine for the taking. *This is a mistake*, I whispered, reprimanding myself for torturing Karen. No one should suffer as I have. Ten minutes from now, let alone ten years, Erika wouldn't matter, so why let her absence continue to define my present? Karen deserved better. Grego too. As my concerned sister repeated herself, I realized all the miles driven between calls to Erika were meant to bring my family and me back together. The previous Friday night, when Erika had wished me dead, should have been my wake-up call. But I had a real chance to turn all of this around if only I would let my sister see what truly had become of me.

"Okay," she said. "Vin's got Grego ready and we're heading out the door, so where are you?"

My heart was pounding. Part of me felt I was being hunted. That my swan song had already been sung.

"You know what?" I said. "How about we do pizza tomorrow, my treat? I'm really not feeling well and just want to go home and sweat whatever this is out." I felt her heart sink through the phone. Her shaky voice was in panic mode.

"Listen," I said. "I promise we'll see each other tomorrow and maybe later this week the three of us can go to the zoo or something. But for now, I really just need some sleep."

I wasn't lying. I really did need some sleep. And honestly, the last thing anybody needed to see was me after having been emotionally raped in Erika's bathroom.

"But why can't you just stop by and see us for a quick minute on your way home? *Mi casa es su casa*, but you already know that, so what gives?"

She was persistent as a toothache. And maybe she was right. Maybe a change of scenery would do me some good. I mean, what could it hurt?

"Deal. But just for a minute because I really don't feel well tonight."

This pleased her. Agreeing to her terms had me standing outside the fire. The last thing either of us wanted was the night to end with more unanswered questions.

"You know," she said, "it's good to hear your voice. I've missed you."

I blinked and nodded mutely. Knowing our goodbye was at hand, a dizzying sensation of sadness came over me. I think Karen felt it too, telling me to hurry up. As the end of our conversation hovered, icy dread washed over me. Suffering in silence, I leaned my forehead against the phonebooths glass shell feeling the color drain from my face.

"Okay, Sis. I'm cold now and have to go, but I promise I'll see you soon. I love you."

"I love you too."

Chapter 40

–

I fell face first. At 7:10 p.m., I simply walked to the edge this time instead of running, leaned forward like falling into bed after a long day, and tore through the night sky until impact.

After speaking with Karen, I knew my only way up was down. It wasn't anything she said that made me jump. It's what I didn't say. The moment my shoes broke free from the pavement and gravity grabbed hold, I knew I'd made the last mistake of my life. The first forty feet felt like slow motion, although I was accelerating. Initially, there was no sound. But once I cleared the bridge's famous blue base, deafening winds created a thunderous back pressure, seeming to slow my fall. I tried turning over, thinking I could claw my way back to safety, but it was too late. The forces of nature were now in control. My feverish struggle to grab hold of anything but air flipped me onto my back, allowing the city lights to bathe my last visions in regret all the way down. This drop was no swan dive. Waiting to break my fall was a disfiguring, traumatic, and dramatic death.

When I reached the bridge's summit for the third time in four days, I calmly applied the brakes and stopped in the middle lane. Along for the ride was dear, sweet Elton. I found his energy beautiful and uplifting. I just wish we could have come together under different circumstances. With the evening traffic slowing around me, I shifted into park, opened the door, and walked to the edge of the bridge, avoiding eye contact with a picture-perfect family in a white Chevelle station wagon, perhaps returning home from an early dinner. Headlights from the west illuminated the utter shock in their horrified faces. The sound of the woman passenger's blood-curdling scream quickly faded with the rush of air drowning out everything I left behind. All that remained was to die.

A tow truck from A to Z Towing heading into Coronado pulled behind my Nova and parked with his yellow safety beacon rotating in step with his flashing hazard lights. Thirty seconds earlier and he might have found himself a hero. But he was too late. A second family who watched me jump drove their Matador red Oldsmobile Cutlass to the tollbooth to report a jumper. Thankfully someone was on duty. Three minutes later, another life forever changed in the tragic wake of my untimely death.

A few miles away Officer Johnson was patrolling a southbound freeway when he received the call he'd prayed would never come. But it was I who forced the dispatcher's hand, shattering the slow night air, turning double-nickel boredom into heart-stopping panic.

"14-DAVID"

"14-DAVID, go ahead."

"14-DAVID, 1031 Coronado Bridge, witnesses report a jumper in the water at 1903 hours."

"14 DAVID 10-4, show me en route from National City code-3."

His first impulse was to run. To free himself of the dark forces I'd introduced to his life. But he'd sworn to serve and protect me at all costs.

"SAM 1, Is this a confirmed jumper?"

"Affirmative SAM."

"SAM 1, 10-4. Please notify the Harbor police and tell them to expedite."

It was all hands on deck. Officer Johnson wanted to pound the steering wheel, but he kept his cool until he confirmed that his worst nightmare had come true. He repeatedly told himself it may not be me because there had already been another jumper earlier in the day. Sadly, the young man who'd died that day wasn't much older than me. Knowing seconds count in an emergency, Officer Johnson floored the accelerator, unleashing 220 furious horsepower towards the off-ramp at Main Street, sliding through the busy intersection, splitting traffic while his lights and siren screamed, speeding left on National City Boulevard towards the I-5 north on-ramp.

With each heart-pounding breath, his excitable speedometer needle rose with purpose. Within twenty agonizing seconds, the 440 cubic inch V-8 accelerated to over a hundred miles per hour, causing his black-and-white cruiser flashing red and blue to race by curious civilians clearing a path for his desperate charge. Drawing closer to the bridge, Officer Johnson began talking to himself. "No, no, no Lori. Don't you do this to me." He could smell the burn of Goodyear rubber carving his path deep into the banked curve that emptied onto the bridge. Locking his brakes to avoid slamming into the traffic jam now stretching into the city of San Diego,

Officer Johnson swerved and continued wailing his siren as he raced west in the span's eastbound lanes.

Showtime! He mashed the brake pedal into the rubber floor mat and speed shifted from drive to park. The violent stop thrust him into the hard-cased steering wheel, leaving his racing heart breathless. A surge of horrified adrenaline unleashed his door, freeing him from 4,460 pounds of screaming black-and-white Mopar muscle. Without hesitating, Officer Johnson launched from the cruiser's tan interior, his quick feet floating with each stride. The bite of winter stung his face first—a stark contrast to the warm cockpit that carried him to my point of no return. The edge was near. There was no stopping him now. Thirty-four vertical inches was all that separated him from the freedom I thought I'd find 246 feet below—his last step towards me, unable to save my life.

Parked directly in front of where Officer Johnson skidded to a stop was my yellow Nova with the driver's side door wide open in the center lane with the headlights on and engine running. But there was no sign of the driver. The red and blue lights flashing across the stunned faces watching the drama unfold signaled to the Calvary that more help was needed. On the front seat were my brown wallet, purse, and the note I wrote to Grandma Vogt. As Officer Johnson turned to approach my car, tears began to stream down his face to the hauntingly poetic words of "Goodbye Yellow Brick Road." The bearded tow truck driver from A to Z Towing frantically tried to calm his utter shock, but he stood blank-faced, breathing rapidly, in his soiled overalls, knowing I was somewhere below him and Elton, floating alone in the fifty-eight-degree ocean, barely breathing, if at all.

Throwing his good-mannered radio etiquette out the window, Officer Johnson raced to his unit, grabbed the microphone, and screamed, "14-DAVID, expedite the harbor police! I have a body in the water!" His heavy breathing told the dispatcher there was no time to waste.

They say a person who falls from a significant height dies mid-flight, before impact. Maybe that's true free-falling from thirty-five thousand feet, but not from the Coronado Bay Bridge. I don't remember hitting the water, but afterward, I watched the night fade as blood filling my lungs squeezed the light from my weary pain-stricken eyes.

When Karen went to view my corpse, the coroner told her I'd died before hitting the water. It wasn't true. Regardless of what anyone says, I was conscious of the last seconds of my life. You would be surprised how slow something this fast happens. I didn't blame the coroner for fibbing to Karen. I understood Mr. Creason, a former homicide detective, was trying to ease the impact of my impact on a grieving sister. He was right to curb her visions of my implosion because I'd slammed into the water at eighty-six miles per hour, conscious of every passing microsecond. The explosive stop was equivalent to being struck by a 226,000-pound weight. There was no magical passing from one realm to another. No fields of swarming butterflies were waiting to welcome me. I died alone, then floated like a waterlogged hunk of driftwood. Death had lied to me all along. My selfish fantasy of a heroic exit ensured nothing more than an eternal curse of guilt for the waves of pain I sent crashing upon those who loved me. Any chance at happiness died the moment I gave up on myself.

After surfacing, I drifted south, towards Mexico. They needed to find me fast, before I washed up on shore or meandered past the next day's tour boats. At about 8:15, the San Diego Harbor Police responded with rescue boat 7177 to "Drag me outta da drink." My death was as Sergeant Joe had described. Fifty-two minutes later, intense searchlights canvassing the rhythmic waves, spotted me floating about two hundred yards south of where I'd powered into the bay's liquid concrete.

As I floated in the crosshairs of intense search lights, three dive-certified officers wearing orange life preservers maneuvered into position before using aluminum lifeguard hooks to pull my soaking, limp corpse to safety at 9:19 p.m.

The marine unit officers struggled to get my dead weight aboard, accidentally bumping my head a few times into a small aluminum step near the aft deck. Once onboard the pride of Shelter Island, my body was laid in a silver rescue litter on the aft deck and transported to the Harbor Police terminal at the Broadway Pier in San Diego. For those who don't know, a litter is a basket stretcher designed for confined spaces and rescues complicated by steep terrain. Mine had an opening at the bottom to prevent water from collecting underneath me. Less water weight would make moving my corpse easier when it was time to lift me out of the boat and into the ambulance.

The ride back to the dock was miserable. I was, of course, dead, and the three officers who recovered me cringed whenever a rogue whitecap banged me into the boat's fiberglass interior. Usually, my teeth would have been chattering because I didn't have a coat on. I was, however, wearing the blue Pickups Limited jacket I'd worn when Karen, Grego, and I had cruised these very same waters three weeks earlier. It had three white stripes down the left front side and our club's name embroidered on the back. Once we reached headquarters, the officers decided to keep my lifeless body on board the boat, away from prying eyes. The Broadway pier shoulders a busy downtown corridor full of motorized life, so the odds favored someone making a gruesome discovery—one they would never forget. All around me, cars, diesel-chugging buses, and people wove a tapestry of movement synchronized by red, green, and yellow signals. Several agitated honks in the distance cried out against the distracted drivers slowing the post-rush hour pace.

Life outside my death was thriving. Yet no one seemed to care that I had extinguished myself. If the population didn't care, then why should I? Across the bay, high atop the bridge, Sergeant Joe reluctantly approached Officer Johnson fighting back tears on my behalf. Both of them struggled to understand the depths of my despair, both were at a loss for words.

Officer Johnson's eyebrows collapsed. "She's gone, sir. She's gone."

"I know, son. I know." Sergeant Joe took a slow breath. He too had feared this day would come. "Hang in there, kid," said the patron saint of the highway patrol.

"Why, Sarge? Why'd she, do it?"

Kicking the bridge with his left toe, Sergeant Joe searched himself for an answer. "That's the million-dollar question, buddy." Both men were in shock, unable to believe I came back for a third time. But I did come back. Only this time with a vengeance. My death stopped them dead in their tracks. We had become fast friends, but they had a job to do, so mourning me would have to wait. There was too much sadness about for any tension to arise. Standing alongside Officer Johnson and Officer Langendorfer, Sergeant Joe pressed his fingertips to his temples before walking closer to the edge where I'd fallen. Looking out into a sea of black, he placed his hands on his hips and began to speak.

"Well fellas, one's thing's fer sure."

"Yeah, Sarge, what's that?" asked Officer Langendorfer, before taking a long drag off a freshly lit cigarette while Officer Johnson looked on in stunned silence.

"Tonight, Lori said da quiet part out loud."

Chapter 41

—

Deputy Coroner Robert Engel and his seasoned trainee Jose Huizar arrived at 10:00 p.m. sharp. It was hard to ignore the glint of 24-karat devotion to Christ around Deputy Huizar's neck. It offered comfort on his walks through life's unfortunate endings. A robust character, he strolled up to me wearing a gray pachuco hat that complemented his thin black mustache with a flare of Mexican pride. He had honed his investigative skills as a police officer patrolling his city's meanest streets. A loner at heart, his imposing presence could be intimidating to those who didn't understand the difference between confidence and cockiness.

Seeing me dead brought no joy to his chocolate-brown eyes. Tasked with a difficult job, he afforded me respect that I appreciated. I was touched by a humble gesture this hardened death detective made before examining me. Standing over my body, he made a subtle sign of the cross and kissed his crucifix before tucking it inside his forest-green sweater vest. He wasn't blessing me. I believe he was asking for the strength to serve me well and the courage to deliver my tragic news with compassion and dignity.

Things heated up once he pulled back the white linen sheet covering my cold, wet body. The first order of business was to confirm that I was actually dead. He checked my carotid artery for a pulse but found nothing. Next, he carefully documented finding the cooling, flaccid remains of a well-developed, well-nourished, Caucasian female adult clad in denim trousers and striped shirt. He noted an area of ecchymosis on my left orbital space, meaning this side of my face slapped the water first on impact. Blinding flashes helped capture the expanding facial bruise darkening my pink hue.

A California driver's license and other papers in my car made identifying me easy. Alongside my purse, on the front seat of the Nova, was a handwritten note I'd penned to Grandma Vogt explaining the reasons I chose to end my life. The suicide note's signature matched my driver's license, supplying enough preliminary evidence to designate my death as an act of self-destruction. With my on-scene investigation complete, a red-over-white Hartsons Cadillac ambulance chauffeured me eight miles north on Highway 163 to the coroner's office in Kearny Mesa. There were no emergency lights flashing on this quiet ride. Once we turned off Overland Avenue, the ambulance pulled around back where the two-person crew pushed me through a wide door marked Examining Room, Incoming. A similar-sized door next to it read Body Release, Outgoing. I traveled through both.

Behind the coroner's office's concrete facade, two attendants dressed in white trousers and black jackets lifted me onto a rolling stainless-steel table and re-covered me. You can bet the bathroom in this death laboratory was neat and tidy without the benefit of nude girls taped to the ceiling. Not only that, but the wall posters were as exciting as watching paint dry. All the surfaces in this joint seemed to either be metal or some other nonporous material. I guess the solid surfaces help keep the bugs down. Right away you notice the smell. It was rank and pungent with a tinge of sickening sweetness, like rotting meat soaked in piss-heavy ammonia, like at Erika's, only deadlier.

A tag was hung on my right toe for identification purposes. In the living world, a smile and polite greeting was my calling card. Now a thin piece of cardboard hung with string introduced me to strangers. My most morbid thoughts were incapable of preparing me for what lay ahead. The brutal honesty of suicide's ugly truth was about to touch me in the worst way.

When I was a child, there was nothing worse than seeing a needle ready to jab me. The intensity of those square alcohol pads was enough to ruin my day. Now I was facing a procedure far more barbaric than some silly shot in the arm.

Once Deputy Huizar had scheduled the autopsy, his team covered me with a fresh white sheet and wheeled me into the cooler. I recognized the sound of an inescapable lock from playing office with Karen at Grandpa's shop. She was the customer and I the proprietor. I would write up phony invoices and store them in Grandpa's oak filing cabinet, which matched the antique rolltop desk where he hid his sweet treats. We would play for hours, sucking on Lemonheads until our mouths turned yellow with sour delight. Never could I have imagined that one day I'd be lying in a chilled filing cabinet built to preserve me. Five other lifeless stiffs were on hand to keep me company through the night, so who was I to complain? Now comfortably on ice, I awaited the coming search for my cause of death down the hall in the lab.

At about 11:45 the next morning, a technician slid my now crisply chilled corpse, with a bag of personal effects balanced on my ankles, onto one of the highly polished rolling chariots and wheeled me past a restroom to an awaiting autopsy table, also constructed of stainless steel, one of five in the operating theatre. Table number 2 was chosen to be my home for the next hour or so. This table had a few distinct features from the rolling ones. First, it was slanted so blood and other bodily fluids could run into a drain at the end, near a washbasin. There was also a scale hanging over its center to weigh each organ. It made a metallic clang whenever a tool struck its shiny surface. And the overhead lights shined brightly as the sun on a clear summer day. Only more intense and without the warmth that shines down from the sky above.

All around me were many drawers filled with surgical tools, and the table next to mine had a plastic tray holding rubber gloves, a shaving razor, and sewing needles. No longer able to define my purpose, I was weighed and measured. I tipped the scale at a healthy 128 pounds. Fingerprinting came next. After the doctor centered me on the table, he placed a rubber block under my neck to keep my head steady during the procedure. A few photographs later had us off and running. My external examination revealed extensive bruising and abrasions covering the backside of my body. This told the pathologist I had landed flat on my back. I had no idea my pinkish hue could darken so profoundly.

At one point during the autopsy the pathologist held my brain in his hands. That's 1,360 grams of my happiest and saddest days. I wondered if he could feel my fears as he ran his skilled fingertips across my brain's gelatin-like structures. The examination revealed no cerebral injuries or abnormalities, proving I died of a broken heart. So, there I lay—cold, dead, and still alone. If only Erika could see me now. Then she would be sorry.

With my exam complete, the only remaining tasks were to bag me up and ship me out. Near the autopsy theatre exit hung a wooden sign reading Silence please, you are now in the presence of a genius at work. Guess those guys and gals had a sense of humor after all. But my tragic end was no laughing matter. In the words of the coroner: "Gross autopsy and toxicological studies revealed the cause of death to be injuries, chest, and abdomen, extensive." And for what?

I was now just another toe tag in an assembly line of death operated by the living comfortable with the science of disease and destruction. It wasn't their job to baby me. They were there to make sense of the broken pieces left behind. Lastly, the pathologist signed my death certificate while I was again refrigerated until a hearse arrived the next morning to transport me home. On paper, I was now a statistic. A suicidal hash mark in the bridge's storied history. Lori, as the world knew her, no longer existed.

Chapter 42

–

Around 10:30 the next morning, two cars driving from opposite directions turned into the Cypress View Mausoleum parking lot on Imperial Avenue, in Central San Diego. One pulled under a wood-beamed carport painted beige and dark brown near the chapel while the other parked by the front entrance facing Greenwood Cemetery, where Mom lives six feet under. Grandma Vogt stepped out of Grandpa's 1969 metallic purple Lincoln Town Car dressed in mourning, unaware that a thin and energetic mortician was unloading me from the rear of the black hearse that had followed her and Uncle Wes onto the property. It wasn't my first ride in a Cadillac, but it was undoubtedly the last. I thought the floppy black hat Grandma wore was a bit overkill, but to each their own, right? Picture dramatic funeral queen meets Kentucky Derby socialite minus the cheerful flowers. The coroner's office had released my remains a few hours earlier, and the mortician at Cyprus View was eager to begin embalming because Grandma was pressing for me to make an early appearance. I'd actually been here several times before today's slow ride south from the 163. Grandpa Vogt was interred here, of course, and he got a vase of flowers hung on his crypt whenever we visited. To me it smelled like an old church full of dusty Bibles. But Karen's face would sour like a rotten apple whenever we swung by to see him. The place is posh though. It reminded me of the Vatican. Everywhere you look fine Italian marble accentuates massive stained-glass windows depicting angelic images of heaven. I often wondered how the striking, brightly glass breathing colored light throughout never fades against the burn of relentless sunshine. Of course, the gleaming white marble statues posed in the grand hall need no explanation. Like the statue of David, they evoke fantasy-rich memories of a life I never lived. I've always believed the beauty of days gone by is something to behold. And now there was plenty of time to dream about places I'd never go and things I'd never see.

Chapter 43

–

There was a bright blue sky everywhere you looked the day I checked into Cyprus View. The kind of blue that made it hard to tell where the ocean ended, and the sky began. Not for my sister Karen, though. How could I know my fall from grace would set her sun forever? My death set off a chain reaction that tore a hole in her heart a mile wide. To this day, she views the phone with trepidation, knowing a single ring can hurl her back in time to the heart-sinking moments of January 21, 1974.

After processing me, Deputies Huizar and Engle reluctantly drove to La Mesa around midnight to speak with my father and share the unpleasant news. No preparation or warning came with this notification.

After knocking several times. "Mr. Vogt?"

Rubbing his tired angry eyes, "Do you have any idea what time it is?"

"Yes Sir, Yes Sir I do. My name is Deputy Huizar, and this is Deputy Engel. Your daughter was involved in an accident earlier tonight. Can we talk?"

"Obviously it was serious or you wouldn't be here in the middle of the night, now would you, poncho?"

"No sir. No I wouldn't. I'm afraid it is serious."

"Wait, which daughter are we talking about here, partner? Lori or Karen?"

"Lori Elizabeth Vogt is who I'm here to represent, sir."

"So, she's not in the hospital or what are you trying to tell me, man? Come on speak up, hombre!"

"No, sir. She died tonight after jumping from the Coronado Bay Bridge at 7:10 p.m. The Harbor Police pulled her from the bay around 8:30, and her remains are in my custody at the coroner's facility in Kearny Mesa."

The glum porch light was not enough to warm the deadly conversation. I admire folks like Deputies Huizar and Engle. How terrible it must be to level families daily with the sobering news of sudden loss. Later, they reflected on their exchange with my father and surmised that he played a hand in the jump that ended my life. Dad even lacked the common decency to invite them inside to discuss the details or the expectations of him in the coming days. Concluding their one-sided conversation, Deputy Huizar hadn't even taken his first step off my father's porch before Karen's phone was ringing on the other side of La Mesa. But she already knew I was gone. I believe she felt me leave.

"Hello?"

"Karen, your sister is dead!"

"I know, Dad."

"How the hell do you know? Some wetback from the coroner's office was just here, and he said no one else knew. See, you can't trust those sonsabitches for nothing."

It would be days before my sister showed the type of emotion one might expect from such intense news. However, she was quick to put our excuse for a father in his place.

In death as in life, she was still trying to protect me at all costs. In a rage, she exploded, screaming into the phone. If only I had followed her example and done the same, I might still be alive.

"Dad!" she roared. "Will you for once in your life shut your face? For Christ's sake, you're married to a Mexican! I know Lori's dead because she called me tonight. She just kept repeating she was cold and had to go but would see me soon. I knew something bad was coming by the tone in her voice. I tried to help her, but she told me not to worry."

Our dad didn't care. All that mattered now was how my lesbian suicide was going to affect his reputation. Especially with the family, considering he was responsible for creating me.

"Never mind all that," he said. "Get yourself dressed because I'm coming to get you right now. I have to identify her body and claim her belongings before anyone gets to her." By anyone he meant Grandma Vogt and Uncle Wes. Karen was in shock at Dad's remarks, standing in her kitchen between a wall and the dining table in a lifeless daze. She should have hung up on the insensitive old bastard. Instead she hurled the phone to the end of the hallway, past Grego's room. It was yellow with a spiraled cord that stretched about ten feet beyond its curled length. The slinky connection allowed her to walk and talk her mama chores whenever I would call to bust her chops about overdoing it with the blue eyeshadow. We'd had the best of times, me and that beautiful sister of mine. Too bad I let the mindless opinions of others kill our future together.

My dad wore these gaudy sterling silver rings loaded

with raw turquoise stones on his fat fingers. Hearing them clank against the door with each knock drove the dagger of my death deeper into Karen's heart. Vinny was speechless. I am thankful he was there to support her because the rest of our family shut down to conceal their guilt-ridden contributions to my demise. In their eyes, the sooner they could distance themselves from the public spectacle of my death, the better. You should have seen our blowhard father standing at Karen's front door, his chest puffed out like a barroom brawler looking to extend his losing record.

After a few tense moments, my loving sister, ravaged by grief, grabbed her brown suede coat for the ride to the coroner's office and stormed outside. Karen rode the entire time in silence, whispering to herself *This isn't real.* After surviving the trip intact, she found the voice on the call box a welcome surprise. It was Deputy Huizar. She thought he might have gone home after talking to dad and she had a million questions to ask him about what happened to me. But he wasn't ready to share just yet. Before Melvin could make it to the front door, Deputy Huizar was inviting them in with routine but kind-hearted condolences.

Having beat Karen and my dad to the office by only about twenty minutes, you can imagine the surprise on Deputy Huizar's face when he saw them standing outside.

Deputy Huizar directed his furrowed brow at my father. "Mr. Vogt, I'm surprised to see you here tonight. I was under the impression you would be coming by in the morning after we processed Lori's belongings. I thought you understood the process."

"I do, but I need to see her now; otherwise, I won't be

able to sleep until I know for sure. Plus, you gotta get me the suicide note we discussed on the porch. Like before anyone else does, if you know what I'm saying, pal."

"As I explained to you before Mr. Vogt, outside of you, Karen would be next in line to claim Lori's belongings, so our office will not be releasing anything without either of your written consent."

As Dad grumbled to himself, Deputy Huizar shifted his concern to Karen.

"We haven't been formally introduced. Hello, my name is Jose."

"Nice to meet you, I'm Karen. Can I please see my sister?" She was beside herself. "No, Lori's not ready to see you yet, sweetheart, but soon."

He was so nice. A ray of hope in Karen's darkest day.

"Is she broken?"

"No, she's not broken, but she wouldn't want you to see her in a place like this. She will see you soon; I promise."

Poor Karen was slipping. Her grip on reality was weakening by the second. "You promise?" she asked, telling Deputy Huizar I had promised the same a few hours earlier over the phone. These were the last words I spoke to Karen before telling her I love you. Hearing them again under these circumstances brought her to her knees. Deputy Huizar sprang into action reassuring her with a comfortable smile. "You bet I promise."

"Thank you," said Karen wiping a flood of tears from her eyes. "Because I have so much I need to say to her."

"As God is my witness, you have my word we'll make her a priority and get her to a more comfortable setting where you can spend some quality time together." For a moment, Karen just rocked back and forth. Recognizing the blank stare of distress, Deputy Huizar helped sweet Karen to a chair in the corner near a travertine lamp table. Dad stood there, shaking his head in disgust at what he considered the weaker sex not rising in the face of adversity.

Turning his attention back to my father, "I'm sorry you folks made the drive up here tonight, but there is nothing more we can do until morning. If you come back after 9:00 a.m. everything will be in order and ready for release. Now please, go home and get some rest."

The next morning, Karen found herself back in the lobby of death. A couple of sleeping pills the night before did nothing to help her sleep. To her, I wasn't dead. There was a misunderstanding somewhere in the system responsible for this madness.

A case of mistaken identity perhaps. Any minute, she thought, I would swing open the screen door with a poorly timed joke ending with "SURPRISE!"

After arguing in the parking lot about my belongings, Karen and Dad walked into the county coroner's office about 9:30 and met a cheerful receptionist named Victoria. An orderly stack of *Life* magazines on the glass coffee table offered a welcome distraction to weary visitors awaiting difficult news. Down the hall from the lobby began the post-mortem half of the building. Left of the main was the hall leading to the bodies. Along the wall to the examination room is a window sunshine never sees. Family members use this portal softly lit in yellow light to identify relatives lost to death's unyielding permeance.

Victoria spoke with the cutest southern accent you ever heard. Her hospitality comforted the harsh reality facing my sister. She took Karen by the hand and personally introduced her to San Diego County Coroner Robert L. Creason. He was the main man in charge and had been briefed on the case and was expecting to intercept Karen before she made the mistake of seeing my blackened face. He was kind to Karen. Convincing her seeing my mortal wounds would serve no purpose nor change the outcome.

After twenty minutes of pleasantries and vague details about my death, Victoria signed over my belongings to Dad, who made sure to snatch everything before Karen had a chance. The paper bag folded at the top and closed with staples, marked Lori E. Vogt, case # 211-74, held my wallet, purse, and suicide note intended for Grandma along with a letter to Erika. That was the last time my private remarks to Grandma saw the light of day. In Dad's quest for perfection, he denied my last opportunity to set the record straight.

A curious thing happened before they left the gray concrete walls of 5555 Overland Avenue. The spunky receptionist called Mr. Creason to her desk situated alongside a busy telephone switchboard, whose lighted circuits stood ready to answer the call. There she discreetly handed him something private. It appeared Deputy Huizar mistakenly forgot to place something in the property bag. After his huddle with Victoria, Mr. Creason walked up to Karen, smiling, and asked her to hold out one of her hands. In it, he placed the seventy-seven cents found on the front seat of my Nova near the brown leather wallet. It was the only property of mine given to her. Without the coroner's staff's thoughtfulness, my beloved sister would have received nothing to represent my physical life on Earth. In the coming days, everything I owned got sold off to remove all reminders of my shameful betrayal to the family name. Grateful, Karen threw her arms around Mr. Creason and let her tears speak for the both of us. Dad, on the other hand, mocked this beautiful moment like only a bully could. "Knock it off, you're making a scene," he said. "Now let's get the hell out of this death trap before someone else ends up on ice."

Chapter 44

–

Yesterday I was alive. Yesterday I was a loving sister named Lori, but then I killed her. And for what? The attention of a transactional love bonded in trauma. Evil had befallen me, disguised as love. I mean, for God's sake, Erika kept track of her good deeds to devalue me whenever it suited her controlling emotional outbursts. Like every dried tear or penny spent on my behalf. But it was I who taught her how to treat me. I thought I needed Erika to need me. I also thought the gift of her smile was worth the occasional slap across the face. But when I got things wrong, I got them very wrong. Only this time there was no going back. This time I was cold from the inside out. For me, there were no more sunny days ahead. No airplanes to watch fly. Only seconds, minutes, and hours of endless time trapped in sheer darkness where only I suffer the wrath of my silent screams.

Outside, the fatigued sky, black as a coal mine, was anything but settled. Karen, restless and hollow, awoke before the first gloomy rays could surface. She intended to sleep away her new reality, but the sound of me crashing into the water shook her every time she closed her bloodshot eyes. It was then I realized that my pain hadn't ended. My death made sure of that. No, it grabbed hold of Karen, ensuring a lifetime of agony would forever hold her hostage.

In the hours to come in somber living rooms around town, memories of me came to life through utter shock mired in profound disbelief. From Erika to the girls and each member of my family, everyone struggled to understand how I could make such a taboo statement. Everyone but Karen, that is. She knew exactly why I chose to publicly execute myself. To her, my death was something no one could take away from me or deny. In death, I silenced my critics once and for all. But in doing so, I sacrificed the greatest gift of all: life.

When I hit the water, everything I loved was lost to me. Including my Grego. I left him behind without so much as a thought. I had many chances to turn back the clock on the dreaded time counting down my end, but that was all water under the bridge now. I was dead and there was nothing anyone could do about it.

The rest of the morning drifted along without so much as a sound against the sporadic drone of the morgue refrigerator's condenser unit. The surprising part of all this was how similar death felt to the darkest, coldest days of my life. Perhaps, but little did I know that though I had survived an autopsy, the worst was yet to come. Later in the afternoon a mortician's assistant rolled me out of the body locker to prepare me for my first showing, scheduled from four to eight. An astringent smell with a sweet twist swayed in the air like alcohol-flavored bubble gum. Perhaps it was the pink formaldehyde embalming fluid used to plump up dead tissue. Don't let anyone tell you it doesn't work, because minutes after the pump kicked on, I went from gray to rosy, lickety-split. But as you know, I never liked attention. Like it or not, though, I belonged to Grandma Vogt's discretion now, and my viewing was going to happen come hell or high water.

As I rolled down a dimly lit hall under a soft white sheet, like a redheaded ghost, Karen made her way to the bathroom down her apartment's narrow hall in preparation to see me one last time. There was no rush, only slow, somber silence. The mood around her only slightly colder than mine. She was still sure this was a mistake. A misunderstanding brought about by mistaken identity or malpractice. Surely her sister couldn't be dead when I was so full of life. But I was dead. Bruised too. Bruised so badly, the disfiguring purple covering my face looked blacker than black. I looked dreadful. Now on a collision course with a heartbroken sister, all I could do was wait while she prayed for a second chance to love me. In the meantime, I was bathed and shoved into a blue dress I wouldn't be caught dead in. Next came hair curlers. The hot kind that burn hair into submission. And brushes caked with colorful makeup and soft pink fingernail polish fit for a priss. Every mother's worst nightmare was about to be front and center for the grieving world to see. I hated this more than anything. But what could I do? With my final transformation complete, it was time to be fitted for a coffin.

The staff was careful not to smudge my makeup, as the extra layers hardly covered the thick discoloration bleeding through on my left cheek. A lacy white veil to mask the emotional wounds smashed into my face would soften the blow of my impact on the living. After placing my prom-ready corpse in a fine copper casket filled with a soft, pillowy, white interior, the funeral director wheeled me into the Chapel of Rest for what would be my first of five showings. As the wheels guiding my lifelessness settled into the lilac-swirled pewter carpet, several large flower arrangements were placed behind me, and a silk drape masked my obvious injury. Grandma, it seems, was having a tough time letting go of her angel.

I never realized how much she loved me until it was too late. I didn't realize a lot of things until it was too late, but that's how it goes when you let emotions take the wheel. Still, it drove me absolutely bananas that she dressed me like a child when I was anything but. I guess doing so was her trembling voice's way of denying the hidden truth of my sexuality.

When Karen arrived, there was no laughter. The sadness spilling over had everyone on alert, even Dad. Appearing somewhat humbled, he stood by, well aware that his oldest daughter might not survive my fall, save for her precious baby boy waiting at home. Like his mom, Grego was waiting for me to appear, flashing my infectious smile. But scrapbook memories of us would be his connection to me going forward. With each step towards the small room at the end of the chapel holding me, Karen braced for the inevitable. Deep down she knew I was gone. But accepting my fate was a demon she fights to this very day. On the walls outside our last moments together, landscapes framed in gold hung on the walls between empty seats awaiting a packed funeral. Soon I would be the eye of everyone's pity. But tonight I belonged to Karen and Karen alone. As she approached, her clammy hands began to tremble. Her quivering lips sounded with a deep resentment for those who pushed me to jump not once, but three times. She knew who was to blame, and so did those responsible. She paused standing before me, trying to reconcile the cold, lifeless reality staring back at her. The funeral director who walked her inside from the parking lot helped her into a padded chair beside me before stepping out. "I'll be right outside," he said. "If you need anything."

My sister is incredibly strong and blessed with a sound mind, but seeing me dead, battered and bruised leveled her deepest sensibilities. She began to cry quietly. Then unloaded as she fumbled about what to do.

Would it hurt to touch me, she wondered? Would my shattered body feel like mush? Unsure of anything but the obvious, she slid her hand under the veil and stroked my hair, dripping tears onto my white-collared knee-length blue dress. Just then a miracle happened. "Come quick," she shouted, sounding a tearful panic alarm that brought a crowd of concerned family and staff rushing to our side. "She's breathing, look!" The stunned onlookers could only watch in horror as Karen pointed at my empty chest waiting for it to rise. "I promise," she said. "I saw her stomach move and everything." Her gasps drew deeper as our future together hung in the balance. "It wasn't like a deep breath," she continued, "but I promise she breathed for me. She really did." Her cries, now more desperate than ever, waited and worried for the impossible to happen. When it didn't, she fell into my casket, ruffling the veil with her limp body. It was as dreadful a sight as you will ever see.

"Please!" she cried out. "Why won't anyone help her?" Her fight-or-flight was in overdrive to save what was already lost. Exasperated, she fell back into the chair and covered her face with her hands. Kneeling down beside her, the funeral director whispered into her ear. Whatever he said helped, because she dropped her hands and acknowledged his efforts with a tearful head nod. When he walked away, she gently poked my arm a few times, begging me to wake up. "Come on, Sis. Wake up and let's get out of here." All around us imaginary midnight roses died listening to my frozen words say nothing at all. My weary secrets were no more. I was a burden now more than ever, with no way to apologize or speak my peace. As Karen combed her fingers through my hair, she said all the things Erika never could.

When it came time to leave, Karen refused. "Leave us alone," she barked, standing to face a wall of worried mourners dressed to impress. More than anything she was protecting me from those entrusted with my well-being. And that, my friends, is why I loved her so much.

Above us the dim lighting caressed the room in a haunting glow. In the grave shadows, meant to hide the unthinkable, Karen pleaded with me for this not to be so. "Wake up, Sis," she continued, inches from my blank stare, studying each masked blemish for signs of life. In her efforts to deny the truth lying dead before her she misread the listless handful of bones resting in hers. There was no touch nor feel on my behalf. Only the severed bond of sisterly love gone too soon.

For the next hour she pleaded for me to come home between fits of apologetic rage for not fighting harder. It wasn't her fault, but I couldn't reciprocate her undying love no matter how much it hurt to see her eyes bleed for me. In a moment reserved for grief, she became a convenient scapegoat for all those involved. After news of my death broke, Dad made sure everyone and their mother knew that Karen ran around with her dyke sister and all her deranged friends. *Blame Karen* became a mantra for those not willing to accept their part in my death. Especially my father. He, more than anyone, took it upon himself to let Grandma know he'd tried to fix me time and again.

As our visit ended, Karen began hyperventilating. She knew once she turned and walked away that she might not have the strength to see me again. A soreness in her lungs suffocated her concentration. She bobbed up and down standing to face me. The soft wood-grained panel walls closed in on her as she prepared to leave me forever. In our final moment together, she shuddered, grabbing hold of the silver handrail running alongside my coffin. It shook with sorrow as she looked to the heavens, asking "Why, God, why?" With her fists clenched tight she surrendered her anger and fell into a state of being unfamiliar to us both. She began to speak without moving her lips. Her face grew pale uttering the last words between us. She spoke each syllable as if it were her last. With her hand in mine, Karen bent down and softly kissed my forehead. A surge of nausea turned her weak limbs heavy and numb. Every ounce of her wanted to scream for me. But she held her tongue, knowing any defenses would only bring further shame my way. The hurt inside her felt violent. It struggled to contain itself, for there is no justice without peace. Before she dropped to her knees, the funeral director, dressed in his Tuesday best, raced to her side and steadied her, walking towards a patio for a breath of fresh air. Heading out the door, she glanced over her left shoulder to see if I had tagged along. Her head dropped for the final time. Our life together was now but a memory lost in a growing statistic that compounds with each crashing splash into the bay.

"Forever and a day," she said placing her hand over her butterfly. "Forever and a day." In a moment that replays day after grueling day, my sister's last "I love you" still matters after all these years. I mean, how could it not when all I ever dreamed of was making her proud.

Chapter 45

–

I didn't have to die. There's no logical explanation sensible enough in this world or the next to justify my being sealed in a blackened tomb for all time and eternity without my life running its full natural course. Yet one simple act could have saved me. If only I had humbled myself enough to ask for help. But I was too proud. I needed to forgive myself and refocus, not die. But I was a love chasing people pleaser for all the wrong reasons. Foolish, because I had security in Ronnie, Karen, and Grego. True intimacy would have come if only I'd have been more patient. There were plenty of other reasons to fight harder as well. Including my beloved Grandma Vogt. I really did love her with all my heart. But I never gave her the opportunity to know the real me. Only the version I wanted her to know. Which inevitably helped guarantee my demise.

In the days after my beautiful casket first discovered the truth about terminal darkness, Karen made Ronnie drive her to Erika's work to confront the madness I never could. At first Erika tried comforting her with stories of our last days together and everything I shared as the other girls gathered to intimidate Karen. But Karen wasn't interested in anymore drama, letting the whole crew have it with both barrels. Surprisingly they went down in flames with little fight. Marsella waddled off first, blubbering half-witted obscenities into the air, followed by the rest of her sackless bullies. Ronnie stood by high-fiving Grego in the cab of his truck, watching Karen scream over the shoulder of the security guard who was pushing her away from the chain link fence standing between her and a trespassing charge. Her final message to Erika was not kind. "Keep the life insurance, you murderer. It's blood money now and of no use to me or my son. You helped kill her, so you spend it, bitch."

Thirty thousand dollars was on the table, which was a ton of money in 1974. But Karen didn't care. She would have no part in any benefit from my death because to her there was none. I think if pushed another inch, she could've wiped out the entire bunch with a single blow. She was that mad. And they knew it too, as not one of them could look her in the eye as she ripped them apart. Ronnie was blown away by her ferociousness. Grego, too, although he was too young to understand the significance of this postmortem assault. Driving away after such an intense release, Karen knew the worst days were yet to come. And all of them were my fault. See, I didn't ease my pain by killing myself. No, I only transferred it to those I left behind. Specifically, my sister. I didn't leave her in peace. I doubled her trouble by adding my grief to hers. In the time it takes to turn light dark, my little blood brother, three-year-old Grego, lost a lifeline to his future. It would be years before he knew I lived because I died before he could remember me.

As I said before, if I was strong enough to die, then I was strong enough to live. I know this because Sergeant Joe told me so. He told me twice, once while smoking his cigar, so I know he was telling the truth. But I thought I knew better. In those times I was unable to listen to reason. For in good times and bad, I pictured only Erika as the reason for my seasons. Boy, was I wrong. It turns out her love was contingent on my usefulness to whatever her needs commanded at the moment. When I stopped being useful, she stopped being in love. The truth is our connection died long before I did because she was looking for an upgrade from the start. Like those who abused Erika before stumbling upon me, she followed suit, compliments of her own antagonistic father. It's the only path she understood, so who am I to judge? I guess that's the price you pay for being one of three gay siblings afloat in a judgmental world blind to parental ignorance. Proving what they say about one person's trash being another man's treasure is true. I don't harbor any ill will towards Erika, though, as we all have our crosses to bear. Some heavier than others, but all demanding in their own right. But then again, don't think I'm sitting around here waiting on her with open arms. I can forgive, but I'll never forget. So now what? Well, for starters, the voice of death I heard night after night, was actually my pain and depression crying out for help. That's right, there was no fallen angel bargaining for my revenge. It was me all along searching myself for an escape to avoid facing the truth of what I mistakenly considered my shameful reality. In the end it seems, I had become more homophobic than my detractors thanks in no part to their loving ways. And I apologize for this not being a more uplifting story.

Sadly, I allowed others self-hatred and projections to contaminate my blessed life. But my reality doesn't have to be yours. As there is hope in every dead end. All it takes is one simple decision to change your life, so make it. Now I don't know much, but I do know that asking for help is critical when it seems there's nowhere to turn. I know doing so would have saved me for sure. I mean, I had Karen right there in the palm of my hand, minutes before the end, begging for me to come home. And instead of opening up, I foolishly turned my back on survival for fear that she too would grow tired of being my number-one fan. And please, don't feel bad for me, as I've learned the value of forgiveness in sharing my deepest darkest secrets. Besides, we've come a long way together, and I'm grateful you gave of your time to hear my story. Plus, pity never looked good on me, anyway. Instead, remember that love more than anything is an action, not a feeling. It needs honesty to live its truths. And most importantly, true love never dies. Trust me, I know better than anyone. How, you ask? Remember Ronnie? Well imagine time traveling to conservative 1972 and being a proud young sailor rushing home to his bride only to find your house overrun with hostile lesbians. Now imagine one of those lesbians is your wife and she leaves you for another woman after ripping out your heart and stomping it into submission. Well, that's exactly what happened to Ronnie. And I'm the one who betrayed his loyalty—a loyalty not even divorce could tarnish. And yet for almost fifty years now, my dear, sweet Ronnie brings me flowers whenever he comes to town. Talk about devotion. Talk about unapologetic love. After my funeral, he made sure to visit me every week for a year before shipping out to sea. Sometimes he came twice. I mean, come on, who does this for someone responsible for such unimaginable pain? Certainly no one I ever heard of before. But he does, he really does. And when he comes, he's careful not to spill any water, as he fears someone might slip and fall on the polished marble floors swirling about the elegant mausoleum. On his last visit, he picked red roses arranged with bright yellow daisies. Feel free to dry your eyes. I'll wait.

Not surprisingly, Ronnie's never seen anyone from my family or Erika's make time to visit, although Grego does regularly. Karen did for a while, but then she moved away to escape the afterlife I left her. In my absence, everything for her became a living hell. Again, not my intent, of course, but I understand and will always love her whether she visits or not. She has my butterfly tattooed over her heart, so I know she's always with me. Just like I hoped she'd be. When the music finally stopped for me, I thought I was the only one. Yet someone dies globally from suicide every forty seconds. Meaning roughly four hundred people killed themselves while we were on this journey together. Staggering, isn't it?

In fact, suicide rates have nearly doubled over the past two decades and continue to climb. But suicide is never the answer, no matter how sad you feel. Annually, tens of millions across the planet will consider suicide and millions of them will make formal plans to carry out these deadly considerations. So, if you or someone you know is hurting, seek help immediately. Please don't delay, as the support necessary to heal is there. I promise. There are even crisis lines today you can call 24/7 staffed with caring people dedicated to your needs no matter how impossible they may seem. And when confronted with an emotional crisis, don't be afraid to ask the tough questions that may just save someone's life. Even your own. This is so important because everyone's worthy of compassion and understanding regardless of their circumstances.

Obviously, I'm no Doctor, and don't pretend to have all the answers. Far from it, in fact. But I know self-care is vital to living one's best life. And my hope is that if you're hiding a secret out of fear of judgement, that you just set it free. Because those that matter won't mind, and the rest can just deal with it because it's your life, not theirs. And to those who've lost love, serve and protect, lost a job, struggle with addiction, bullying or the nightmares that come with fighting a foreign war, please know the hope your suffering craves is everywhere, and probably closer than you think. You just have to look and be brave enough to surrender when you find it. Even battle tested Navy Seals, who train in the shadows of the bridge and are known for their world class pain tolerance, sometimes fight suicidal thoughts and depression. And no, asking for help does not make you weak. Now I know you're probably thinking nope, not me, Lori, because I'm too strong to faulter. But remember my friends, I was once in your shoes and thought I knew better too. So please, don't ever forget that it's okay not to be okay. Because the world is counting on you to thrive in your own beautiful uniqueness. I'm counting on you as well. And together, maybe we can end this plague of suicide if only we open our hearts and minds to those in need hiding behind walls only love can tear down.

Oh, and one more thing: Be nice. Be nice to everyone you meet. Even people you don't like very much. Especially the perfect ones with perfect lives. Because often, those of us with the happiest smiles already have one foot in the grave.

Made in the USA
Middletown, DE
25 May 2022